"Do we have a firm agreement?"

Rikki accepted the hand Max held out to seal the deal. "We do. Carter will be so excited."

At the mention of her son's name, Max's expression turned a bit sly. "So, say someone... me, for instance...might want to work on another model whenever he needs to take a break from his research to ponder things. So, as an experienced mother, do you think the assistant I have in mind would prefer building a pirate ship or a Viking longship?"

She knew when she was fighting a losing battle. "What five-year-old doesn't love pirates?"

Max was gracious in victory. "Thank you, Rikki. I promise I won't be a troublesome guest."

He already was that, but at that moment, she couldn't bring herself to care.

Considering the potent power of Max's earnest blue eyes and hopeful smile, she could only hope that this arrangement didn't turn out to be a huge mistake.

D0776442

Dear Reader,

I'll let you in on a little secret—as with most writers I know, over the course of writing a book, the characters who started out as rather vague ideas soon become real people to me. From the moment I first "meet" them, they grow and change, becoming more three-dimensional as their story unfolds.

This was especially true with Maxim Volkov. When Max appeared in the first Heroes of Dunbar Mountain book, *The Lawman's Promise*, he caused quite a stir, and not in a good way. In fact, about the only person who made him feel welcome was Rikki Bruce, owner of the bed-and-breakfast where he stayed. I think Max was just as relieved as the citizens of Dunbar were when he left town at the end of the book.

But people change, and Max's experiences in Dunbar had had a profound effect on him. So even as he left, I knew that he wouldn't stay gone for long. On his first visit, he was focused on his family's past. But this time, Max is in town to figure out his future.

I hope you enjoy watching the sparks fly as Max and Rikki figure out if they've both just found their happily-ever-after.

Happy reading!

Alexis

HEARTWARMING

To Trust a Hero

Alexis Morgan

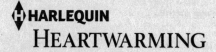

If you purchased this book without a cover you should be aware
that this book is stolen property. It was reported as "unsold and
destroyed" to the publisher, and neither the author nor the
publisher has received any payment for this "stripped book."

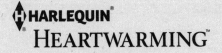

ISBN-13: 978-1-335-47542-8

Recycling programs
for this product may
not exist in your area.

To Trust a Hero

Copyright © 2023 by Patricia L. Pritchard

All rights reserved. No part of this book may be used or reproduced in
any manner whatsoever without written permission except in the case of
brief quotations embodied in critical articles and reviews.

This is a work of fiction. Names, characters, places and incidents
are either the product of the author's imagination or are used fictitiously.
Any resemblance to actual persons, living or dead, businesses,
companies, events or locales is entirely coincidental.

For questions and comments about the quality of this book,
please contact us at CustomerService@Harlequin.com.

Harlequin Enterprises ULC
22 Adelaide St. West, 41st Floor
Toronto, Ontario M5H 4E3, Canada
www.Harlequin.com

Printed in U.S.A.

USA TODAY bestselling author **Alexis Morgan** has always loved reading and now spends her days creating worlds filled with strong heroes and gutsy heroines. She is the author of over fifty novels, novellas and short stories that span a wide variety of genres: American West historicals; paranormal and fantasy romances; cozy mysteries; and contemporary romances. More information about her books can be found on her website, alexismorgan.com.

Books by Alexis Morgan

Harlequin Heartwarming

Heroes of Dunbar Mountain
The Lawman's Promise

Love Inspired The Protectors
The Reluctant Guardian

I want to thank everyone at Heartwarming for all of their amazing support and hard work in helping to make my books the very best they can be. This is especially true of my wonderful editor, Johanna Raisanen. Her enthusiasm and responsiveness make my job so much easier!

CHAPTER ONE

MAXIM VOLKOV PULLED over to the curb a block short of his destination to study the large Victorian house that had been home to him for a short time earlier that summer. He loved its mix of elegant lines and curious oddities, especially the curved turret room perched at the top like a crown. Painted a soft yellow with dark green trim, the house had a warm and welcoming look about it. He couldn't wait to check in, to the point he'd arrived hours before his room was supposed to be available.

As he contemplated what to do next, a car drove past, and the driver slowed to give Max a long look. No surprise there. In a place the size of Dunbar, Washington, strangers stood out. The instant the guy recognized Max, his expression morphed from merely curious to disapproving in a heartbeat. He immediately hit the gas and tore off down the street. Considering how fast gossip traveled in the small town, it would be less than thirty minutes before all six hundred citizens would know Max was back in town.

Okay, that was an exaggeration. It might take up to an hour before the ripple of news reached the outskirts of town.

All of which meant it was time to get moving. The only question was what would happen next. He could hardly blame Rikki if she was having second thoughts about renting him one of her rooms for an extended stay. On his previous visit, she'd ended up with local residents marching up and down outside of her B and B protesting her decision to provide Max with a safe refuge in town. Offering to move out had only made her madder at him than she had been at the crowd out on the sidewalk.

That memory had him smiling. What the woman lacked in size, she made up for in sheer pigheaded determination. He liked that and so much more about her. Even so, when he'd finally left Dunbar behind, he hadn't expected to return. After all, his short stay in town hadn't exactly been fun, especially considering most of the townspeople had hated Max with a passion.

They'd had reason to, he supposed. After all, he'd shown up out of the blue to announce that the Trillium Nugget, a chunk of gold worth a small fortune, didn't actually belong to the town at all. He'd set off a firestorm the day he'd strolled into the chief of police's office and plunked down his file of research that proved the nugget had really belonged to Max's family.

It had come as a great relief to all of the locals when the combined efforts of the police chief and the curator of the town's museum uncovered the complete story. As it turned out, Max's great-grandfather, Lev Volkov, had indeed discovered the nugget over a hundred years ago in his mine at the base of Dunbar Mountain. But when thieves had beaten up Lev to get his gold and then left him for dead, the good citizens of Dunbar had taken him in and nursed Lev back to health. To repay their kindness, he'd donated the immense chunk of gold to his benefactors to use as they saw fit. Sometime later, the Trillium Nugget became the centerpiece of the town's local history museum and a source of great civic pride.

The facts had left Max no choice but to

withdraw his claim. All he'd asked for in return was that the display of the Trillium Nugget be updated to include his great-grandfather's story. The curator of the museum, Shelby Michaels, had recently sent him an invitation to come view the newly renovated display. That had given him the legitimate excuse he'd needed to return to Dunbar. It had also solidified his plans to take up residence in town for the foreseeable future while he researched the town's history and his great-grandfather's role in it for a book he wanted to write.

How long he'd be staying all depended on what kind of welcome he received when he finally worked up the courage to knock on Rikki Bruce's front door. Financially, she might appreciate having a long-term guest staying at her bed-and-breakfast, but that didn't mean she would be happy that it was Max. For now, he'd check in, unpack his bags, and then maybe go back out for a late lunch. During his last stay, he'd taken most of his meals at the only eatery in town and had grown quite fond of the place.

The owner, Titus Kondrat, was a genius in the kitchen. Thanks to his many tattoos and solitary nature, the man was the source of much speculation about his life prior to moving to Dunbar. The most popular rumor was that Titus had personal experience in life behind bars, and that's where he'd learned to cook.

Max found it amusing that no one seemed to have the courage to actually ask Titus about his past or what had brought him to Dunbar in the first place. It was hard to tell if their reticence was due to Titus's intimidating personality or if they simply didn't want to risk being banned from his café. No one in their right mind wanted to lose access to arguably the best chicken and dumplings in the Pacific Northwest.

Max had his own reasons to appreciate Titus Kondrat. While the man hadn't exactly gone out of his way to befriend Max, at least he'd allowed him to hang out in the café as long as the table wasn't needed for other customers. While Max could've also worked in his room at the B and B, the protestors had left Rikki alone whenever he left the place. Those brief respites had eased his conscience at least a little for bringing the problem to her doorstep in the first place.

Meanwhile, the same car that had driven by a few minutes ago was back. Somewhere along the way, the driver had picked up several passengers, none of whom were even making a token effort to disguise their curiosity. One even leaned out of the back passenger window to snap a picture of Max as the car rolled past at a snail's pace.

What was up with that? Were they about to dust off their old protest signs and hit the pavement again? If so, it was definitely time to get a move on. As soon as the other car turned the corner, Max drove the short distance to the bed-and-breakfast. After parking, he grabbed his overnight bag and a couple of surprises out of the trunk. Then he took a deep breath, crossed his fingers, and knocked on Rikki Bruce's front door.

RIKKI SHUT OFF the vacuum cleaner and let the silence settle around her. She could've sworn she'd heard a knock at the front door, but it could have just as easily been the sound of her young son thumping around in his room overhead. She was about to give up and resume vacuuming when the pounding started up again, this time a little louder and longer.

She wiped her hands on her jeans and then touched her hair to make sure it was neat and tidy. It never hurt to make a good impression, especially when her bottom line currently hovered just above the dividing line between making a profit and having to eat ramen for dinner until business picked up again. She had no current guests in residence and wasn't expecting anyone until later in the afternoon. However, there were those rare occasions when someone drove through town and decided to stop for the night.

Pasting on her friendliest welcome-to-my-home smile, she opened the door. After one look at the man with his fist poised to knock yet again, she jettisoned the smile and almost decided eating ramen noodles for the next month held a certain appeal. Regardless, her unruly pulse kicked it up a notch, and she wished she was wearing a less faded pair of jeans and maybe a shirt that didn't have streaks of dust on the front. If Rikki had known Maxim Volkov would arrive so early, she wouldn't have spent the morning sweating up a storm while she took advantage of a high vacancy rate to do some heavy cleaning.

She gave his suitcase a pointed look. Next

to it was a large shopping bag with a box peeking out the top that looked suspiciously like a giant Lego set. "Mr. Volkov, I'm pretty sure I told you that check-in time wasn't until after three o'clock."

He got the same guilty look on his handsome face that her son, Carter, had when she caught him sneaking an extra cookie before dinner. "I thought it would take me longer to get here. Traffic can be pretty bad along the I-5 corridor."

She crossed her arms over her chest and arched an eyebrow. "Seriously? Is that the best you can do?"

It was hard not to laugh when she noticed he also had the guilty five-year-old foot shuffle down pat. "Okay, fine. Shelby Michaels invited me to see the new display about my great-grandfather at the Dunbar Historical Museum. I was so excited about seeing how it turned out that I left home extra early."

"So why aren't you on her doorstep instead of mine?"

"Because she doesn't rent rooms and you do. I also forgot the museum is closed on Thursday afternoons. I had planned to go there first before checking in here." He offered her a hopeful smile. "That is, unless you've changed your mind about letting me stay."

While Rikki could really use the money, she wasn't sure she needed the aggravation that having Max Volkov under her roof brought with him. She also didn't believe for an instant that the man had forgotten a darn thing about the Dunbar Historical Museum. One couldn't spend ten minutes in Max's company without noticing the sharp intelligence in those bright blue eyes. Surrendering to the inevitable, she left the door open for him and retreated to the glass-fronted counter where she normally greeted new guests. "Do you want the same room?"

He waited until he was inside with the door closed before answering. "Actually, I was hoping I could have the one in the turret. I'm guessing the view of the mountains from that room is rather spectacular."

He chewed his lower lip as his expression turned more serious. "I mentioned that I planned an extended stay last week when I made the reservation. The thing is that I would like to rent your turret room for what could easily be several months while I do the research for a book I want to write about my great-grandfather's life. There will be times when I'll have to leave to do research elsewhere, either for the book or for the handful of freelance articles that I'm already committed to writing, but I won't be actually checking out when that happens. I think that would only complicate things for both of us. So, would you consider letting me pay on a month-by-month basis? Or, if you prefer, I could even pay all at once for…say five months with an understanding that I can extend my stay if it becomes necessary."

Rikki sat down in her desk chair as she tried to absorb everything he'd just said. When he'd mentioned an extended stay, she was thinking in terms of weeks, not months. He must have been really worried about how she'd respond to his request from the way his words had picked up speed there toward the end. Maybe he thought she'd cut him off before he'd finished explaining the situation.

That said, there was no way she would turn him away. Even if his presence caused her undue stress, she couldn't afford to turn down a booking of that magnitude. After a few seconds, she said, "I don't think charging you for several months at once would be a good idea.

If something were to change and you needed to leave earlier, I'd have to refund the difference. It makes more sense to pay one month at a time until you have a chance to see if it's all going to work out the way you want."

He was looking much happier by that point. "Whatever works best for you, Rikki. Just let me know."

"I will."

Looking relieved, he silently handed her his platinum card. Once she'd processed the payment, he returned the card to his wallet. "Thanks for letting me stay, Ms. Bruce."

His use of her last name probably meant he'd picked up on her mixed feelings about having him as a long-term guest. Before she could decide if she should apologize, her son came pounding down the steps from the second floor. "Mom, can I have a granola bar? I know we just ate lunch, but I'm still—"

He went silent the second he spotted Max, but she could guess what he'd been about to say. No doubt he was hungry again. Carter had hit another growth spurt and was eating Rikki out of house and home. But instead of finishing his demand for food, he coasted to a stop on the bottom step to stare at their guest. For the longest time, neither man nor boy moved or spoke a single word. Then, between one second and the next, they both launched into action. Carter jumped high as Max captured him in midflight to swing the giggling kid around and around.

"Mr. Max, you're already here!"

Max stopped mid-twirl to set Carter back down on his own feet. Then he went down on one knee to put himself on the same level as her son. "I am. Is that okay?"

Carter didn't hesitate. "Yep. I have so much to tell you! I was really hoping you'd come back 'cause we missed you a whole bunch when you were gone."

Rikki winced, not that Carter was wrong about that. The whole house had seemed too quiet and too empty after Max had returned to Portland. Yeah, it had been a long time since she'd last spent so much time with an attractive man. He was handsome, but there was more to Max than that. She might have a weakness for men with wavy blond hair and sky-blue eyes, but she valued character and intelligence even more. The bottom line was that he checked every box on her list. If she were the type given to indulging in wild flings, Max Volkov would've been the perfect candidate.

But there was someone else whose needs she had to put ahead of her own—Carter. Her ex-husband was no kind of father at all. In fact, Joel had mentally divorced his son at the same time he'd divorced her. Considering what a jerk he'd turned out to be, they were both better off without him. Carter had only been a year old when Joel disappeared from their lives, so it wasn't as if he'd ever known what it was like to have a reliable male role model in his life.

That didn't mean that he didn't want one. That's were Max Volkov came in. Unlike most of her guests, he'd gone out of his way to spend time with Carter. He seemed to enjoy building models as much as Carter did. They'd done art projects together, played catch in the backyard, and read books before Carter went up to bed. One part of her had appreciated the way Max had made her son feel special, and she'd secretly hated the day he'd gone back home to Portland.

Like Carter had just said, they'd missed the man a whole bunch. It was hard enough to admit that truth to herself. There was no way she'd admit it to him. Right now, he was patiently listening to everything Carter had to say. When her son finally ran out of steam—or at least breath—Max glanced at her.

"I can't wait to hear more. But for now, provided your mom says it's okay, I have a surprise for you."

Her son's face lit up with excitement. Carter gave Max a quick hug before turning his puppy-dog eyes in her direction. "My chores are done. I picked up my toys, put my clean clothes away, and even carried the basket back down to the laundry room."

Now she had both Max and Carter staring at her with hopeful expressions. How was she supposed to resist that? "Since you did everything I asked you to, I suppose it's all right if Mr. Volkov wants to give you the surprise now."

"Thanks, Mom."

Meanwhile, Carter greedily eyed the nearby shopping bag. She wasn't the only one who recognized the logo on the corner of the box. Her son's eyes widened as Max pulled the present out of the bag and handed it over to him.

Unless she was mistaken, it was one of the

fancy spaceships from the *Star Wars* universe. Having bought several smaller sets for Carter for his birthday and Christmas, she strongly suspected this one would've been way out of her price range. Max shouldn't have sprung for such an expensive gift for Carter, but she couldn't bring herself to rain on his parade. Carter tended to be shy around strangers, especially men, but he'd taken to Max from the moment they'd met.

She was about to nudge her son to remind him of his manners. Before she could, he gently set the box aside to give his favorite guest another huge hug. "Thank you, Mr. Max. Would you work on it with me?"

"I'd love to, Carter, whenever your mom says it's okay."

"Let's let Mr. Volkov get settled first, Carter. While he does that, we'll bake the cookies you promised to help me with this afternoon. Afterward, the two of you can take over the big table in the library to work on the project."

Carter looked disappointed, but he knew better than to argue. For his part, Max ruffled the boy's hair. "She's right, kiddo. I need to put my suitcase upstairs in my room and then head over to the café for lunch. I shouldn't be gone all that long, though. After that, we can get started."

"Okay, Mr. Max."

She thought they had everything settled, but then Max peeked into the shopping bag. "Huh. There seems to be one more present in here. I wonder who that could be for?"

He pulled a gift-wrapped box out, this time offering it to Rikki. "Looks like this one has your name on it."

Rikki stared at the package. She knew she should do something, but she couldn't bring herself to take it from his hands. Max rose to his feet and stepped closer. "It's just a little present, Rikki. I saw it and thought of you. It's no big deal."

But it was, at least to her. She couldn't remember the last time anyone had surprised her with a gift of any kind. Well, other than the handmade projects Carter made for her. Granted, she always displayed his macaroni art with great pride, but still.

She finally managed to reach for the present. "Thank you, Max. I mean that."

Max nodded, but her son had lost patience

with her. "Open it, Mom. That's what you do with presents."

He was right, of course. With shaky hands, she set the package down on the counter and started the painstaking process of unwrapping it without tearing the paper. Both males stared at her as if she'd lost her mind. "What?"

Carter shook his head. With a stage whisper, he told her, "You're doing it wrong, Mom."

Showing his solidarity, Max put his hand on Carter's shoulder and offered her a hint of a smile. "He's thinking you're supposed to get excited and tear into it."

Rikki was flashing back to her own childhood. "I don't get many presents, and I like to savor the experience. Besides, my grandmother always saved wrapping paper to use again."

Max grinned at her. "Where's the fun in that?"

"Fine, I'll do it your way this time."

When she tore off the paper in one quick yank, Carter applauded. "Good job, Mom! That's how it's done."

She lifted the lid off the box and tossed it aside. Her breath caught in her chest as she studied Max's gift. "You shouldn't have. But I'm glad you did."

Carter was bouncing in place. "What is it, Mom?"

She lifted the book out of the tissue paper with care. "It's a cookbook. One I've admired for a long time. A famous chef named Julia Childs wrote it, and it's all about French cooking."

"But you already have a bunch of cookbooks." He frowned, looking at his friend and then back at her. "And it looks old."

Rikki gently traced the title with her fingertip. "That's what makes it special, Carter. The original edition came out seventy years ago. It's one of the most famous cookbooks ever."

When she opened the cover, she was shocked to realize that it was actually a first edition. Not only that, it was autographed. "Max, this had to cost a fortune. It's too much."

"It didn't cost me anything, Rikki. It belonged to my grandmother, who passed it along to my mom. She wasn't much of a cook, so it's pretty much been collecting dust on a shelf. I was clearing out some stuff in my garage and ran across it. You were the first person I thought of, and I knew you'd give it a good home."

What should she do now? They didn't exactly have the kind of relationship that included hugs, but he deserved that and more for this. Finally, remembering his sweet tooth, she settled for something less intrusive but that he'd still appreciate. "Thank you, Max. And for being so thoughtful, you get to pick what kind of cookies Carter and I bake this afternoon."

Her offer clearly hit the bull's-eye. He rubbed his hands together greedily, a big grin on his face. "Wow—what are my choices, and how many do I get?"

She paused briefly to consider what ingredients she had on hand. "Sugar cookies, chocolate chip, snickerdoodles, oatmeal raisin, or cream cheese spritz."

He turned to Carter for advice. "What do you think? The chocolate chip or the cream cheese?"

How like him to make sure her son's opinion mattered. It was one of many reasons she'd missed Max more than she should have when he'd checked out the last time he was in Dunbar. If he continued in this same vein, it would be even harder to watch him walk away again.

Carter didn't hesitate. "Chocolate chip is my favorite."

"Then chocolate chip it is." Turning back to Rikki, Max asked, "Will they have nuts, too? I like walnuts, but not pecans."

"Walnuts are doable. Do you prefer milk chocolate, bittersweet, or white chocolate?"

Once again, he consulted Carter. "What do you think?"

Her son gave her a quick look and shrugged. "I like them all."

Max's blue eyes twinkled when he met her gaze over her son's head. "Me, too. We want some of each."

She surrendered without even putting up a token fight. "It's a deal."

CHAPTER TWO

MAX STOPPED OUTSIDE of the café and took a calming breath. So far, everything was going his way, and he didn't want his good mood destroyed by somebody's thoughtless comments. Bracing himself for the worst, he opened the door and stepped inside. He remained by the door long enough to let his eyes adjust to the dim interior.

Luck was with him. Only about half of the tables were occupied. That gave him a chance to scope the place out, and no one even glanced in his direction while he waited to be seated. Two seconds later, Titus himself picked up a menu and headed his way. His expression wasn't exactly welcoming, but then that was typical of him. "I heard you were back."

"I am."

"For how long?"

"A while."

The other man gave him a considering look.

"Why? Are you here to lay claim to something else in town?"

Rikki's image immediately flashed through Max's head, but she was a *someone*, not a *something*. That wasn't anyone else's business, so he settled for a different truth. "Nope. Shelby Michaels invited me back to tour the new display in the museum."

Titus crossed his arms over his chest and leaned against the counter. "Yeah, that might take all of fifteen minutes, tops. That barely justifies an overnight stay."

The man wasn't wrong about that. He also was unlikely to buy Max's explanation that he'd forgotten the museum wasn't open on Thursday afternoons. They both knew Shelby Michaels wouldn't hesitate to open the museum to give Max a private tour.

"Fine. I could've driven in from Portland tomorrow morning to see the display, but the truth is I didn't want to miss out on the Thursday special here at your café. Please tell me you have at least one helping of the chicken and dumplings left."

Titus snorted at the idea. Everybody in town knew they had to get to the café extra early on Thursdays if they wanted to score some of that savory goodness. "It's usually all gone by now, but I'll check. If we're out, I'll bring you something else. Take that four-seat table in the back corner."

At any other restaurant, Max would've pointed out that he preferred to choose his own lunch, but there was no use in provoking Titus. During his prior stay in town, he'd eaten at the café almost daily and never had a bad meal. The real issue was that he would've preferred to sit closer to the door so he could make a quick exit if it became necessary. He wasn't in town to cause trouble, but past experience said it might come looking for him anyway.

But rather than ignore an edict from Titus, he'd take his assigned spot and hope for the best. He'd survive even though it meant he'd have to parade across a room full of people who weren't all that fond of him. Bracing himself for whatever might happen, he calmly strolled across the café, head up and shoulders back. He had every right to be there, and Titus had made his welcome clear by taking Max's order himself.

Once he was seated, he checked his email and answered a few messages. He'd also gotten a text from the editor of an online magazine acknowledging he'd received and approved the article Max had written for him. The funds would be transferred into Max's account by Monday at the latest.

So, job done. He still had several other articles he was working on, enough to keep him busy and financially afloat for the next few months. He might have to make an occasional trip to do research, but he'd built enough time into his schedule to allow for that while still working on his new project.

A shadow fell over his table, drawing his attention back to the present moment. He looked up to thank his server for the quick service, but the words died unspoken. Instead of someone delivering Max's lunch, the man looking down at him was Dunbar's chief of police, Cade Peters.

"Chief Peters, how can I help you?"

The other man tossed his hat on the table and sat down. "Titus thought you might like some company."

Right.

"So he took the time to let you know I was back before bringing me my lunch?"

Cade laughed. "He didn't have to. I heard

about you moving back into Rikki Bruce's place within minutes of you parking your car. A concerned citizen felt it was his duty to report the renewed threat to the town."

Yep, the gossip grapevine was alive and thriving in Dunbar. "Let me guess. This concerned citizen drives an old Chevy sedan and had three companions with him, one of whom had a blurry photo of me."

"Pretty much. I told them you were here in response to Shelby's invitation to see the new display at the museum."

"Did that calm them down?"

Cade huffed a small laugh. "Not particularly, but I told them to leave you alone and to stay away from Rikki's place this time."

Hopefully they'd listen to Cade. Even if they didn't, at least the man had tried. "Thanks, I appreciate it."

"Anytime." Cade leaned forward, elbows on the table. "So, do you have any big plans for the rest of the day?"

Max mirrored Cade's actions, meeting his gaze head on. "Nothing set in stone. Why?"

"I wanted to invite you over to my place for dinner tonight. Say around seven o'clock, if that works for you."

The invitation was unexpected, but not unwelcome. Max had a lot of respect for Cade. The man had risked his own career by defending Max's right to a fair hearing when he'd presented his claim for the Trillium Nugget. "I'll be there. Can I bring anything?"

"It will just be the two of us and Titus. He already offered to bring the food, and I'll provide the beer."

"Sounds great."

Before Max could say anything else, one of the servers arrived with a folding stand and set it up next to the table. She made a second trip to the kitchen, this time returning with a large tray piled high with food. After settling it on the stand, she quickly distributed the plates. It was hard not to laugh when Cade realized that Max had gotten the highly coveted chicken and dumplings while he had to settle for a bacon cheeseburger with sweet potato fries. A third plate matched Cade's. Maybe it was for Shelby Michaels, the curator of the local museum. She and Cade had fallen in love while investigating the history of the nugget.

Max gave the plate a pointed look. "Is Ms. Michaels joining us?"

Cade looked disgusted. "No, she ate earlier to make sure she got the special. I had a scheduled video conference with the county sheriff and couldn't get away in time."

He glared at Max's plate. "So how did you rate the last serving of the special?"

By that point, Titus had arrived. "Because he got here before you," he said, settling into the chair beside Cade. "If you'd gotten here first, you'd be the one lording your good fortune over him. Now eat before your food gets cold."

Max didn't need to be told twice. The savory chicken and fluffy dumplings were every bit as good as he remembered. Even so, the best part of the meal was knowing that his two companions had gone out of their way to make him feel welcome. Their acceptance might go a long way toward convincing the citizens of Dunbar to do the same.

So far, checking into the B and B and then venturing out to the café had gone smoothly. However, if the protests started up again at Rikki's place, he would have to leave. But maybe, just maybe, with Cade and Titus on his side, he'd be able to execute the rest of his plan.

"When is Mr. Max coming back?"

Rikki joined her son at the front window. "I don't know, Carter. He said he was going to the café for lunch, but maybe he had other errands to run."

She hated the look of disappointment on her son's face when he looked up at her. "He promised to help me with the kit he brought me. The cookies are ready and everything."

"I'm sure he hasn't forgotten."

But if he had, she and Max would be having words. She didn't expect guests to entertain her son, but Max was different. He'd gone out of his way to befriend Carter on his last stay. If he wasn't interested in maintaining that friendship, then he shouldn't make promises that he didn't want to keep. Carter deserved better.

Rikki did, too, but her son's needs came first. Too many people had disappointed him—his father and her former in-laws were all on that list. Why would she expect any better treatment from a passing stranger than she had from Carter's own family members?

She'd been on the verge of calling Max to read him the riot act when Carter started bouncing in place as he pointed down the street. "There he is, Mom! Max didn't forget."

"That's great, Carter."

From the way Max was hustling, the man was well aware that he was late. Good. She might not have to tear into him for disappointing her son. "Why don't you go wait in the library? Now that Mr. Volkov is back, I'll go fix a plate of cookies and drinks for the two of you."

Carter reluctantly headed for the library while she waited for Max to arrive and gave thought to exactly what she wanted to say to him. At the very least, he should have called to let Carter know he was running late. Before she got it all straight in her mind, the phone rang. By the time the front door opened, she was at the front counter verifying a new reservation for one of her regular visitors.

Rather than heading for the library to find Carter, Max stopped at the counter and waited for her to finish the call.

"We'll look forward to seeing you this weekend, Ms. Billings. Have a safe drive over the pass."

When she hung up, Rikki finished typing in the last few details on the reservation before turning her attention to Max. "Was there something you needed?"

"I apologize for being late, but lunch ran longer than I expected. I didn't notice the time until I was on my way back."

He frowned. "I'm not sure why, but both Cade Peters and Titus decided to join me. I know it's too little and too late, but I should've called to let Carter know I hadn't forgotten about my promise to help him. I will apologize to him, too, but I wanted you to know I'm sorry if I kept him waiting."

It was nice that he recognized his error. Her frustration disappeared as she offered him the barest hint of a smile. "Apology accepted. Carter is in the library, but I can tell him if you need a minute to catch your breath."

"No, that's fine. I'm looking forward to helping him. He's not the only one who likes working on models."

Then he gave her a sly smile as he sniffed the air. "Just so you know, I turned down a piece of Titus's apple pie knowing there would be chocolate chip cookies waiting for me here. I'm betting Carter and I both work up quite an appetite by the time we get done."

With some effort, she mustered up a stern

look. "You're an adult, so I can't set a limit on how many cookies you consume in the process. However, as Carter's mother, I have to say too much sugar isn't good for him. The cookies are small, so he can have three, total."

"Ordinarily I would point out that leaves all the more cookies for me, but I'm guessing what you're actually saying is that I should set a good example for him."

"That would be nice."

He didn't bother to hide his disappointment. "I'm pretty sure three cookies aren't equivalent to one piece of apple pie, but I'll have to trust your judgment on the matter."

Rikki couldn't help but laugh. "Max, I never said you couldn't have more after Carter goes to bed."

"I'll hold you to that." He started down the hall but turned back. "By the way, Cade invited me to his place for dinner tonight. I'm not sure how late I'll be, so I'll take a raincheck on the extra cookies until tomorrow."

"Okay. And just so you know, I got a new reservation from another regular customer. Mrs. Billings will be arriving tomorrow afternoon, and she likes a pot of tea and a little dessert after her long drive over the pass from where she lives in Spokane. I'll make sure to set some cookies aside for you, though."

"That's great. Now I'm off to hang out with Carter."

Rikki watched as he disappeared down the hall and wondered why his dinner plans left her feeling a bit…she guessed *disappointed* was the word she was looking for, which was kind of silly on her part. After all, she ran a bed-and-breakfast. Just as the name implied, breakfast was the only meal included in the price of the room. It was to be expected that Max would make arrangements to eat dinner elsewhere, while she fixed a simple meal for herself and Carter.

The trouble was that during his prior stay, Max had brought back food from the café for the three of them several times. Not only had she gotten a break from having to cook, but she'd also enjoyed sharing a meal with another adult. Carter was the center of her universe, but the topics of their dinner discussions didn't often qualify as stimulating conversation.

Until Max had called to make his reservation, she'd had no idea if he would ever visit Dunbar again. But now that he was back, she found herself remembering how much she'd enjoyed spending time with him. Not only had they shared a few meals, but there'd been a couple of nights they'd shared a bottle of wine and a cheese tray after she tucked Carter in for the night. They'd also watched a few movies together and spent other evenings reading in the same room.

It wasn't that she really needed—or wanted—a man in her life. No, it was more that she sometimes felt starved for adult company: people who were personal friends, not simply guests there for a brief stay. Her mind immediately thought of Shelby Michaels and her friend, Elizabeth Glines. Shelby ran the town's post office as well as the historical museum that was housed in the same building, while Elizabeth was a stay-at-home mom. She had two kids, and her husband made his living as a fishing and hunting guide. Rikki didn't know either woman well, but she liked them both.

They came to her bed-and-breakfast at least twice a week to use the small gym in the sunroom along the back of the house. The previous owner of the B and B had set it up for guests, but she'd also allowed the local women to make use of it for a small monthly charge. Rikki had decided to continue the practice when she bought the place. While it didn't earn her a ton of money, every little bit helped the bottom line. That was especially true in the winter months when the tourist industry was a little more hit-and-miss.

She'd already started joining Shelby and Elizabeth when they stopped by for a workout. They didn't get to talk much, but it had been a place to start. Shelby had recently invited her to check out their book club that met once a month. If Rikki decided to join, she'd need to find a sitter for Carter, but it might be worth it. Since moving to town, she'd been too busy settling into her job here at the B and B to have much time for socializing. That became even more true when she bought out the previous owner and started on the long process of renovating the place.

There was still a lot of work left to do, but exercising on a regular basis with friends was good for her physical health. Discussing books with other adults would also be a step up from the picture books that she and Carter read together. Logic said she shouldn't feel guilty about wanting a little time for herself. When she and Carter stopped to pick up their mail tomorrow, she would ask Shelby what book her group was reading next and go from there.

For now, though, she'd better go fix the treats she'd promised Carter and Max before her son started complaining. She stacked six cookies on a plate and set it on a small tray. After fixing her son a cup of apple juice, she filled a mug with coffee for Max.

Rikki stopped short of the open library door to listen briefly to the conversation coming from inside the room. Both Carter and Max were laughing about something, so they were clearly enjoying themselves. While her son was often a bit shy around new guests, he'd taken to Max from the first day. Since taking over the B and B, Rikki made sure her son knew the breakfast buffet in the dining room was for their guests. He had to wait until they had finished eating before he could help himself. However, Max had been eating alone and invited Carter to join him, saying he would appreciate the company.

The rule was there for a reason, but Max had gradually convinced her to let Carter join him as long as there were no other guests around. She'd made a point of reminding her son that Max would eventually leave and not to get too attached. The warning hadn't prevented Carter from moping around for a few days after Max checked out.

Eventually he'd leave again, this time for good. She only wished she didn't find that thought so depressing. Telling herself that was a problem for another day, she pasted a smile on her face and carried the tray into the library. One look at the table where they were working had her laughing. The small blocks were scattered over the entire surface.

"Carter, when you opened the box, was it set to explode?"

He looked confused by her question, but Max grinned. "We spread everything out so we could start sorting the blocks by type, size and color. Once we finish doing that, we're going to check to make sure we have everything we need."

Her son gave her a superior look and explained. "Yeah, Mom. With a model of this size and complexion, you have to be organized."

Max leaned in close to Carter and whispered, "That's complexity, not complexion."

Her son frowned and then nodded. "Sorry, I meant complexity. That means there's a whole lot of parts that we have to keep track of. Complexion is how your skin looks."

It was hard not to laugh at her son's definitions. Max must have already had to explain the difference to Carter once before. "It's nice you have a plan of action, Carter. I can't wait to see it when it's done."

He reached for his juice and a cookie. "We're only going to get everything organized today. We won't start putting stuff together until tomorrow, right after breakfast. Mr. Max had a long drive to get here today, and he's already tired. I guess it's because he's old and not young like me."

Max wasn't the only one who winced at her son's last comment. After all, although she didn't know exactly how old the man was, she and Max were probably around the same age. "Well, I'll let you two get back to work."

She stopped to ruffle her son's hair and stage-whispered, "Take it easy on the old man here, Carter. He's supposed to meet some friends for dinner, and we don't want him to be too tired to go."

Carter was busy picking the red blocks out of the piles. "He already told me, Mom."

Max shot her a dark look that promised retribution. But then he grinned at her and winked, his blue eyes twinkling with amusement and a hint of something else that kicked her pulse up a notch. Deciding that beating a hasty retreat was the wisest move, she picked up the tray and started for the door.

"Have fun, boys."

Her son called after her. "I'm a boy, Mom. Mr. Max is a man!"

Yes, he was, and a handsome one at that, not that she was going to admit it to either Carter or Max. "Sorry, kiddo. You're right, of course. He is a man."

As she left the room, Max mumbled something under his breath that sounded an awful lot like he was glad she'd noticed. Before she could decide if she was right about that, someone knocked on the front door. Maybe she had more unscheduled guests. She hoped so. Not only could she use the extra business, but they would also serve as a distraction to keep her from thinking too much about Maxim Volkov's easy smile and broad shoulders.

CHAPTER THREE

MAX HAD NEVER been to Cade Peters's house before, but he had no trouble finding it. The rustic log cabin sat at the edge of a peaceful meadow surrounded by huge Douglas firs and tall cedars. Although the place was located only a short distance from the center of town, the trees blocked the view of any neighboring houses, offering Cade a great deal of privacy.

After parking his car, Max got out and looked around. The temperature was pleasantly cool, and the air smelled fresh and clean. Smiling, he walked over to the porch and dropped into the chair next to Cade's. "You've got a nice place here. I bet you enjoy the peace and quiet a lot."

Cade nodded. "I do. I've been renting, but I recently reached out to the owners to see if they might be willing to sell. If they won't, then I'll start looking for a piece of property and build something similar."

He pointed toward the woods. "The only problem with that is that I'll have to find a new bunch of four-legged neighbors to hang out with."

It took Max a second to spot a small group of black-tailed deer skirting the edge of the trees before slowly walking farther out into the clearing to graze. When a pickup pulled up behind Max's car, they didn't even look up. Max was pretty much a city boy, so his experience with living close to nature was pretty limited. Regardless, it seemed odd that the deer weren't at all skittish about being so close to humans.

"Are all deer so tame?"

Cade shrugged. "This particular bunch has acted that way ever since I moved in. Stranger yet, they don't even take off running when Titus shows up with his dog in tow. Ned scares some people, but the herd doesn't seem to be bothered by him."

As if to prove Cade's point, Ned hopped out of Titus's truck and trotted over to explore the clearing. He got within sniffing distance of the deer before finally heading for the porch. He stopped to greet Cade before moving on to Max. It was understandable why some people might find the dog intimidating. He was huge and looked to be a mix of German shepherd and maybe golden retriever. Max let the dog sniff his hand to see if he remembered him from when he'd spent time in Titus's café on his last visit to Dunbar. When the dog leaned into his touch, Max stroked his soft fur. "He's gotten friendlier."

Titus was busy filling Ned's water bowl and then setting out a second one already filled with kibble. "He's always easier to get along with when there's food in his immediate vicinity."

Cade laughed. "That's true of me, too."

"Well, in that case, I'd better feed you." Titus paused to look around. "I thought you said something about beer."

"I didn't want it to get warm while I was waiting for you to show up. I'll be right back."

When Cade stood, Max started to get up, too. "Can I do anything to help?"

"Nope, I'll get it."

Titus handed Max a paper bag and set one just like it on Cade's chair before taking his own seat. "Hope you like corned beef."

"I do."

Just to be polite, Max waited until Cade returned and passed out the drinks before opening the bag that Titus had given him. Wow, the man's gift for providing excellent meals obviously extended beyond the stuff he offered the customers in the café. The corned beef was piled high on dark rye bread, the side salads were Max's favorites from the lunch menu, and there were two different flavors of mini pies.

"Thanks for all of this, Titus. It looks wonderful."

His response was typical for the taciturn café owner. "Don't talk. Eat."

Max offered him a quick salute. "Yes, sir."

That earned him an eye roll accompanied by the merest hint of a grin before Titus turned his attention to Cade. He held up his beer and studied the label. "Have you been out scouting for more new microbrews again?"

Cade nodded. "I had a meeting last week over near Seattle. I'd heard about this brewery and thought I'd pick some up on my way home. I bought three different types. They're all good, but this is my favorite."

After taking a swig, Titus smiled in approval. "I can see why."

Max made a mental note to pick up some

of his own favorite microbrews the next time he made a trip back to Portland. If Cade and Titus made a habit of including him like this, it would only be polite to contribute his fair share when it came to the refreshments. He spent so much time on the road that he couldn't remember the last time he had friends to hang out with like this. It felt good.

"You're thinking awfully hard over there, Max."

Cade was too observant. Rather than risk sounding pitiful, he lied. "I'm just thinking about the new display at the museum. I'm looking forward to seeing it."

That much was true, but there was a lot more riding on this repeat visit to Dunbar than just seeing his great-grandfather's name on a display case.

"Shelby did a bang-up job on the new layout."

Considering how Cade had fallen hard for Shelby Michaels while they'd worked to prove the Trillium Nugget should remain in Dunbar, the man might be a bit prejudiced when it came to anything Shelby did. Regardless, Max believed him. Cade hadn't been the only one who had been impressed with the woman's fierce determination to protect the town's heritage. Shelby was as smart as she was beautiful, not that he'd mention his opinion on that last part to Cade.

Besides, Max's own interests lay elsewhere.

"Shelby offered to let me tour the museum tomorrow before it opens to the public. She's going to act as my tour guide rather than asking one of the other docents to do it. I really appreciate that."

Titus put his feet up on the porch railing. "What's the matter, Max? You afraid one of those octogenarians will try to exact a little revenge for all the trouble you caused the last time you were here? Like maybe conk you on the head with the nugget?"

Heck, yes, he'd prefer Shelby's company over the rest of the museum's board members. "I wouldn't put it past a couple of them. I don't know about you, but I'd think long and hard before taking on Ilse Klaus."

Both the other men grinned, but he noticed they didn't dispute his assessment of the threat that woman presented. No one with a lick of sense would deliberately provoke Ilse. She'd been the longtime mayor of Dunbar and a force to be reckoned with in local politics. But in a surprise move, her husband Otto had decided to run against her in the last election and won. He'd even made good on his sole campaign promise—to prevent his wife from painting the town's official vehicle to match the VW hippie van that she and Otto had owned back in the day. The couple was still given to wearing tie-dyed clothes on occasion, but even Otto had admitted that a flower-power van was a bit over the top for a government vehicle.

As far as Max could tell, Otto had pretty much run out of steam as a politician after briefly basking in the glow of having won that particular battle. For sure it had taken a lot of effort on the part of Cade and Shelby to help him deal with the threat Max had presented to the town's beloved nugget. Even before Max had left Dunbar, rumor had it that Ilse spent much of her time plotting her comeback campaign to oust her husband from office. If Max had to guess, Otto would be only too glad to hand the reins back over to his wife.

"Shelby mentioned that you might be sticking around for a while."

Cade seemed awfully interested in Max's

plans. Of course, he'd almost cost the man his job, so he had good reason to be concerned about what Max was up to now.

"Yeah, my reservation at Rikki's is open-ended. Shelby is going to show me the new exhibit tomorrow, but I'm planning on spending a lot more time at the museum in the foreseeable future doing research for something I'm working on."

When Cade frowned, Max set his drink aside. "For the record, I both like and respect Shelby, Cade. However, I do know you two are dating. I don't poach."

The man's answering smile was nothing short of smug. "Not just dating. We're engaged."

Max sat up straighter. "I hadn't heard that, but I can't say that I'm surprised. Congratulations to you both. Have you set a date?"

"Thanks, and we have." Cade sighed. "I was all for eloping, but she said there would be a lynch mob after me if I even suggested it."

Even Titus looked shocked by that revelation. "Seriously, Cade? What did you expect? The woman grew up here. You'll be lucky if everybody in town doesn't try to sneak into the church."

Max tried not to laugh at the glum look on Cade's face. "So I've been told. The only reason I even suggested it was that the church was already booked out for ten months. We took the first date available even though neither of us wanted to wait that long. The church secretary put us at the top of the waiting list in case there's a cancellation, even a last-minute one. Shelby's already got her dress, and I bought a tux just so we can be ready at the drop of a hat."

"I'll keep my fingers crossed for you."

At the same time, Max wondered if the couple wasn't seriously underestimating how much work would be involved in organizing such a big event. The few weddings Max had been dragooned into participating in over the years had involved a lot more work than merely changing into a tux and wedding gown. But if anyone could marshal her forces to pull off a successful wedding campaign with little or no notice, it would be Shelby.

Meanwhile, Cade smiled as he removed the lid from one of his mini pies and picked up his fork. "On another subject, I liked the piece you wrote on the national parks in our area. I've added a few of the trails you mentioned to my list of ones I want to try."

"I'm glad you found it helpful. I've got a couple more articles like it scheduled for later in the year. I'll let you know when they're published."

"Do that." Cade popped the top on another beer and passed it over to Titus before opening one for himself and another for Max. "I'll look forward to reading them."

"Must be interesting to be able to pick and choose what you write about," Titus said. "How did you get started as a freelance writer?"

Titus's question surprised Max. For a man who was pretty closemouthed about his own past, he seemed awfully curious about Max's. "I majored in journalism in college, envisioning myself doing cutting-edge reporting out on the streets or maybe in whatever war was raging at any given moment. However, my parents developed health issues and needed my help."

That had been eight years ago, and the nightmare of all that it had entailed remained a dull ache in his chest. "I ended up taking a job at a local paper. It didn't pay much, so I started taking on small side jobs to make ends meet. One thing led to another, and I ended up making more money as a freelancer. After my parents were gone, well, traveling for my job gave me something else to think about."

"Sorry, man. I didn't mean to hit a raw nerve."

"It's okay. You didn't know." He watched as the deer gradually made their way back into the trees, a reminder that it was time to head back to Rikki's. "Anyway, I sort of got in the habit of spending almost as much time on the road as I do at my place in Portland. I try to organize things so that I do the research for several articles on each trip before heading back home."

He finished off his drink. "Lately, though, I've been thinking it might be nice to stay in one place for a while."

"At least with the internet, I'm guessing it's possible to do a lot of your research remotely."

That came from Cade. "Yeah, it is. I already do most of my preliminary work that way. But I've found there's nothing like seeing and experiencing something firsthand to make my writing come alive."

"So are you thinking of making a career change?"

"More of a change in focus." Not wanting to reveal too much about that subject until he had all the pieces in place, Max decided to turn the tables and ask Cade a few questions of his own. "Why did you leave the military to become a cop in the civilian world?"

The man shrugged. "Bouncing all over the world got old. I grew up in the Midwest, but I fell in love with the Pacific Northwest when I was stationed at the joint bases up near Tacoma. My last overseas deployment was a rough one, and I decided enough was enough. I wanted to stay in law enforcement, but on a smaller scale. That's why I took the job here in Dunbar."

"I can see why that would appeal."

Max wondered if their discussion would spur the third member of their group into revealing something of his own past. From the way Cade was watching his friend out of the corner of his eye, Max guessed that he was having the same thoughts. For his part, Titus stared out across the clearing where the deer were still grazing, his expression somber. If Max had to guess, the man was looking into the shadows of his past, not even aware of the peaceful scene in front of him.

Ned had been dozing at Titus's feet, but he abruptly lurched to his feet with a soft whine and laid his head in his owner's lap. When that didn't spark a response, Ned gave Titus's hand a soft nip and followed it up with a loud bark. That did the trick, dragging the man's mind back to the porch. He blinked and then glared down at the dog. "What's your problem, Ned?"

Max hadn't realized that dogs were capable of rolling their eyes when their human companion said something particularly ridiculous, but Ned managed to pull it off. Stepping away from Titus, the dog turned in a circle twice before lying down, his back to his owner.

Cade carefully averted his own gaze, and Max followed suit to give Titus a chance to gather himself. A few seconds later, the man in question stood up. "I should get going. I've got prep work to do to get ready for tomorrow. Thanks for the beer, Cade. I'm guessing I'll see you tomorrow, Max. I'm trying a new recipe, and I'd appreciate your feedback."

"I'll be there."

When Max started to stand up, Cade motioned for him to hold off on that. Both men remained seated to give Titus some space as he gathered up Ned's bowls and stowed them back in their bag. "Come on, dog."

Still looking much put-upon, Ned took his time stretching before reluctantly following Titus over to the truck. As they walked away, Max called after them. "Thanks for feeding us tonight, Titus. If we get a chance to do this again, I'll pick up barbecue from that place over on Highway 2."

Titus didn't look back, but he raised his hand to acknowledge he'd heard Max's offer. When he was inside the truck with the door closed, Max asked, "Is he okay?"

Cade remained silent until the pickup disappeared from sight. "I'm not sure. He's a hard nut to crack. The quintessential mystery man."

As he spoke, he collected the empty beer bottles. Max took that as a signal that it was time for him to be going as well. "We all have our secrets."

Cade didn't dispute that, but he stared off at the woods with much the same expression on his face as Titus had. "Yeah, but I worry that his—whatever they are—might come back to bite him one of these days."

Did he know something about Titus's past or was he just guessing? Either way, it was none of Max's business. "Thanks again for inviting me. Tell Shelby I'll see her in the morning."

"I will. Maybe I'll join you at the café tomorrow. I'm curious what new dish Titus is adding to the menu."

Max would appreciate the company. "I usually get there after the lunch rush is over, but my schedule is flexible."

"I'll text you tomorrow."

"Sounds good."

As Max backed out of the driveway, he was aware that Titus wasn't the only one whose secrets continued to haunt him. He had a few of his own. Cade, too. And then there were those shadows that sometimes appeared in Rikki Bruce's pretty eyes when she thought no one was looking. Like Titus, she was incredibly tight-lipped about her past, so Max had no idea what might have left its mark on her.

But he had every intention of finding out.

CHAPTER FOUR

THE FLASH OF headlights had Rikki on her feet and looking out the front window for the fourth time in the past hour. When the car kept going, she sighed and returned to the computer behind the counter. After getting an unexpected guest settled for the night, she'd decided to get caught up on paperwork since Max still hadn't returned from his dinner with Cade Peters and Titus Kondrat. She wasn't his keeper but she still checked every time someone drove past her bed-and-breakfast. It was a waste of time, and what Max did when he left the premises was none of her business.

Her concern was left over from his last stay in Dunbar, when he was at the epicenter of a major controversy in the town. Not that she'd ever admit it to her friends and neighbors, but she'd thought their reaction to his assertion that the Trillium Nugget actually belonged to his family had been way over the top.

Yeah, she got that it was part of the town's history and everything. Maybe it was because she hadn't grown up in Dunbar, but she hadn't been able to get all worked up about it. The truth was that she had sympathy for both sides. As the showpiece of the town's museum, the nugget brought more than its share of tourists to Dunbar. The money they spent while they were there helped keep the town's economy stable.

Even though Max had actually been right about his great-grandfather discovering the nugget, Rikki worried that a few people in town would neither forgive nor forget the whole affair. For that reason, she wouldn't retire to her private quarters for the night until she knew he was back. Not that she wanted him to know she'd been waiting up for him like a parent counting down the minutes until their teenaged kid returned home with the family car.

She entered the last few bills in her spreadsheet. It was a relief to see that, barring any unexpected expenses, she should make it through the end of the month with a positive balance in her account. While she really loved owning her own business, it wasn't easy knowing its success or failure rested squarely on her shoulders. That's why she kept a small cushion set aside in case it all went horribly wrong. It wasn't much, but it would keep a roof over their heads and meals on the table long enough for her to find a job.

Not that she wanted to go back to working for someone else. However, she was all Carter had, and she took the responsibility seriously.

With the bills paid, she did a quick check of several of the online review sites to see if any of her recent customers had taken the time to post comments about their stay at the bed-and-breakfast. As much as any business owner hoped for all five-star ratings, that wasn't realistic. All she could do was provide the best service possible and keep her fingers crossed that her guests would post good reviews.

The first two places she checked hadn't changed since she'd looked the previous week, both showing a good solid four stars. The third site, though, had dropped down into the low threes. She reluctantly forced herself to read the sole new review. Someone had given her a single star with no explanation given. How was she supposed to improve her service if the unhappy customer couldn't be bothered to say what had gone wrong in their review?

Stewing over it wouldn't help, so she held her breath as she checked one last site. It was a huge relief to see the only new review was a five.

It was time to be done for the night. After she had logged off the computer and was gathering up the receipts to put away, another set of headlights flashed in the front window. This time the car slowed and turned into her driveway. She quickly finished the filing as she listened for the sound of footsteps coming up the sidewalk. The front door swung open just as she closed the file drawer and turned to greet her prodigal guest.

"Welcome back. Did you enjoy your dinner with Chief Peters and Mr. Kondrat?"

Max locked the door before joining her at the counter. "I did. Titus brought some really great corned beef sandwiches and his usual excellent desserts. Cade served a microbrew he picked up when he made a trip over to Seattle. A good time was had by all."

"Sounds nice."

"It was. I'd never been there before, but

Cade lives in a log cabin with a huge porch that faces a meadow. He even has his own herd of deer that comes out to graze there every night. I always thought deer were pretty skittish, but this bunch didn't mind having an audience, not even with Ned there."

She frowned. "Who is Ned?"

Max grinned. "He's that eighty-pound stray dog that moved in with Titus a while back. The mutt is scary-looking, not unlike his owner. But once Ned takes a liking to you, he's okay. And like I said, the deer didn't mind him hanging around."

He stopped to stare up at the ceiling for a second, his head cocked to the side as if he were listening for something. "Is Carter down for the night?"

"Yeah, he fell asleep halfway through the second book I was reading to him. He had a pretty exciting day working on the model with you. I want to thank you again for thinking of him like that."

"He's a good kid. Besides, I wasn't lying. I like working on models, too." He leaned closer and dropped his voice as if about to share a state secret. "I've got my eye on two more sets. Think Carter would enjoy building a pirate ship or maybe a Viking longship?"

She bought herself some time to think over what she should say by locking her laptop in a cabinet behind the counter. Carter would be thrilled for the chance to build either one. The problem was that it wouldn't do to let her son get even more attached to a man who would only be a short blip on their radar in the grand scheme of things. Her decision made, she stood up in order to meet Max's gaze head on. "I'm sure he'd love to put together either of those kits, Max. The only question is if he should."

Her guest frowned, his excitement extinguished in an instant. "I don't understand."

"He likes you, Max. Maybe a little too much, especially considering you'll eventually leave again. I can't in good conscience let you gift him with more expensive toys."

After a moment's silence, he nodded. "You're right, of course. I let my enthusiasm run away with me. Carter's a great kid, and I wouldn't want to hurt him."

He took a step back from the counter. "I'd better head up to my room now. I'm supposed to meet Shelby Michaels before the museum opens in the morning."

She'd been about to ask if he would like to join her for a glass of wine, but Max was already walking away. Had she hurt his feelings? She hoped not, but Carter had to come first in her life. Rather than let them end the evening on such a low note, she said, "I'm sure you're looking forward to seeing the new display about your great-grandfather. I'm betting Shelby has done a great job on it."

He paused on the first step. "Cade said she did, but I suspect he's a bit prejudiced considering he's engaged to the woman. See you in the morning."

"Good night, Max."

Once he disappeared upstairs, she made her rounds. After double-checking to make sure the front door was locked, she took care of a few chores in the kitchen to prepare for making breakfast in the morning. With that done, she turned off all the lights except for the ones in the entryway and out on the front porch.

Upstairs, she checked on Carter. He was a restless sleeper and, as usual, had kicked his blankets off. She tugged them back up in place and kissed his cheek before slipping back out of his room. A few minutes later, she settled into her own bed with the book she'd picked up at the bookmobile on its most recent visit to town. While it would be nicer to have a real library in town, at least the bookmobile allowed her access to an endless selection of books for her and Carter.

She plumped her pillows and opened the latest book by her favorite cozy mystery writer but lost interest after only a few pages. It wasn't the writing; she just couldn't stop thinking about the man sleeping one floor above her. It had been two months since his last visit, but it felt as if he'd never been gone. Strange how he seemed to fit seamlessly into their lives.

Finally, she gave up for the night and turned off the lamp. And as she curled up under the covers, it struck her that for the first time in recent memory, her bed seemed a little too big and a whole lot too empty.

BREAKFAST HAD BEEN a lonely affair. Normally, Carter slipped in to keep Max company, but he hadn't been able to do that today. He was upstairs playing in his room while Max was stuck eating breakfast burritos with an older man who must have checked in late last evening. The guy never stopped talking on his phone the whole time he was at the table.

At least he hadn't tried to engage Max in conversation. For Rikki's sake, he would've done his best to be polite, but he had other matters on his mind and no desire to get involved in a meaningless discussion with someone he didn't know. For sure, he hadn't enjoyed hearing all the details about some stranger's gallbladder surgery while he was eating. Finally, Max had grabbed his laptop and headed out the front door.

Since he had a little time to kill before his appointment at the museum, he decided to drop by the bakery in town for a cup of coffee and hopefully one of the owner's highly prized apple fritters. He also planned to pick up a couple of extras to share with Shelby and Cade. She was the one giving him a personal tour, but Cade would probably drop by if he could.

On Max's last visit to Dunbar, he'd actually avoided Bea O'Malley's bakery for two reasons. First, he hadn't been welcome much of anywhere in town as long as he was trying to reclaim the Trillium Nugget as his family's legacy. The second was Bea's reputation for being the town crier, as Titus was known to describe her. There wasn't a thing that went on in Dunbar the woman didn't consider fair fodder for her gossip mill. At least from what Max had heard, the news she passed along was only rarely mean-spirited.

She'd made an exception in his case. Hopefully, she and the rest of her fellow citizens had moved on now that the crisis had passed. Bracing himself, he opened the door and paused long enough to inhale the heady aroma of cinnamon and yeasty goodness.

Shuffling forward in line as the people ahead of him were served, he finally reached the counter. The smile Bea had offered everyone else was missing when she faced him. "You're back."

"Yes, I am. Shelby Michaels personally invited me to come see the new display at the museum." Not that he actually needed anyone's permission to return to town. It was a free country and all of that. "I thought I would buy three coffees and three of your fritters as a thank you gift for Shelby. The extra fritter and coffee is in case Chief Peters joins us."

The woman was obviously a hard sell, but Max was only willing to go so far to get back into the town's good graces. Finally, she nodded and slipped three of the fritters into a bag. After a brief pause, she added a fourth. "No charge for that one. My mother is scheduled as the docent on duty today, and she'll appreciate a treat."

Max knew a hint when he heard one. "In that case, please add a coffee for her, too."

With his purchases in hand, he smiled and nodded at a few familiar faces as he made his way to the exit. He might not have completely won over Bea, but at least he'd made a start. That would make his life easier now that he'd returned to Dunbar for an extended period of time.

As he headed the short distance down the street to the ramshackle building that housed both the town's small post office and the museum, he thought back to the unsatisfactory conversation he'd had with Rikki last night about Carter. Would she be happier if he found somewhere else to stay for Carter's sake? If so, he'd do his best to honor her wishes no matter how much he hated the very idea.

That was a discussion for later.

A familiar figure appeared down the street. Cade Peters had just walked out of the police department and was headed his way. Max knew the man had a habit of making a trip down to Bea's place every morning for coffee. If Titus was to be believed, the ladies in town used to make excuses to be out and about in time to watch Cade pass by. Evidently, there was a dearth of eligible men in town, and they had all been vying for the new police chief's attention. There had also been a steady parade of ladies dropping off casseroles so Cade didn't have to cook for himself.

How had Shelby felt about her competition? From what he knew of her, he bet she'd found a way to put a stop to their efforts. He also wondered if the women had found a new target for their culinary flirting. Not that Max was interested. Somehow, he doubted Rikki would appreciate him loading up her refrigerator with a bunch of casseroles from random women.

Meanwhile, he and Cade met up at the door to the post office. Max held up the tray full of cups and the bag containing the fritters. "I thought Shelby would appreciate coffee and a fritter."

Cade eyed the grease-stained bag with greedy interest. "That's a pretty big bag for just one fritter."

"Obviously I bought one for myself, and Bea asked me to bring one to her mother, too."

Then he grinned at the other man. "There was still room in the bag, so I added one for you. No one wants to see you looking all pitiful while Shelby and I pig out on ours."

"Don't be a jerk. Besides, Shelby would've shared hers with me."

The door opened to reveal the woman in question. "What would I share with you?"

Max held up the bag. "The fritter I brought for you."

She gave Cade an incredulous look. "Aren't you the same guy who once told me a real friend would never ask me to share a fritter?"

Cade looked a bit insulted. "I'm not just a friend. I'm your fiancé. Engaged couples share important stuff all the time."

Max surrendered the bag to her outstretched hand. "This is the exact situation

I was hoping to avoid. That's why I bought one for him, too. Bea sent along one for her mother if she's here…"

"I knew I liked you, Max."

She might now, but she sure hadn't when he'd first come to town. He was glad the three of them were making an effort to put all of that behind them.

"Why don't we go eat these in the break room? After that, we can head over to the museum. Helen hasn't come in yet, but she should be along any minute."

The three of them settled in at the small table in the break room. Shelby grabbed napkins for all three of them, and then sat down. "How was your drive over from Portland?"

"There was a brief slowdown in Olympia, but I've seen worse. At least it was a nice day for the drive."

As she distributed the coffee and pastries, Shelby asked, "Is Rikki happy to have you back as a repeat customer?"

He thought back to the boy leaping into his arms as soon as he spotted Max waiting at the bottom of the steps, and he smiled. "Both she and Carter seemed glad to see me."

"Carter sure is a cutie. I don't know if she

told you, but Rikki is thinking about joining our book club. I hope she does, because it would give me a chance to get to know her better and vice versa. My friend Elizabeth and I both work out in the small gym at the B and B, and Rikki has started joining us whenever she can."

That was good to hear. On his last stay, he'd noticed that Rikki rarely interacted with anyone other than her guests. She should have friends that she could depend on here in Dunbar if she and Carter intended to make the town their permanent home. That left him wondering what Rikki did with Carter when she couldn't take him with her. He'd have to tell her that he'd be glad to keep an eye on him for her if he was around. Surely she'd trust him with her son for a few hours. The two of them could watch a movie or even hole up in the library to work on another model.

Shelby and Cade took turns entertaining Max with a few stories about things that had happened since he'd left town.

Once all three of them had devoured their fritters, Cade checked the time. "I'd better head back to the office. Thanks for the fritter and coffee, Max."

A few seconds later, he reappeared. "I think Helen just came in. Do you want me to send her this way?"

Shelby stood up. "No, that's okay. We're heading over to the museum in just a second."

"I'll pick you up after I get off work."

"Until then." She wrapped her arms around Cade and gave him a quick kiss. Evidently, that wasn't enough to satisfy him, because he tightened his hold on her and deepened the kiss.

To afford them some semblance of privacy, Max finished off his coffee and headed to the sink to wash the sticky remains of the fritter off his hands. They were both good people and a perfect fit for each other. He was truly pleased for the couple, but it was hard not to envy them. He'd like a little of that kind of happiness in his own life, but he spent too much time on the road to make that kind of connection with anyone. He'd never wanted to stay put in one spot long enough to really try.

But the truth was that wanting to honor his great-grandfather wasn't the only reason he wanted to take up residence in Dunbar for the foreseeable future. There was something else that had tempted him to return—the chance to get to know Rikki Bruce a whole lot better.

CHAPTER FIVE

BY THE TIME Cade walked away, Shelby looked thoroughly kissed and not a little embarrassed. "Sorry about that, Max. That was probably unprofessional behavior on my part."

"Cade's, too." He grinned and mimed zipping his lips. "Luckily, I had my back turned and didn't see a thing."

"Yeah, right. Regardless, are you ready to start your tour?"

"I'm looking forward to it. I also really appreciate your letting me see the new display before the museum opens for the day."

"I thought you might want some privacy. Besides, one of the local tour bus companies recently added a stop here in Dunbar to their route. Not everyone visits the museum, but we sometimes get quite a crowd. It's been a nice boost to the local economy. They usually pull up out front about half an hour after we open."

She smiled. "I just hope you like what we've done with the display. Earl Marley and Oscar Lovell worked hard on the design and layout. Your assistance with writing the narrative was a huge help. A lot of the locals who've read it have commented on how much they learned about our town's history."

As she spoke, she led the way back up the hall and through the door into the museum. "Do you want to go straight upstairs or look around down here first? I suspect you didn't really get much out of your first visit."

That was putting it mildly. He'd been too intent in seeing the nugget his great-grandfather had discovered. "Let's go upstairs first. I can always look around the rest of the museum on my own."

"Sounds like a plan."

When they reached the top of the steps, Shelby looked around. "Helen, are you up here? Mr. Volkov bought you some coffee, and your daughter asked him to bring you a fritter."

A door in the back corner opened, and the older woman stepped into sight. While Cade and Shelby had both been welcoming, it was clear Helen Nagy had very different feelings about Max's return.

He held out the bag with the fritter and the cup of coffee. "They're both still warm."

She jerked her head in a quick nod toward the cluster of desks in the corner. "Just set them down over there."

He did as ordered before joining Shelby in front of the glass-fronted case that held the nugget. They'd moved it out of the center of the room and nearer the wall that now held a display of photographs that had all been taken around the same time the nugget had been discovered. Lev, his great-grandfather, was featured in several. Max stood back to study the display in its entirety before moving closer to start reading the already familiar text.

When the phone rang, Helen answered it and signaled Shelby it was for her. "It's the mayor, Shelby. Don't worry, I'll keep a close eye on Mr. Volkov for you."

There was no missing the barely veiled suspicion in the older woman's voice, but Max didn't respond. Nor did he acknowledge her presence when she stalked across the room to hover just at the edge of his peripheral vision, sneering at him with her hands on her hips. Clearly forgive and forget wasn't in the cards when it came to the elderly docent. As he finished the first part of the display and moved to his right, she stood her ground until the last second before backing up just far enough to allow him to stand in front of the second panel.

Unfortunately for Helen, he wasn't the only one who'd noticed her hostile behavior. As soon as Shelby finished talking to the mayor, she took matters into her hands. "Helen, what do you think you're doing?"

Not for a second did the woman take her eyes off Max. "Like I said, I'm keeping an eye on him."

"Oh, for Pete's sake." Shelby stalked closer. "No one has to keep an eye on Mr. Volkov. He's here at my invitation to view the new display."

Still not ready to surrender, Helen pointed at him. "The last time he came to town, he wanted to steal our nugget. What makes you think he isn't here to try again?"

"That does it, Helen. Get your purse and go home. I won't stand for you insulting our special guest."

The older woman stood her ground. "I don't trust him, and you shouldn't either. How do you know that he won't destroy the display as soon as you turn your back?"

"Because he footed the bill for all of the changes, Helen. Didn't you wonder where we suddenly got the money to redo not only this display but several of the others? Even if Max hadn't done that, he wrote all of the text for the display. I will remind you that he makes his living as a writer, but he did it for free to honor his great-grandfather."

By that point, the other woman looked a bit sick. "You never said a word about the money or about him helping Oscar with the writing."

"That's because he asked me not to." Shelby glanced in his direction. "Sorry about that, Max, but I lost my temper."

"No problem." He finally faced Helen directly. "I would appreciate you not sharing that information with anyone else. I prefer to work behind the scenes."

"I will, Mr. Volkov, and I apologize. I'll go home now."

Before Helen had gone three steps, he made a snap decision. "Please don't leave, Helen. Stay and enjoy your coffee and fritter. No use in letting them go to waste. I understand why you were concerned, but you have my word that I have no further designs on the nugget. Far more people will learn about Grandpa Lev with the nugget here in the museum where they can read about his life."

"Thank you, Mr. Volkov. I'll do that if it's all right with Shelby."

He'd done his part to diffuse the situation. Turning his attention back to the photos on the wall, he let Shelby hash things out with her recalcitrant volunteer. A few minutes later, Helen headed downstairs to restock the small gift shop in advance of the museum opening for the day.

"That was nice of you, Max, especially since Helen isn't the easiest person to get along with. I'm not sure I could've been as forgiving as you were."

That was the opening he'd been waiting for. "About that. I have to admit that my reasons for trying to make peace are actually selfish ones."

"How so?"

"I'd really like to write a book based on Lev's adventures when he emigrated from Russia to this country. In order to do that, I would need to utilize various resources here in the museum and would be in and out a lot. Things will go more smoothly if I can make peace with everyone concerned."

"True enough." Shelby hesitated before adding, "Just to be clear, I can't let you take anything out of the museum. It's against our policies. I'm sure you can understand why."

That was disappointing. After a second's thought, he nodded. "I do understand. Maybe I could work here in the museum if you have a spare desk or even a table I could use. I wouldn't want to be in the way when you have people coming through. I could always come before the museum opens or limit my time here to the afternoon that you're closed."

Shelby studied him. "So you'll be staying at Rikki's, not going back and forth to Portland?"

"Yeah. She agreed to rent me her best room on a month-to-month basis. There'll be times where I have to leave for short periods of time to do research for my freelance articles, but otherwise I'll be right here in Dunbar."

While he hadn't actually expected Shelby to jump up and down in excitement over the prospect, he also hadn't expected her to be frowning so hard. Finally, she nodded. "I'll run your request to work here by the rest of the board. You have my vote, but the others should have a chance to weigh in on the subject."

At least she wasn't rejecting his request outright. "Any idea when you might have an answer?"

"The board won't meet for another couple of weeks, but I'm guessing you'd rather we didn't wait that long. I can ask Helen what she thinks and then call the others. I'll try to let you know one way or the other by tomorrow. If they have questions, I'll get in touch."

"That's all I ask."

He turned back to the display. "This all turned out really well, Shelby. I've reached out to several local papers and online magazines about the possibility of doing some articles about the museum and its history. No promises, but a couple asked for more information about what I have in mind."

Her eyes lit up. "That would be terrific. If I can be of any help with that, let me know. It would be great promo for the museum as well as the rest of the town."

"Like I said, there's nothing definite, but I'll keep trying."

Their conversation was cut off when Helen bellowed at Shelby from the bottom of the steps. "You're needed over in the post office."

Shelby rolled her eyes. "I'd better go see what's going on. I'll come back up as soon as I can."

"No need. I'll be fine up here on my own, and then I want to revisit the displays downstairs, too, if there's time before the bus arrives. I can always come back later if necessary."

"Okay, but stop by on your way out if you have any questions. I'll also start calling the board members as time allows. If I had to guess, Helen would've been the toughest sell, but I think maybe she's had a change of heart when it comes to you."

When she disappeared down the stairs, he smiled. Everything was falling into place rather nicely. Not only would he be able to write his book, he could also figure out why Rikki Bruce had haunted his dreams every night since he'd left Dunbar.

RIKKI STOPPED IN the dining room long enough to set out a tray of freshly baked cookies. Even though she only had two guests at the moment, she wanted to make sure neither one had reason to find fault with the service she provided. Seeing the coffee pot was half-empty, she filled a travel cup for herself and put a fresh pot on to brew.

"Oh good, I thought I smelled cookies."

Somehow Rikki hadn't heard Debra Billings walk up behind her, which startled her into bobbling one of the cups she'd been setting out on the buffet. At least she managed to catch it before it hit the floor. After adding it to the tray on the buffet, she turned to face the other woman. "Yes, I tried a new recipe that calls for butterscotch bits and macadamia nuts. Carter gave his approval, but then, that boy has never met a cookie he didn't like."

Debra smiled as she eyed the cookies rather greedily. "Well, if they taste as good as they look, I'm betting they're delicious."

"I'd appreciate your feedback. I just started the coffee, but it should be ready in just a couple of minutes."

Like Max, Debra was a repeat visitor to the bed-and-breakfast. Rikki didn't know much about the woman other than she was a semiretired nurse in her late fifties. She always dressed neatly and wore her hair in a short bob, the color a bit on the brassy end of the bottle-blond spectrum. Judging from the quality of her clothes, she must have money.

From what the woman had told her on her previous visits, she still took the occasional job as a private duty nurse. She lived on the other side of the state, somewhere near Spokane, but was considering moving back to western Washington where she grew up. She'd mentioned that Dunbar was sort of in the middle of where several of her relatives lived, which is why she stayed with Rikki whenever she came to visit them.

"Would you have an extra travel cup that I could borrow? I forgot to bring mine, and I'm heading off to visit my cousin today. I should be back by early evening. I don't really like driving after dark these days."

"Sure, I'll get one for you."

She returned with the cup and a plastic sandwich bag so Debra could take several of the cookies with her. "Help yourself to as many of the cookies as you'd like. I have more in the kitchen."

Debra wrinkled her nose. "I shouldn't, but I was going to spend some time on the treadmill when I get back anyway. These cookies are definitely worth doing a few extra minutes. Besides, it's not like my cousin is into healthy cooking. I don't think that woman has a single recipe that isn't deep-fried. It's all delicious, of course, but none of it is good for you."

Her complaints about her cousin's cuisine didn't stop Debra from cramming at least a dozen of the cookies into the bag Rikki had given her. That didn't include the two she'd eaten before Rikki left to fetch the travel cup. She'd have to refill the plate before Max returned.

After tucking the bulging bag in her oversized purse, Debra asked, "In case my plans change and I can't make it back until late, should I take a key with me?"

Rikki always hesitated before loaning out one of the house keys, but Debra had borrowed one before and had proven to be reliable about returning it. "Sure, I'll get one for you."

They walked through to the foyer, where Rikki kept the keys locked up in a small safe. "Here's your key. If I've already gone upstairs for the night when you get back, you can drop it into the same slot where you leave your room key when you check out."

"Thanks for trusting me with it."

"Anytime. I hope you have a nice evening."

A few seconds after Debra closed the door on her way out, the doorknob turned. She could see Debra walking by the front window, so it wasn't her at the door. Rikki ignored the sudden flutter of her pulse and resisted the urge to check her appearance in the mirror mounted on the entryway wall before Max walked in.

He looked to be in a good mood. His time with Shelby must have gone well. "Did you enjoy your visit to the museum?"

"I did. The display was everything I could have hoped for. They did a really nice job and found the right balance between celebrating the town's history while explaining the impact Lev's generous gift has had on Dunbar."

She was happy for him. Max had never shared many details about his past or why celebrating a man he'd never met had been so important to him, but she had no doubt that it had been nothing short of an obsession for some reason. Not that she was going to press him for details. She had her own secrets, ones that she had no desire to share with anyone. By moving to Dunbar and buying the bed-

and-breakfast, she'd turned the page on her past. All that mattered now was providing a stable future for her son.

Max looked as if he had something else to add to the conversation but wasn't sure if he should. Before he could make up his mind, her son hollered down the steps, "Is Mr. Max back?"

"Yeah, Carter, I'm back. You ready to get started on the kit?"

No matter how many times Rikki told her son to walk—not run—down the stairs, he'd never gotten the message. She wasn't sure how one small boy could make that much noise clomping down the steps. A few seconds later, he appeared, still charging full speed ahead. Before she could snap out a warning for him to slow down and be careful, Max stepped in to take charge. He held up his hand, "Whoa, there, Carter. I know your mom doesn't like you running down the steps, and I'd rather spend the afternoon playing with blocks instead of making a trip to the emergency room."

Carter came to an abrupt stop, grabbing on to the railing before his momentum could send him tumbling to the floor. When he'd regained his balance, Max issued one more order. "Now, go back up and show us that you do know how to come down the steps like the smart boy you are and not like a wild animal."

Rikki's temper flashed hot and furious. It wasn't that what Max had ordered her son to do was unreasonable. In fact, she would've done the same if given a chance. That was the point—it wasn't Max's place to discipline Carter. It was hers. Period. No one else's.

Meanwhile, her son trudged back up the steps before turning around to head back down, moving at a snail's pace. His lower lip jutted out just enough to make it clear what he thought of his hero calling him on the carpet. When he reached the bottom step, he sighed. "Can we work on our project now?"

Max shot her a considering look before answering. "Yes, but I think your mom has something she wants to tell me."

Smart man.

"While Mr. Volkov and I talk, Carter, why don't you go into the kitchen and fix yourself a glass of water to take into the library with you. Make sure you put it on a coaster."

He gave her a hopeful look. "And can I get

us some of the new cookies? You said you wanted Mr. Max's opinion."

She waited for several seconds before answering. No use in letting her son suspect that she was a pushover who could be bought and paid for with a flash of puppy-dog eyes. Finally, she nodded. "Yes, you can get some cookies. Two for you—" she gave Max a dark look to let him know he wasn't out of her bad books as yet "—and three for your friend here. Now go before I change my mind. He'll be along in a minute."

As soon as Carter disappeared into the kitchen, she turned on her guest. "I know you meant well, Max, but Carter is *my* son, not yours. I don't want him learning that it's okay for strangers to order him around. Most of my guests are nice people and probably trustworthy, but it's not as if I really get to know them. I would appreciate it if you would respect my wishes and not take it upon yourself to parent my son. As I said, that's my job. Please don't do it again."

He flinched as if her words hurt him in some way, but she wasn't going to apologize.

Max nodded but didn't say a word. He simply walked away. Was he rethinking his decision to stay at her B and B for the next few months? She'd hate that, but maybe it would be for the best. It wasn't as if he had mentioned any plans to return to Dunbar once he finished his research. Why would he?

A small voice in the back of her mind whispered, *Maybe because you and Carter live here*.

She waited until Max joined her son in the library before heading upstairs to change out the towels in her guests' rooms and make their beds. On the way, when that little voice started whispering again, she told it to shut up.

CHAPTER SIX

MAX HUNG OUT with Carter until Rikki told her son to get washed up for dinner. That left Max on his own and trying to decide if he wanted to walk back to Titus's café or check out a different restaurant in one of the nearby towns. Neither option held much appeal.

At least he and Carter had finished the model. Max seriously couldn't remember the last time he'd had so much fun. The kid was bright and easygoing. In fact, there was a lot about Carter that reminded Max of Rikki. They both had the same silvery-gray eyes and light brown hair. There were differences, though, which Carter had likely inherited from his other parent.

Max couldn't help but wonder about Carter's father. Rikki had never mentioned the man, and Max hadn't asked. If he were to guess, he figured the guy was no longer part of their lives and most likely hadn't been for a while. For starters, Rikki didn't wear a wedding ring, and while there were several pictures of her and Carter on display around the place, there was only one photo that featured a man. An older gentleman, perhaps one of Carter's grandfathers.

Another reason Max thought Carter's dad wasn't a major player in their lives was that Carter had never talked about him. Considering the way the kid chattered about anything and everything that crossed his mind, that particular omission stuck out. Again, Max had never brought up the subject since it really wasn't any of his business. As curious as he was to learn more about his pretty hostess and her past, grilling her son for information wouldn't be the smartest way to go about it. While Rikki hadn't kicked him to the curb when everyone else in Dunbar wanted to run him out of town, she wouldn't hesitate to toss him and his baggage out the front door if she thought he was any kind of threat to her son.

As if he'd conjured her up, Rikki appeared in the doorway. "Look, Max, I think I probably overreacted earlier, and I'm sorry."

"No problem. I understand your need to protect Carter, and I was out of line."

She shook her head. "No, you weren't. Not really. You even handled the problem the same way I would have, and we both know you're not really a stranger. Max considers you a friend, and you've never done anything to make me doubt your good intentions when it comes to my son."

All of which left Max wondering how Rikki herself felt about him. Did she only see him as a customer, or had he managed to slip across the line to being something more? Now wasn't the time to ask. Especially when Carter poked his head into the room. "Did you ask him, Mom?"

"I was about to, but remember, he might already have plans."

Two pairs of gray eyes stared at Max. While Rikki looked amused, her son's expression was more...hopeful, maybe. "Carter thought you might like to join us for dinner tonight. We're having his favorite meal—grilled cheese sandwiches with tomato soup."

"Yeah, and it's not the stuff from a can." Then Carter frowned. "Well, the tomatoes come out of a can, but they aren't soup yet. Mom has to do stuff to them first. It's really good, though. I promise."

The offer was definitely more appealing than his other options. "If you're sure. I know dinner isn't usually included."

Rikki didn't hesitate. "We're sure. Just know it's nothing fancy."

Max rose to his feet. "I don't need fancy, Rikki. I'd really love to eat with friends instead of alone at the café."

By that point, Carter was bouncing up and down. "Mom said we could each have a scoop of ice cream for dessert if we're on our best behavior."

Max didn't even try to hold back his laughter. "Thanks for the heads-up, Carter."

The boy took off for the kitchen, leaving the two adults to follow in his wake. When he was just out of hearing, Rikki whispered, "I was talking about Carter, not you."

"Good to know. Regardless, I'll be on my best behavior." Then he grinned and waggled his eyebrows as he added, "Well, unless a little bad behavior would earn me a second scoop."

He wasn't sure how she would react to the small flirtation. Even though her fair skin had turned a bit pink, she gave him a long look from his head to his toes and back up again to meet his gaze head on. Then she offered him a smile that held just a touch of heat. "I guess we'll have to wait and see how it goes. But just so you know, I'm pretty picky about who gets a second scoop."

Then she walked away, leaving him staring at her back and wondering just how picky she was.

FANCY OR NOT, Max couldn't remember when he'd enjoyed a meal more. Rikki had used really good cheese in the sandwiches, and the tomato soup was delicious. Carter was extra chatty, so neither adult had to contribute much to the conversation. Mostly they smiled and nodded as he gave his mother a blow-by-blow description of how he and Max had managed to finish the Lego model.

About the time he ran out of steam, Rikki broke out two cartons of ice cream. Carter immediately engaged Max in a heated discussion about which flavor to choose since they each only got one scoop. In the end, Carter went for the chocolate while both Rikki and Max picked the vanilla.

When she handed him his bowl, Max winked and asked, "No second scoop?"

"Not tonight." But she was smiling when she broke out more of the cookies he and Carter had shared earlier. "You'll have to be satisfied with these."

He offered her a more innocent smile than he had earlier. "I'll be satisfied with whatever—"

His phone rang, bringing their conversation to an abrupt halt. As much as he wanted to ignore it, he couldn't. There was only one reason that Shelby Michaels would be calling him this late in the evening.

"Sorry, guys, but I have to take this."

He didn't wait for a response, preferring to take the call out of their hearing. He had a lot riding on what Shelby had learned in the time since he'd left the museum.

"Sorry to take so long in answering, Shelby. I was in the middle of something."

"No problem. I knew you would want to know as soon as I had an answer for you. The board agreed to allow you to work at the museum. And like I already told you, I can't let you take anything off the premises. I will try to get them to ease up on that restriction at some point, but I can't guarantee that will happen."

"That's all great. I really appreciate that you went to bat for me."

"Anytime."

After he hung up, he noticed he'd missed seeing a text from a person he'd been trying to set up an interview with for weeks. To make things worse, the old guy insisted they talk in person—something about having some photos and other materials he was willing to share with Max. The last thing he wanted to do leave right now, but there was no getting around having to make a quick trip back to Portland. He sent a quick text back confirming that he could meet with the guy tomorrow afternoon. Then he returned to the kitchen with the intention of helping with the cleanup, but he was too late. "I was going to help with the dishes."

"No problem." Rikki wiped her hands on the dish towel. "Your ice cream is in the freezer, and the cookies are on the counter."

"Thanks for saving my ice cream for me. That was Shelby calling to say I can do my research at the museum." He reached for a couple of the cookies and retrieved his bowl from the freezer. "But something else has come up, and I need to leave really early in the morning. I have an appointment tomorrow to interview someone I've been trying to talk to for weeks. I'll be gone for a couple of days. Will you tell Carter that I'm sorry that I won't be able to play catch with him tomorrow like I promised? I feel bad about that."

"He'll understand."

Max wasn't so sure about that, but there wasn't much he could do about it. "I'd also like to talk to you more about my plans here in Dunbar."

"Can it wait a little while? I need to go supervise Carter's bath, and I promised to read him an extra book before lights-out. After that, though, I can come back down, unless that's too late."

Max shook his head. "Do whatever you need to in order to get Carter all squared away. In the meantime, I'll eat my ice cream and then read in the library."

"See you in a few."

"WHY CAN'T MR. MAX stay here all the time?"

It wasn't the first time Carter had asked Rikki that question. He hadn't liked her earlier answer and wasn't likely to like this one any better. "Because this isn't his home. Mr.

Max is a writer, Carter. It's his job and how he makes his living. That means sometimes he has to go to other places in order to do his research. That's why he's here in Dunbar right now instead of in Portland, where he really lives. And like I said, he promised to be back in a couple of days."

"But I like doing things with him, Mom. Guy things." Carter tossed aside the book they'd just finished reading together. "I don't want him to leave."

She didn't either, but it served as a reminder that eventually he would leave for good. Back when she'd first considered buying the bed-and-breakfast, the former owner had given her some advice on the ins and outs of running the business. Maude had cautioned Rikki to draw a hard line between her professional life and her personal one. Basically, the relationship between host and guest should be cordial but remain businesslike.

Until Max, maintaining that separation hadn't been a problem for Rikki. It had started eroding during his first stay. By this point, there was little or no hope of resurrecting it.

Back to the matter at hand. "I owe you one

more book, kiddo. Which one do you want me to read?"

He didn't look at all excited by the prospect. Instead, he turned away from her and pulled the covers up to his shoulders. "That's okay. I'm tired."

She suspected he was more sad than tired, but there wasn't much she could do about it right now. "Sleep tight, big guy."

As she turned out the light and slipped out of the room, she stopped to take a deep breath. She understood Carter saw Max not just as a friend, but also as…well, a father figure was probably the best description. Try as she might, she couldn't fill that particular need in his life. That should've been Joel's job.

It wasn't the first time she'd wished that her ex-husband had been a better man. It wasn't that Joel was bad. It was more that he had never grown up. As far as she could tell, he'd had no interest in transitioning from a good-time guy to a responsible adult. In the end, he'd simply abandoned his wife and son in search of excitement with no responsibility. Carter hadn't even started to walk when his father disappeared from their lives.

It had been tough learning how to be a single parent, but Rikki had no regrets. Carter was worth every sacrifice she'd made. Right now, though, she wanted to do exactly what her son had just done—crawl into bed and pull the covers up over her head.

But before that could happen, she needed to find out what Max wanted to talk about. He hadn't acted as if it was particularly serious, but something in his voice or maybe the look in his eyes said that it was still important. Maybe he wanted to apologize for flirting with her earlier. She really hoped not, but there was only one way to find out.

Max was right where he'd promised to be. But instead of reading, he was sitting at the table and frowning at the spaceship he and Carter had built together. Unsure that he even realized he was no longer alone, she hovered in the doorway. He answered that question a second later.

"Carter is such an amazing kid." Max finally looked at her. "This set was designed for adults and much older kids, but he would've been able to build it even without my help."

She ventured closer. "He's already reading even though he hasn't started school yet. I worry that he'll find it boring when he starts kindergarten in September. On the other hand, he spends too much of his time with me, so I'm really hoping he will at least make some friends."

"I'm sure he will."

Max pushed the model farther away. "I have something I need to ask you."

He paused as if waiting for her to respond, but he still hadn't told her what was going on. "I can't say yes or no until you actually ask me a question."

"That would help, wouldn't it?" He turned to face her more directly. "I really want to write about my great-grandfather's life, focusing on after he moved to the Pacific Northwest. I haven't decided if it will be nonfiction or if I'll write a fictionalized version of his life. You know, more of an adventure story."

He briefly paused and ran his fingers through his hair, maybe trying to organize his thoughts. "It's complicated, mainly because I've never written a book before. I figure I'll start with what I do know how to do—gather the facts and then go from there."

Rikki walked farther into the library and

took a seat at the table. "Have you always wanted to write a book?"

He shrugged. "I think a lot of people who love to read think that they'll write a book of their own someday. All I can say is that with everything that's happened, I feel pretty darn motivated to give it my best shot. I obviously find the subject fascinating, and I love doing research. Only time will tell if all of that translates into a book people might want to read."

"That's so cool. I'm glad Shelby said you could use the resources at the museum."

For the first time, his eyes gleamed with excitement. "Me, too. The board, however, ruled that I can't take anything off the premises, which is understandable since most of it is irreplaceable. I'll have to do most of my research on site."

He chewed his lower lip as his expression turned more serious. "Which brings me to what I wanted to talk to you about. The problem is that I have no idea how long all of this will take. I've already told you that I'd like to rent your turret room for what could easily be several months. There will be other times when I'll have to leave to do research elsewhere, either for the book or for the handful of freelance articles that I'm already committed to writing."

Rikki leaned back in her chair as she tried to absorb everything he'd just said. He must have been really worried about how she'd respond to his request from the way his words had picked up speed there toward the end. Maybe he thought she'd cut him off before he'd finished explaining the situation.

"So what's the problem?"

"I have no idea how long all of this will take, and I know you're concerned about Carter getting too attached to me. Would it be better if I looked for somewhere else to stay?"

At least he understood that she had good reason to be worried about how entangled Max was becoming in their lives. That said, there was no way she would turn him away. "I've already agreed to let you stay here."

He looked much happier after she said that. "Whatever works best for you, Rikki. Just let me know if it becomes a problem."

"Will you still be leaving in the morning?"

"Yeah. It could be Tuesday or even Wednesday before I head back this way. I also need to buy a few things to set up a sort of mini office in my room. You know, like a printer. If it's okay, I'd like to have the stuff shipped directly here."

"That's fine. I'll keep an eye out for it. Carter will miss you while you're gone, but I assured him you'll be back soon."

At the mention of her son's name, Max's expression turned a bit sly. "So, say someone…me, for instance…might want to work on another model whenever he needs to take a break from his research to ponder things. It's obvious I would need a special assistant to help me with that. So, as an experienced mother, do you think the assistant I have in mind could possibly be allowed to help me build a pirate ship or a Viking longship?"

She knew when she was fighting a losing battle and ran up the white flag. "What five-year-old doesn't love pirates?"

Max was gracious in victory. "Thank you, Rikki. I promise I won't be a troublesome guest."

He already was that, but at that moment, she couldn't bring herself to care. Half an hour later, she was once again in bed staring up at the ceiling. Now that she'd put some distance between herself and the potent power of Max's earnest blue eyes and hopeful smile, she could only hope that this arrangement didn't turn out to be a huge mistake.

Because Carter wasn't the only one who would be counting the hours until Max came back.

CHAPTER SEVEN

THREE DAYS LATER, Max walked into the Dunbar Police Department and asked to speak to the man in charge. Unlike the first time he'd done that, he wasn't about to set off a firestorm of trouble for Cade or the town itself. Sergeant Oscar Lovell was manning the front desk. He didn't smile, but at least he didn't immediately order Max to vacate the premises. The two of them had worked together on the new display at the museum, which had gone a long way toward convincing the older man that Max wasn't out to rob the town on this visit. It was a small victory, but progress nonetheless.

"The chief is in his office, but he might be busy. He doesn't usually shut his door unless something important is going on. He may not have time for a social call right now."

Then Oscar frowned and leaned forward over the counter to study the paper grocery bag Max clutched in his right hand. "It is a social call, isn't it? It's department policy that I need to inspect whatever it is you've got in that sack."

Praying for patience, Max did his best to maintain a friendly attitude as he lifted up the bag so Oscar could see its contents. "Yes, it's a social call. I promised to bring Cade some of my favorite microbrews from Portland. I'm here to deliver them, but then I'll be heading over to the museum to see Ms. Michaels."

"Yeah, I heard about you wanting to root through our records. Shelby promised you would treat everything with care. I figure that's true considering you're wanting to write a book about that Lev Volkov fellow."

"That's my plan."

"Good luck with that." Oscar pointed back over his shoulder. "Go on back. You know the way."

"Thanks, Oscar."

Seeing that Cade's door remained closed, Max briefly considered leaving the six-pack with Oscar to deliver later. However, Max had a quick question for Cade, so he knocked on the door and waited for an invitation to enter.

"It's unlocked."

When he walked in and saw Cade's face, Max set the bag down. "Hey, man, are you all right? You're pale and looking pretty shaky."

"I'm fine. Well, sort of anyway." Then the other man blinked and shook his head. "On second thought, not really."

"What's happened?"

"I just talked to Shelby." Cade held up his phone for Max to see as if that explained everything.

"Is she okay? Should we go across the street and check on her?"

"Maybe. As soon as I'm sure my legs will support me."

It had to be some really bad news to have rattled the former soldier. Seriously, Cade looked as if he'd just stared his worst nightmare in the eye and had been the first to blink. Maybe a distraction would help. Max pulled the six-pack out of the bag. "Would one of these help? It's a mix of several different microbrews I bought in Portland. I know you're on duty, but I won't tell if you don't."

Cade stared at the bottle in Max's hand as if he was about to lunge across the desk to grab it. Finally, he leaned back into his chair.

"I can't, but I'll definitely be having a few of those when I get home tonight."

They both sat quietly for a few seconds until Cade's coloring returned to normal. Figuring the worst of the crisis had passed, Max made himself comfortable in one of the two guest chairs that faced Cade's desk. "If you don't mind me asking, what happened?"

"Shelby and I are getting married."

He said that as if to reassure himself that was true. Had it ever been in doubt? Max feared he was about to tread on thin ice with his next question. "That's a good thing, isn't it?"

"Yeah, it is. Really good."

But then Cade went back to looking a bit spooked. "We had a date reserved at the church, but it was a lot farther out than either of us wanted. Like I told you the other night, we asked to be notified if a closer date came available."

"I'm guessing one did."

"Yeah, that's the good news."

"And the bad?"

Cade launched right back into panic mode. "The wedding is less than three weeks from now. And it can't be something small and intimate. Oh, no. It has to be a full-blown formal affair with who knows how many of our friends, family and neighbors. Shelby is freaking out about how we're going to break the news to people that the church only holds a hundred people, including the wedding party."

Before Max could think of what to say to that, Cade held up his hand and started counting off a litany of problems. "I won't meet the in-laws until the day before the wedding. What if they think I'm not good enough for her? Shelby will meet my parents then, too. I'm sure they'll love her, but they're not happy we live all the way out here instead of moving back to the Midwest. Meanwhile, we have to find a caterer, a DJ, and a florist. What on earth were we thinking?"

Max couldn't help him with most of the stuff on the list, but he knew the answer to that last question. "You were thinking that you love Shelby, she loves you, and you both want to start your lives together as a married couple as soon as possible. Now you can. I'm sure your parents will adore Shelby. Seriously, who wouldn't? And if your future in-laws have a lick of sense, they'll be thrilled that Shelby has found a man who loves and respects her."

He gave Cade a few seconds to process that much before adding, "And I used to DJ when I was in college, so you've got that covered. I'm sure there are others who will step up to help out. Maybe Titus can handle the food or at least the desserts."

Cade grabbed a pen. "I should write some of this down."

"While you do that, I'm heading across the street to meet with Shelby." He stood up to leave but remembered the question he'd wanted to ask Cade. "Last week I promised to pick up barbecue for Titus, you and me. What night would work best for you?"

After giving it some thought, Cade said, "Shelby has a meeting tomorrow night, so I should be free. I'll check with Titus and let you know."

"Sounds good. I'll understand if the wedding stuff has to take precedence. I'll be in town for the foreseeable future, and my schedule is flexible."

Looking decidedly desperate, Cade shook his head. "No, I'd like to get together with the two of you. It may be a while before things calm down again."

The poor guy was probably right about that. "I'm looking forward to it."

As Max passed by the front desk, Oscar asked, "Is everything okay back there?"

It wasn't Max's place to spread the news. "He got an unexpected phone call. He told me to leave the door open when I left."

That last part seemed to reassure the older man. "Good to know."

Max hustled across the street to the post office to catch up with Shelby. It would be interesting to see how she was handling the change in their wedding plans. He got his answer as soon as he walked into the post office. She was nowhere to be seen, but he could hear her voice coming from down the hall. "Shelby, can I come back there?"

"Sure."

She was shuffling through a stack of papers and frowning big-time. "Have a seat. I'll be with you in a minute."

It was closer to five before she finally re-membered he was there. Looking apologetic, she straightened the papers and set them aside. "Sorry, Max. My mind is a bit fried right now."

He grinned at her. "Actually, compared to Cade, you're looking pretty good. Regardless, I'm really happy for both of you."

She wrinkled her nose. "This sudden change in plans has thrown him for a loop."

"Pretty much, but he was doing better by the time I left. He was making a to-do list, and I told him I could DJ the reception if you'd like. That's how I earned money when I was in college."

That set off another round of paper shuffling. "You wouldn't mind?"

"I wouldn't have offered if I did. If you want to check my references, let me know. It won't hurt my feelings, and it might give you one less thing to worry about."

He borrowed her pen and jotted down several names and numbers. "And just so you know, there's no cost to you. Nowadays I do this for people I consider friends, not to make money."

Shelby immediately stood up. When Max did the same, she surprised him by giving him a rib-crunching hug. "Even checking one thing off the list is a huge relief."

"Glad I could help."

"Now, let's go get you situated. I've cleared out a desk for you to use upstairs, and I'll show you where we keep the journals and other files you might find useful. After you have a chance to look around, let me know if there is anything else you need."

"I appreciate this, Shelby."

More than she could know. He never expected to go from being viewed as a threat to the town and its heritage to having an increasing number of friends in Dunbar. He wasn't exactly sure how it had happened, but he liked it. He followed Shelby upstairs. The sooner he got the lay of the land, the sooner he could get to work.

RIKKI CLIMBED DOWN off the ladder to refill her paint tray. It was tempting to call it a day, but she really wanted to finish the last two walls. If she got that much done, tomorrow she could start moving the furniture back into the room. Once that happened, she would have one more room completely refurbished and ready to rent.

She did her best to only fill the house with paint fumes when she didn't have any guests in residence. Now that Max had moved in for an indefinite length of time, that wasn't possible. Well, unless she put all of the renovations on hold for the length of his stay, but she really didn't want to do that. Of course, it would all go faster if she gave in and hired a contractor to do the work, but she actually liked doing a lot of it herself. It not only gave her a sense of accomplishment, but it allowed her to make the best use of her limited funds.

So far, she'd only had to hire someone to deal with electrical and plumbing repairs. Slowly but surely, progress was being made. It helped that the previous owner had done the necessary upgrades on the main floor and the exterior before putting the place on the market. It was only the smaller guest rooms on the second and third floors that had been sliding downhill from shabby chic to just plain shabby.

"Oh, so this is where you're hiding."

Max poked his head in the door and looked around. "Looks like you could use some help. I swing a mean paintbrush."

Her first instinct was to turn down his offer. It would be one more step across that line between host and guest. "You don't have to."

"I know, but I've been sitting all morning. It would do me good to do something more active."

He was wearing what looked like new jeans and a navy Henley shirt that brought out the color of his eyes. "Okay, but do you have any work clothes with you? It would be a shame to ruin what you have on."

Max gave her a long look, a grin tugging at the corners of his mouth. "Nothing as cute as those striped overalls you're wearing. The paint-splattered pink baseball cap is a nice touch, too."

She threatened him with her paintbrush. "Watch it, buddy."

He laughed and made a beeline for the door. "I'll be right back."

Rikki was back up on the ladder when he returned, this time wearing a pair of jeans that had holes in both knees. He'd coupled his jeans with a faded T-shirt from some bar she'd never heard of. Even his shoes were a ratty pair she hadn't seen him wear before. "Boy, when you decide to go grubby, you really go grubby."

He bowed, waving his arm with a flourish.

"Thank you, ma'am. I pride myself on dressing for the occasion."

Cute, but it was time to get back to work. When she stretched as far as she could to paint the top edge of the wall, Max came closer and looked up at her. "I could do that part for you if you'd like. I've got a steady hand, not to mention I'm taller."

Considering edging was her least favorite part of painting, she didn't hesitate. Climbing back down, she surrendered the paintbrush and picked up a roller. "I'll start on the next wall."

Max studied the two remaining unpainted walls and then bent down to run his fingers over a row of small repairs she'd made in the plaster. "What's with all these patched holes? They're not at the height where you'd hang pictures."

"No, they're not. All I can figure is that the previous owner might have had some kind of vermin infestation or something in this room and the exterminator was looking for signs of damage. I'd never noticed them until I moved the furniture out of the room. To be honest, I'd hardly set foot in here until I decided to paint. It's not one of the rooms Maude rented out to guests when I took over the job managing the place for her. She never said anything about any problems, and the house passed inspection with flying colors. Unfortunately, she died not too long ago, so I can't ask her."

His curiosity apparently satisfied, Max started up the ladder and got to work. "Where's Carter?"

Rikki waited until she'd picked up more paint on her roller before answering. "I don't know if you've met Shelby's friend Elizabeth, but she has a daughter who is now old enough to do some babysitting. I've started hiring her to watch Carter for me here at the house. It gives her some experience, and I don't have to worry about what he's up to when I'm in the middle of something like this. The last time I checked, they were in his room doing an art project."

"Being a single parent must be hard at times, but you make it look easy."

Even though he didn't phrase his comment as a question, she figured it was Max's way of expressing his curiosity about Carter's father. He didn't push her to respond, instead leaving it up to her how much, if anything, she wanted to share on the subject. She rarely discussed her past and for good reason. However, for some reason she didn't mind filling Max in on at least some of the basics.

"My divorce was finalized about a week shy of Carter's first birthday. I was given full custody, so he hasn't seen or heard from his father since the day Joel moved out of our apartment. His excuse for leaving was that life was too short to be tied down to a wife and dirty diapers."

She kept rolling paint in wide swaths across the wall, covering up the depressing dark gold color with a soft shade of green. Too bad the pain from her past wasn't as easy to eradicate. For the longest time, Max remained silent. It was almost a relief. She and Carter didn't need his pity. But when he finally spoke, his voice held nothing but the sharp edge of anger.

"What a fool."

At first she wasn't sure if he was talking about her or Joel, but then he muttered a few words she suspected she wasn't supposed to hear. "What kind of man has everything and simply throws it away?"

Max clomped down the ladder and headed straight for her. "Tell me that he at least pays child support."

She propped her roller against the wall and turned to face him. "Why is that any of your business? I'm not in the habit of sharing my personal finances with a guest."

He winced and backed away. "My apologies. You're right. Should I go back to my room?"

Rikki reined in her anger. She wasn't mad at the man standing in front of her. "I apologize, Max. To answer your question, no, he doesn't. While the extra money would be nice, I can support my son without Joel's help or interference."

"And if he ever shows up on your doorstep and demands access to his son, what then?"

"I'll deal with it. I can't imagine any judge looking favorably on a man who deserted his family and never made any effort to support his son." She brushed her hair back from her face. "Having said that, there are nights that I can't sleep for worrying about that very thing."

Max stared out the window to the street below, his face set in harsh lines as if he expected Joel to come marching up to the door any second. "Do you know where he is?"

"California, the last I heard, but that was two years ago. Before that, I think he was in

Hawaii. He likes to surf and moves around a lot."

Looking a little more calm, Max asked, "Isn't Carter curious about him?"

"Not really." Which she found sad in a way. "On the rare occasion he asks about him, I tell him that his father had to move away. So far, he's been satisfied with that, but I'm not sure what I'll say when he wants to know why we never hear from Joel. I don't want to bad-mouth him to Carter. Regardless of how I feel about the man, he's still Carter's father. I don't want my son to grow up hating half of himself."

Max looked surprised by that last comment. "Good thinking. People should have more care in dealing with such things. The kids are stuck in the middle at the best of times. They shouldn't have to take sides."

That sounded like the voice of experience to her, but she didn't want to pry. Instead, she picked up the paint roller and got back to painting. When Max was back up on the ladder, she asked, "How did your meeting with Shelby go?"

"Really well. She set up a small area for me to use when I'm there. Which reminds me, I ordered another printer to use at the museum. It'll probably show up on your doorstep any day now."

"I'll keep an eye out for it."

He climbed down to reposition the ladder. "I think I should tell you something I learned today, but I would appreciate it if you kept it to yourself for a short time. I'm sure the news will spread like wildfire the minute Bea at the bakery finds out about it and sounds the alarm. I'm not in the habit of gossiping, but I think this situation may end up impacting you in a good way."

What could it be? "Okay, I won't tell anyone."

"The church had a cancellation two weeks from Saturday, so Cade and Shelby will be getting married a whole lot sooner than expected. Both of them have family coming from out of town and probably some friends. Shelby's parents will probably want to stay at her house and Cade's at his, but there may be others needing a room."

Wow, that was big news. "I'm happy for them, but that's not much time to pull together an entire wedding."

Max's laugh was a bit wicked. "No, it's not, but it will be fun watching them try."

She gave him an admonishing look. "That's not nice."

But he wasn't wrong.

CHAPTER EIGHT

MAX TRUDGED UP the front steps of the B and B. It had been a long day. Since Shelby preferred he didn't hang out at the museum once it opened, he'd gotten up far earlier than normal to get some work done before she shooed him back out the door. He'd worked for several more hours in his room before driving to a nearby town to pick up the barbecue feast he'd promised Cade and Titus.

He'd enjoyed hanging out with them and pigging out on smoked pork deliciousness. Both men had also appreciated the microbrews he'd brought from Portland. He found it interesting that Titus had seemed a bit taken aback when Max presented him with a selection to take back home with him. It was almost as if no one had ever given the man an unexpected gift.

Since all three of them had to work tomorrow, they'd made an early evening of it. He figured he'd do some more reading and then head to bed. When he walked through the front door, Rikki was at her desk talking on the phone. She held up a hand to signal that she needed to talk to him. He leaned his elbows on the counter and waited to see what she wanted.

He could only listen to her side of the conversation, but what he could hear made him angry. It was tempting to jerk the phone out of Rikki's hand to demand whoever was on the other end of the line treat her with more respect, but that would only make Rikki mad at him, too. He was smarter than that. Besides, unlike the customer she was doing her best to placate, Rikki wouldn't hesitate to tear into him for interfering in her business.

"I'm sorry, Ms. Billings, that room is still spoken for. However, you can have your choice of any of the other rooms." After a brief pause, Rikki tried again. "The blue room that you had last time is available. So is the rose room. I also just put the finishing touches on the green room, so you could be the first person to stay in it."

She met Max's gaze and rolled her eyes. "Okay, that's great. I'll reserve it for you, and

I'll put you on the waiting list for the turret room. As I said, it is rented for the foreseeable future, but I will let you know if that should change. Have a nice evening."

After disconnecting the call, Rikki took several deep breaths before speaking. "Sorry about that. If I'd known she'd go on so long, I wouldn't have asked you to wait."

"Is there a problem with my room?"

"Not at all." She leaned back in her chair and bit her lower lip as if considering how much she should share. "On your first stay here, you said you preferred to make your own bed and stuff like that. You said that as idiosyncrasies went, that wasn't such a strange one."

He still preferred to do it himself but knew that didn't sit well with Rikki. He'd compromised this visit by letting her do a thorough cleaning once a week. "What does that have to do with Ms. Billings?"

"For some reason, she likes to stay in a different room every time she stays here. Until now, it hasn't been a problem, but she wasn't happy that she can't have the turret room on her next visit. Evidently, she had her heart set on it even though I already told her that you booked it for an extended period of time. At least I had the new green room to offer her, so problem solved."

Max nodded. "Good. So what did you want to talk to me about?"

She pointed toward the library door. "Several packages arrived late this afternoon. I would've carried them up to your room, but I thought maybe they were for your office at the museum."

"Let's go see."

She laughed as he tore off down the hall. "You're as bad as Carter at Christmas."

As he disappeared into the library, he called back, "Gotta love presents even if you buy them for yourself!"

She caught up with him as he was inspecting the first box. "Good call," he said, giving her a thumbs-up. "I bought this to use at the museum."

Then he picked up the second box and shook it. Pulling out a small pocketknife, he cut through the packing tape and produced something that would have Carter whooping with glee. Max held the pirate ship up for her to see. "Aye, matey, she be a fine ship."

Shaking her head, she said, "You two will have fun with that."

At least she was smiling. He wasn't so sure how long that would last when he opened the third box. As soon as she saw the picture of a longship on the box, she frowned. "I thought you were only going to buy one of those two sets."

"I did, but then I couldn't decide which one I liked the best. It was easier to order both than to always wonder if I made the right choice."

"Carter would've been happy with either one."

He studied the two sets with greedy glee. "But maybe I wouldn't have been."

Finally, he moved on to the fourth box with even more trepidation. She was already unhappy about him spending money on Carter, even though the models were as much for him as for her son. Seeing what else he'd bought was bound to only make the situation more volatile. Regardless, he was no coward. Taking a deep breath, he offered her a large gift-wrapped box.

Her smile was a bit uncertain as she took it from his hands. "Max, you shouldn't have."

At least she didn't shove it right back at him. Still, he clasped his hands behind his back in case she changed her mind. "Go ahead, open it."

"Do I really have to rip the paper to pieces this time?"

He grinned. "Sorry, ma'am, but them's the rules."

Rather than getting down to business, she pulled out a chair and sat down. Max walked around to the other side of the table and did the same. Sitting across from her gave her a little space, which she seemed to need. It also afforded him a clear view of her face as she pondered the package. She gave it a little shake and smiled. "Well, at least I know it's not a model for me to put together. I was afraid it was the village for your pirates and Vikings to plunder."

That was funny. "I'll keep that in mind for the next time I get the urge to shop."

"Don't you dare, Mr. Volkov."

She finally started unwrapping the package. While she wasn't exactly trying to save the paper, she still took her time as if savoring the process for as long as possible. That was okay. He enjoyed watching her. When she finally lifted the lid, her expression was everything he'd hoped for. She looked across at him, her eyes glistening with a suspicious sheen.

It was a basket of bath oils, scented candles and a few other goodies he thought she'd like. "A while back, Carter told me you liked things that smell good like air freshener, but for people."

He loved her laugh. She set the bath oils aside and reached for another box in the basket. "That comes from a shop that's known for its specialty chocolates. The smaller one in the basket is a custom-blend tea. I hope you enjoy them."

His main worry had been that she'd think a few of the things like the bath oils were a little too personal. Knowing that she poured every ounce of her energy into caring for her son and keeping a roof over their heads, he figured she rarely indulged in luxuries for herself.

She sniffed one of the candles. "I shouldn't accept all of this, Max, but that's not happening. Especially after the day I've had."

There was a note in her voice that he didn't like. "What happened besides that Billings woman being unhappy that she can't have my room?"

"It's nothing. Don't worry about it."

"It's something, Rikki, or you wouldn't be holding that candle in a death grip. Tell me."

She slowly nestled the candle back down in the basket. "There's nothing you can do, and it's my problem."

"I know that, but maybe talking about it will help."

"Let's just say that social media is a great way to advertise my business, especially when people take the time to leave good reviews. But sometimes something goes wrong."

"Such as?" Because he couldn't imagine anyone being disappointed with the service Rikki provided to her guests.

"There was one couple who didn't understand that a bed-and-breakfast was exactly that. No lunch, no dinner. But honestly, they didn't seem all that upset at the time. I don't even know for sure that they're the ones who left a one-star review, but I can't think of anyone else who seemed disappointed with their stay here in town."

"Has this been happening a lot?"

"That's just it. Up until the last couple of

months, it hadn't happened at all. I get an occasional three-star review, but I also get enough fives so it averages out to four stars overall. I'm happy with that. One bad review doesn't have much of an impact, but I've had a couple lately. If it keeps up, it could hurt my business."

Her chin came up in a show of stubborn pride. "But what really makes me mad is that neither of the one-star reviews gave any kind of feedback. How can I fix the problem when they don't tell me what's wrong?"

"I'm sorry that happens, especially when I can't imagine anyone finding fault with this place." The only thing he could do to help was post a review of his own. She hadn't mentioned which site was the problem, but he excelled at research. He'd find it. Heck, he'd leave reviews on them all.

"Well, I'm going to head up to bed. I need to get an early start at the museum."

Rikki stood up at the same time he did and circled around to his side of the table. To his surprise, she set her basket down and gave him a quick hug. "Thank you for my goody basket and for being such a good listener. It means a lot."

It was tempting to hold her closer and test the waters with a kiss, but he wasn't sure either of them was quite ready for that.

But soon. Really soon.

THE NEXT COUPLE of days were quiet, which was fine with Rikki. Several unexpected guests had shown up at her front door, but it hadn't been a problem to accommodate them. Carter was a little on the mopey side, mainly because Max had left again two days ago to do research for one of his articles. Right now, her son was holed up in the library working on the pirate ship. He was capable of doing the whole thing by himself, but it wasn't as much fun without Max there to help.

She knew exactly how he felt, not that she'd admit it to him or Max. She could barely admit it to herself. Rather than ponder that scary thought, she did her best to concentrate on the multiple shopping lists she was working on.

When the front door opened a few minutes later, her wayward mind hoped that Max had come back earlier than expected. Instead, it was Debra Billings, back for another stay to visit with a family member. "Welcome back. Did you have a nice time with your cousin?"

"I did. We went out for lunch and browsed a few of the gift shops." She held up a couple of shopping bags. "I managed to find a few Christmas gifts for my friends back home, although it's awfully early to be thinking about the holidays. However, once the passes become unpredictable, I might not be back this way for a while."

"Sounds like you had fun."

"We did." Debra checked her watch. "Well, I'm going to take a nap before I head over to the café for dinner."

"You should take a key with you." Rikki had already gotten one from the safe just in case. Setting it on the counter, she added, "My book club is meeting tonight, so Carter and I will be out later than normal."

Picking up the key, Debra thanked her. "On another subject—I couldn't help but notice that the guy who was renting the turret room isn't staying here any longer. Since he's gone, I would like to book it for two nights a week from now. I have a family dinner to go to, so I'll be back in town."

Seriously, why was the woman so determined to sleep in every bed that Rikki had to offer? While she thought Debra was a nice enough woman, she found this particular idiosyncrasy perplexing. Not to mention a bit irritating since she'd already explained more than once that Max had paid for the room in advance.

"I'm sorry, Debra, but Mr. Volkov is due back shortly. As I've told you, he's booked the room for an extended period of time. He never actually moves out even if he gets called away for a day or two."

Not that it was any of the woman's business. Rikki figured if she kept repeating the same explanation, eventually Debra would give up her quest to rent the room.

The other woman's smile didn't quite reach her eyes. "Well, it doesn't hurt to ask. I figure that it offers a nice view of the mountains."

"It does." Rikki couldn't blame her for wanting to enjoy the beauty of the Cascades. "Hopefully you'll get a chance to see it for yourself at some point."

"Thanks again for the key. I'll drop it in the slot when I get back from dinner."

As she walked away, Rikki called after her, "Enjoy your nap."

"I will."

Deciding she'd worked long enough, it was time to check on her son in the library. He was concentrating so hard on getting the bow of the ship put together that he didn't notice her approach until she was standing next to him. She started to run her fingers through his hair, but he ducked out of the way. "I'm too big for that."

No, he wasn't and never would be. He'd always be her little boy no matter how big he got. It was a mom thing, but he wouldn't want to hear that. Instead, she backed away to give him a little room. "You've made a lot of progress on the ship."

"I had to take some of it apart again to fix it. I should've waited for Mr. Max to come back." He sat back, looking frustrated. "It's a lot harder than the other set we did."

"I'm sure the two of you will get it figured out. He should be back tomorrow or the day after. But right now, we need to have an early dinner. My book club meeting starts at seven."

Carter gave her a hopeful look. "Can we eat at the café?"

It was tempting. No cooking and no dishes

sounded good to her. "Why not? We don't have any more guests coming tonight, and Ms. Billings has a key to get back in. There's no reason we have to stick around here until it's time to leave."

"Do I have to go to the book club, too?"

"Yes, we're meeting at Shelby's house. She said you can watch a movie in her living room while the grownups hang out in the family room."

Even the promise of a movie did little to make him any happier. She'd tried to hire Elizabeth's daughter to stay with Carter, but Liza had already been booked to babysit for someone else. That left Rikki only two choices—stay home or take Carter with her. It might be hard for him to understand, but she occasionally needed to spend time with other adults. "Go wash your hands and comb your hair while I get my purse. Then we'll go to the café. And if you eat whatever vegetables Mr. Kondrat serves you, you can have dessert."

"Does that go for me, too?"

The familiar voice had both mother and son spinning to face the door. Carter yelled, "Mr. Max, you're back!"

"I am." Max crossed over to the table to

admire the model. "Wow, you've gotten a lot done. Nice job."

Her son beamed with pride. "I worked hard. Now we're going to the café for dinner. Are you going to come with us?"

"That's up to your mom."

Both males turned hopeful eyes in her direction. "Sure, it's fine. I'll give you a key to get back into the house after dinner. Carter and I will be going directly to my book club meeting from the café."

Her son made no effort to hide his lack of the enthusiasm for that last part. "Yeah, I have to watch a movie while she talks with the other ladies."

Max looked at her and then at Carter. "Is there any reason why Carter can't come back here with me? We can work on the model while you're at the meeting."

Darn the man. Why hadn't he gotten her alone before even suggesting such a thing? She would've appreciated the chance to think things through before mentioning the possibility to Carter. While she'd also had misgivings about leaving Carter alone with Liza, she'd made up her mind to do it. Would allowing Max to take responsibility for her son for a few hours be any different?

It might not be logical, but it was. The only question was why she felt that way, although she could hazard a guess. Liza would never have a long-term role in Carter's life except maybe as a friend. If she moved away, it would hardly cause a ripple in her son's life.

But Max…somehow he'd already become the second most important adult in Carter's life. If he walked out the door tomorrow, never to return, it would hurt her son in ways she didn't want to consider. Every inch the man crept deeper into their lives would only heighten the impact he had on both of them when he checked out for the last time.

Suddenly, that small voice was back, whispering temptation in the back of her mind. *But what if he doesn't disappear? Not all men are like my ex. What if Max stays not just in Carter's life, but mine as well? What then?*

There was so much about the man that she liked, which meant there was a whole lot about the man to fear. Meanwhile, Carter continued to plead his case. "Please, Mom? Working on the pirate ship is way better than a movie."

One he would have to watch alone. She couldn't blame him for wanting to opt for a more enjoyable way to spend his evening. When she still didn't respond, Max offered her a smile tinted with disappointment. "It's all right, Carter. We can have dinner together if that's still okay with your mother."

She hated that she was hurting all three of them. Could she put her fears aside long enough to give Max a chance to prove he wasn't like her ex-husband? Or was she going to make him pay for crimes he'd never committed in the first place?

"No."

The single word slipped out, hanging in the air between them. Her son looked furious. Max looked hurt. And she…well, she now knew what cowardice might feel like.

CHAPTER NINE

"MOM, THAT'S NOT FAIR!"

Carter bolted out the door. She needed to go after him, to explain things. That would have to wait until she dealt with the man who currently stared at her as if he'd never actually seen her before. "I wasn't talking about dinner, Max. If you and Carter are still willing to go with me, that is."

He folded his arms across his chest. "I'm not so sure that's a good idea, Rikki. Not when it's clear that you don't trust me anywhere near Carter. Not when it really counts."

His words jabbed at her like a sharp knife. "That's just it, Max. Before this, I've never had anyone I *could* trust him with."

She pointed to her head. "In here, I know you would never hurt Carter." Then she thumped her fist over her chest. "But my heart says I need to protect my son at all costs. It's not your problem. It's not Carter's, either. It's mine.

When I said no, I was asking myself if I really wanted to be the kind of woman who would judge all men by my ex-husband. The answer was I don't."

She offered him a tremulous smile and took a deep breath. "If you're willing to watch Carter for me, I would greatly appreciate it."

Max stepped close enough to cradle the side of her face with his hand, his touch so gentle. "I would be honored."

Feeling marginally better, she said, "Thank you. Now I'd better see if I can make peace with Carter."

She found him up in his room. He immediately flopped onto his bed and turned to face the opposite wall. "Go away."

"I will, but I would like to apologize first. I'm sorry I upset you and Max. I was being a scaredy-cat." She sat on the edge of his bed and risked laying her hand on his shoulder. "I'm not used to leaving you with strangers, and I panicked."

He peeked back over his shoulder at her. "Mr. Max isn't a stranger. He's my friend."

"Yes, he is. Mine, too, and I've already apologized to him downstairs. He's still willing to go to dinner with us. After that, I'll go to my book club while he brings you home. You can work on the model until I get back, even if it's way after your bedtime."

Carter sat up and swiped a few stray tears off his cheeks. "Really?"

"Yes, really."

Then he launched himself into her arms. "Thanks, Mom. I'll go tell him."

"Wash your face first, and then we need to hustle. I don't want to be late for my meeting."

And even though she probably shouldn't, she called after him, "And just this once, you can have dessert even if you don't eat all your vegetables!"

IT WAS RIKKI'S first time attending the book club meeting, and she didn't want to be judgmental. However, if this was how little they actually discussed the current month's selection, she didn't know why they bothered reading the book in the first place. Although, to be fair, she could understand why everyone might be more interested in how Shelby's wedding plans were coming along.

"We have the pastor, of course, and the DJ for the reception. I have my dress, and Cade has his tux. I have calls in to several photographers, so that's still up in the air."

Her friend Elizabeth topped off Shelby's glass of wine for the third time in the last hour. "When do your mom and dad get in?"

"Not until the day before the wedding. The same with Cade's parents." Wobbling a bit, Shelby suddenly went on point as if she'd only just then realized Rikki was there. "I've been meaning to call you. I need to ask how many rooms you'll have available."

Thanks to Max's early warning, Rikki could reassure her on that count. "All of them except the one Max Volkov is using. I won't book any of them until I know how many you might need and for how long. Do your parents or Cade's need a place to stay?"

Shelby's laugh held more than a hint of hysteria. "Nope, but reserve them all for me and Cade. I'm pretty sure we're going into hiding. My mom wants things done one way, and his mother wants them done another."

Ilse spoke up. "And what do you want?"

"I want to marry Cade." Shelby sighed. "That's it. That's all I want."

The older woman nodded in obvious approval. "Then what everyone else wants doesn't matter, does it? Otto and I were married at a folk music festival by a shaman. And we've lasted fifty years."

Bea leaned forward to better see Ilse, who was seated on the other end of the couch from her with Helen Nagy in between them. "Was that even legal?"

Ilse rolled her eyes. "Probably not, but Otto later insisted we also go to city hall and have a judge marry us. He said he wanted to make sure he had me lassoed. We still celebrate our anniversary on the date of the festival, though. That's the one that really counts."

Like most people in town, Rikki found the relationship between Ilse and her husband to be both confusing and entertaining. Whatever they had together, it obviously worked. It was hard to argue with five decades of marriage; harder still not to be a little bit jealous.

Bea turned her attention back to Shelby. "What kind of food are you going to serve at the reception?"

"Under the circumstances, we need to keep things simple." Shelby held up her wineglass. "You know—local wines, local beers, and some stuff to eat."

"What kind of stuff?" Bea spoke slowly,

enunciating each word carefully as if that would increase the likelihood of getting any kind of useful information out of the somewhat tipsy bride-to-be.

"Cade said he wanted good stuff, but nothing fancy." Then she frowned. "Not sure what that means. Somebody write that down, and I'll ask him."

Bea waited until Elizabeth grabbed a pen and paper. "Write it down, but also write down that Titus and I will handle the food."

Elizabeth's eyebrows shot up. "He volunteered?"

"He will if he knows what's good for him."

Rikki bit her lip to keep from laughing at the thought of tough-looking Titus facing off against Bea. All things considered, she'd put her money on Bea. Rikki had never been part of a close-knit community like this, but she had to admire how everyone seemed ready to jump in and help Shelby and Cade.

The meeting broke up a few minutes later, mainly because their hostess had dozed off shortly after Elizabeth had taken away Shelby's empty wineglass. Everyone pitched in to wash the dishes and pack up the leftover food.

As they filed out the front door, Ilse stopped Rikki. "Did you walk or drive here?"

"I walked from the café."

"Come on, I'll give you a ride home. I've got room."

Rikki didn't hesitate. While she could easily walk the short distance back to the house, accepting the offer of a ride felt like she was one step closer to being truly accepted as a member of the group. Of the town as a whole.

It was as unexpected as it was gratifying. At long last, maybe she and Carter finally had a real home.

DESPITE RIKKI'S PROMISE that Carter could stay awake until she returned home, the boy had lost the battle to keep his eyes open that long. He and Max had worked hard on the model right up until Carter spent more time yawning than he did snapping pieces together. To encourage the boy to give up the battle, Max stopped working himself and complained that he needed to quit for the night, using the excuse that he needed to rest his eyes after such a long day.

He gently coaxed Carter into getting ready for bed and then read to him until he finally fell asleep. Tucking a kid in for the night wasn't something Max had any previous experience with, but he could see why both mother and son might love the routine. He tried to remember back to his own childhood and couldn't muster up even one memory of anything like the ritual that obviously meant so much to both Rikki and her son. Lucky them.

When Carter was down for the count, Max crept out of the boy's bedroom, looking back one more time before closing the door. He had to wonder if he'd been the first person other than Rikki to put Carter to bed. The thought that it was even possible warmed a part of Max that had been cold for…well, most of his life.

On his way back downstairs to wait for Rikki, he heard a noise. Cocking his head to the side, he waited to see if he heard it again. There…it sounded like footsteps coming from the third floor near the staircase that led up to the turret. He reversed course and headed up the steps in stealth mode, pausing every few seconds to listen.

All was quiet. Maybe he'd only imagined that someone was creeping around where they didn't belong. After all, the old Victorian had its fair share of creaks and groans that were common in a house of its age. No matter what it had been, he wasn't hearing it now. Satisfied that all was well, he went back downstairs and grabbed the book he'd left in the library. After foraging in the kitchen for a late snack, he parked himself at the front desk to read until Rikki got back. Two chapters in, a car briefly stopped in front of the house. A minute later, Rikki stepped through the front door.

He tried not to take personally that she looked a bit disappointed to find that Max was the only one who had waited up for her. "Carter fought a gallant fight to stay up this late, but I was afraid he was going to doze off on top of the library table. I can't imagine sleeping on top of all those little blocks would've been very comfortable."

Rikki laughed, just as he was hoping she would. "Was he good for you?"

"He was great. He got ready for bed all by himself and then picked out a couple of his favorite books for me to read. He fell asleep before I finished the second one. I promised you'd check on him when you got home."

"I'll do that."

She started to walk away, but he wasn't quite ready to let her go. "How was your meeting tonight? Was the discussion interesting?"

"We had fun, but we actually spent most of the time talking about Shelby's wedding plans. Don't tell anyone, but I was actually a little disappointed about that. We ended up postponing the discussion about the current book until next month after the wedding hubbub is over."

"Good idea." He picked up his plate and glass. "I'm going to go put these back in the kitchen and head up to bed myself."

Rikki frowned. "Do you know if Debra Billings has returned?"

Oh yeah…there was another guest in the house. That's who he heard moving around upstairs. Although, come to think of it, her room wasn't located in that part of the house. "I didn't hear her come in, but she might have arrived while I was in Carter's room or back in the kitchen. I've been sitting here at the desk for the past half hour or so."

"Let me check something."

He stepped away from the desk while she unlocked the box where guests dropped off keys. "She's back. Since I was going to be gone for the evening, I gave her a house key to use."

Mystery solved. Everyone was home.

"Good night, Max."

"Good night. Just so you know, I'll be up early again tomorrow. Shelby promised to let me root through some files in the basement of the museum." He chuckled. "She did warn me that I'd be on my own if we ran across any creepy crawlies. Something about spiders the size of a dinner plate. I suspect that was a bit of an exaggeration. At least I hope so."

Rikki paused on the second step and shivered. "I don't blame her. I'm not overly fond of spiders myself."

As she headed up the stairs, he debated telling her about the noise he'd heard earlier, but decided against it. No doubt it had been Debra Billings heading up to her room. Putting it out of his mind, he returned his dishes to the kitchen and retired to his room. He tried to read a little more of his book. But just like Carter, he fell asleep before he finished another chapter.

TOO FEW HOURS had passed for Max to feel fully rested when his alarm went off. It was tempting to go back to sleep, but he rarely allowed himself to veer from the schedule he set for himself. As a self-employed writer, he was the only one responsible for making sure that he met his deadlines and produced the amount of work he demanded of himself.

He rolled out of bed, got dressed, and gathered up his laptop and other things he would need for his time at the museum. Locking the door as he left his room, he trotted down the narrow staircase to the first floor. He sniffed the air and picked up the heady scents of bacon and coffee. Rikki varied the fare that she offered her guests for breakfast. It was all good, but her hobo scramble made with eggs mixed with bell pepper, onion, hash browns, and bacon was his favorite. Topped off with one of her muffins, the meal would carry him through the morning.

The museum opened at twelve on Sundays, but he could work until then. After Shelby booted him out at noon, he'd continue his research online over lunch in the back corner of Titus's restaurant or perhaps by the front window in Bea's bakery. Either place would work, and it gave him time to indulge in some people-watching, his favorite hobby. Luckily for him, for a town its size, Dunbar had more than its fair share of characters. Eventually he hoped to coax several of them into sharing their family stories with him to use as background for his book.

But right now, it was time eat and hit the road to maximize his time at the museum. He wasn't at all surprised to find Carter lurking right outside of the dining room. He wasn't allowed in there if a guest other than Max was eating breakfast. Unfortunately, there was a woman at the buffet dishing up a plate.

"Sorry I can't eat with you this morning, Mr. Max."

Ruffling the boy's hair, Max considered the possibilities. Finally, he leaned in close to whisper, "Meet me in the library. I'll bring enough for both of us."

Carter was off like a shot while Max continued on into the dining room. As he picked up two plates, the woman turned to face him. "Oh, you must be the writer Rikki has told me about. I don't think we've been formally introduced. I'm Debra Billings."

"Maxim Volkov. Nice to meet you." He held up the two plates to show why he wasn't offering to shake hands.

"You must be extra hungry."

He wasn't about to admit that he was sneaking off to the library to share the bounty with the owner's son. "It's my favorite breakfast, and it's a long way until lunchtime."

"So true." She nodded to her own plate piled high with food. "I'm checking out and driving back over to Spokane this morning."

He checked the weather outside the window. "It should be a nice day for it. Enjoy the drive."

"Thanks, I will."

She took a seat at the table while he served himself and grabbed two sets of silverware before leaving the room. As planned, Carter was waiting for him in the library. He'd already moved enough of the blocks out of the way to make room for them to eat. Max handed Carter his plate and sat down.

Before diving in, Carter scrunched his face, looking a bit worried. "Think Mom will get mad that we're hiding in here?"

Max's own conscience kicked in. "I like eating with you, but I don't want to get you in trouble. Ms. Billings is leaving today. So unless someone else checks in, we can eat together tomorrow."

Carter nodded and stood up. Before he could make his escape, the door opened. Rikki stepped inside and gave them both a mad mom look. "Gentlemen, care to explain?"

Max spoke up before Carter could. "It's my fault. We both know Carter can't join me in the dining room when you have other guests, and I thought this was a reasonable alternative. But as soon as we sat down, Carter decided that I was wrong about that. He was about to leave when you came in."

"Is that true, Carter?"

It stung that she doubted Max's statement, but he kept his mouth shut. This was a problem of his own making. When her son nodded, she smiled at him. "I'm glad you figured out that you'd made a mistake all on your own."

Her words to Max were a little less friendly. "You should've known better."

"Yes, ma'am."

Carter giggled but then slapped his hand over his mouth. Rikki's mouth twitched just enough to let them both know the crisis was over. "Don't do this again. For now, eat your breakfasts, gentlemen. Carter has chores, and I'm guessing Shelby is expecting you at the museum."

"Thanks, Mom."

Max waited until Carter wasn't looking to wink at Rikki. She rolled her eyes and left the room, quietly closing the door on her way back out. When the two of them had polished off every bite, Max gathered up their dishes. "Off you go, kiddo. Like your mom said, you've got chores, and I have to work."

"Will we get to work on the pirate ship today?"

"Later this afternoon or else after dinner."

"Promise?"

"I promise."

Happy that all was well in his world, Carter bounced out of the room with a smile on his face. It was hard not to envy the little boy's belief that the adults in his life kept their promises, that his happiness mattered to them. Max knew firsthand what it was like when a kid couldn't depend on anyone, and he devoutly hoped that Carter never experienced how much that kind of betrayal hurt or the scars it left behind.

CHAPTER TEN

RIKKI WENT ABOUT her morning chores more
out of habit than any sense of accomplishment. She wasn't exactly bored, but she was
out of sorts for no particular reason that she
could pinpoint. Normally, she took great pride
in caring for the home she shared with her
guests. Right now, though, she'd rather be
doing anything other than dusting and weed-
ing out old magazines. Carter was playing
upstairs in his room, probably counting the
hours until Max returned to work on their
project again.

The man himself left for the museum
shortly after he and Carter had finished their
breakfast in the library. She'd never admit it
to him, but the house seemed too quiet and
empty as soon as he walked out the door.
With the living room all polished up, she
paused to consider where to turn her attention next. She couldn't clean Debra Billings's

room until after the woman actually checked out, which should be anytime now.

Maybe it was time to take a quick coffee break. No sooner had she started for the kitchen than her phone rang. She hustled to the front counter where she'd left it plugged in to recharge. The name on the screen surprised her. "Max, did you forget something?"

"Nope, Shelby asked me to call you."

He went on to explain that Shelby was hosting a pizza and movie night for a group of kids of varying ages, something she did on a regular basis. She wondered if Carter might like to come. Rikki's first instinct was to say no, but that wouldn't have been fair to Carter. If they were going to make Dunbar their permanent home, he deserved to make friends and connections of his own.

Instead of agreeing immediately, she told Max that she would ask Carter and then call him back. She made a quick trip upstairs to explain the invitation to him. Needless to say, her son was thrilled with the prospect of hanging out with other kids even if he didn't know many of them. At least he knew Liza, and Rikki figured the girl would watch out for her little friend.

On the way back downstairs, she realized that she now had an entire evening free of responsibilities. Maybe she'd put some of those scented candles and bath oils Max had given her to good use. Yeah, a long soak in the huge bathtub with a glass of wine and a good book was just the ticket. Her own plans made, she called Max back.

"Is Shelby sure she wants to do this so close to the wedding?"

Max laughed. "I guess some of the parents asked her the same thing, but she didn't want to disappoint the kids. Besides, she said it would give her something else to think about other than the wedding for a few hours."

"Well, in that case, Carter would love to go. What time should I drop him off?"

"She said anytime around five would be good and that you should pick him up no later than ten."

"That's nice of her."

"So, what are you going to do with your evening?" Before she could answer, he kept right on talking. "I was thinking the two of us might have dinner somewhere nice. I know you won't want to go too far since it's Carter's first movie night."

She couldn't find the words. When was the last time she'd been on an actual date? Not that Max had called it that. But even if it was simply an outing between two friends, it was as close to a date as she'd had since Joel walked out of her life. Should she risk it? And if she did, what should she wear?

Those were both foolish questions and easy to answer. Yes, she should definitely risk it. Even if it was simply dinner with a friend rather than a date, it was a chance to simply be herself, not just Carter's mom. All things considered, Max probably wouldn't care what she wore. It wasn't as if they were driving all the way into Seattle to a five-star restaurant.

"Look, forget I asked."

Oops, she'd been dithering longer than she'd realized. "No, Max, I'd really love to go."

A second of silence followed, but then he spoke. "We can drop Carter off on our way."

"I'll be ready."

As she hung up, Rikki was hard put to describe how she was feeling—buzzy, excited, and a little bit terrified. It was ridiculous to get so wound up about a simple outing. She wasn't even sure why she'd agreed to go, but something about dinner with Max had her pulse racing and a big, silly grin on her face.

She had hours to kill until it was time to go, but right now she needed to go root through her closet for something to wear. Before she could put that plan into action, she realized that she wasn't alone. Her other guest was hovering on the other side of the counter, her luggage at her feet. "Oh, hi, Debra. Are you on your way out?"

The other woman handed over her key. "Yes, I am. I wanted to thank you for all your usual great service. It's nice to know I have someplace so comfortable to stay whenever I want to come visit my family. Actually, I was about to extend my stay, but I got a call about a job and need to get back home."

"Another private duty job?"

"Yes, a previous client of mine had another surgery and will be getting released from the hospital in the next couple of days. Melody is going to need some care for a week or two while she recuperates at home. I think she's hiring me to give her kids some peace of mind. They don't live close and would worry if she was on her own too soon."

"I bet she really appreciates your help."

"She does." Debra grabbed the handle of her suitcase. "Well, I should be going. I always like to get back home before dark. I'll see you again soon."

After she walked out the door, Rikki headed upstairs to check on her son and her wardrobe. She'd pick an outfit, make her son lunch, and then she might just take that bath she'd been looking forward to.

MAX LEFT THE museum and drove twenty miles to the car wash in a nearby town. His car tended to get cluttered up with empty burger wrappers and drink cups on his research trips. Rikki probably wouldn't comment, but she deserved to be driven in style, not a rolling dumpster.

He also didn't want to disappoint Carter by not getting back in time to work on their ship. Hopefully the boy was still excited about hanging out with Shelby and the horde of kids she'd invited over. But if he'd changed his mind, Max would simply invite Carter to join Rikki and him for dinner. It might mean a change in restaurants to one that was more family friendly, but that was okay. Sort of. He was really looking forward to having Rikki all to himself for a few hours.

His young friend bolted out the front door and headed straight for him at a dead run as soon as Max pulled into the driveway. Max left his laptop case in the car as he got out to greet Carter. It was a good thing he had, because the boy launched himself into the air, and Max needed both arms to catch him.

"Did you hear? I'm going to a movie party at Ms. Shelby's house. There's going to be a bunch of kids and pizza. I hope there's mushrooms and pepperoni. That's my favorite."

Max gave him a quick squeeze before setting him back down. "I did hear. I bet you'll have a great time."

Carter frowned. "We were going to work on the ship, but I won't be home. Did you want to come, too? I know it's for kids, but I bet Ms. Shelby wouldn't mind."

Such a generous little heart. "No, that's okay, Carter. Your mom and I are going to go out for dinner."

"Oh, that's right. She told me."

Max grabbed his pack and let Carter lead the way into the house. Once they got inside, Max checked the time. "I have a couple of hours before I need to get ready. Do you want to work on the ship now?"

Carter nodded enthusiastically. Meanwhile, Max couldn't help but notice that Rikki was nowhere in sight. "Where's your mom?"

Carter pointed toward the ceiling. "Upstairs taking a bath. I don't know why. She took a shower this morning. Weird, huh?"

Max struggled to keep his thoughts on that subject PG-rated. "Sometimes grown-ups take baths to relax sore muscles or ease a headache."

It was hard not to laugh at the incredulous look Carter gave him. Clearly the habits of adults were a mystery to him. He took Max's hand and towed him down the hall. "Come on, I got more work done on the masts."

Max followed his young friend into the library and did his best to not think too much about the woman upstairs. He hadn't lied to Carter about why some people took a long soak in the tub. That didn't keep him from wondering if the ritual was actually Rikki's way of getting ready for their date, the first of what he hoped would be many more to come. The possibility that she was as excited about the evening ahead as he was had him smiling.

HOURS LATER, Max was sitting across from Rikki at the restaurant, thinking that he couldn't remember the last time he'd enjoyed an evening out as much as he had this one. Starting out, Rikki had been a little nervous about leaving her son at Shelby's, but Carter had marched in the door and headed straight for Liza. She was older than most of the other kids, so Shelby had hired her to help ride herd on the younger ones. Thanks to her efforts, Carter had been quickly absorbed into the group.

That had allowed Rikki to relax and enjoy the evening. They'd driven thirty miles to a steakhouse, one that offered good food without being too fussy. The conversation between them had flowed easily as they discussed the usual getting-to-know-someone topics—books, movies and sports. From there, they'd moved on to what Max had learned so far from his research at the museum. At first, he wondered if Rikki was asking him about it just to be polite, but it quickly became apparent that she was genuinely interested.

It was his usual habit not to discuss his personal history, so he couldn't help but notice that he wasn't the only one who didn't share a lot of details about the past. Maybe Rikki thought she'd already told him enough about her marriage and subsequent divorce. That was fine. Max didn't particularly want to learn intimate details about her life with another man.

But if he put together all of what he knew about Rikki's past, not much of it predated her marriage and the birth of her son. He found that interesting. What was she hiding? And how did she go from a single parent receiving no child support to the owner of her own business? He could simply ask, but he'd rather she decide on her own to share the information with him without being prodded into it.

That didn't mean she wasn't above asking a few pointed questions of her own. At least she waited until they were in the car and driving through the darkness back to Dunbar. "Have you ever been married?"

"No."

When he didn't continue, she gave him a considering look. "Well, that was succinct. I'm betting there's a lot more to the story."

How much did he want to share? The honest answer was as little as possible. "I came close once. We were together a little over a year when she walked away and didn't look back. That said, if Marti hadn't ended things when she did, I would have."

Rikki cringed. "Sorry if I brought up a sore subject. I didn't mean to pry."

Max grinned at her. "Sure you did, but that's okay. It isn't as if I haven't asked questions about you and your ex."

"That's right. You did."

He knew a hint when he heard one. He remained silent as he slowed to turn onto the narrow two-lane highway that led to Dunbar before adding more to the narrative. "Fine, if you want the gory details, you can have them. Marti and I met right after college. She was a reporter, and our paths crossed when I did a feature article for the newspaper she worked for. We shared a lot of the same interests, and one thing led to another. But, as it turned out, we didn't actually like each other, at least not enough to risk anything as serious as marriage."

Honesty was painful, but Max couldn't blame it all on Marti. "It was mostly my fault. At least, that's what she said. Looking back,

I can't say that she was wrong. I don't open up to people easily, and she wanted that. She said she couldn't build a life with a man who never let her close enough to see who he really was. Then there was something about being cold at the core."

"Really? She actually said that?"

Rikki sounded angry, as if Marti's assessment of Max made her furious. Her next words confirmed that. "What was wrong with her? Because she was way off base. Look how good you are with Carter. Kids are often great judges of character, and he took to you right away."

Her defense of him pleased Max to no end, but then, she didn't know the details of his past any more than Marti had. "I'd like to think I've grown up some since then."

At least, he hoped so, considering Rikki had already been hurt enough by one man's immaturity. She reached over to pat him on the arm. "Life somehow forces all of us to grow up at some point whether we want to or not."

"Truer words were never…"

He let the words drift off as they rounded

the last corner and the bed-and-breakfast came into sight. "What the heck?"

Rikki turned to see what had caught Max's attention. She gasped when she realized there was a Dunbar police car parked in her drive-way with its lights on and flashing. It also worried him that every light was on in the house. That certainly wasn't how they'd left it. "What's happened?"

Max's phone rang before he could even hazard a guess. "What's going on, Cade?"

"I heard Rikki was out with you. Are you anywhere close?"

"We went out to dinner, but we're right down the street." He slowed to a stop, not willing to approach the house until he knew if it was safe. "The call is on speakerphone, so we can both hear you."

"Come on ahead. I'll explain things when you get here."

Max hit the accelerator. "We're on the way."

He couldn't help but think that it was a good thing Carter wasn't with them right now. They'd thought about picking him up on their way, but the party wasn't due to break up for another hour. Neither one of them had wanted to make him leave early, so Max had offered to go back out to retrieve him closer to the ten o'clock deadline.

Meanwhile, Rikki had Max's hand in a death grip. "What do you think has happened?"

"Only one way to find out."

He parked in his usual spot and walked around to the other side of the car, intending to open the door for Rikki. It wasn't surprising that she was already out and heading straight for Cade Peters.

The man obviously had years of experience in dealing with situations like this, because the first words out of his mouth were, "Everything is fine, Rikki. No damage except to the lock on the back door."

The flashing red-and-blue lights on Cade's vehicle painted everyone's face in stark relief. Even so, Rikki managed to look pale and not a little scared. "Someone broke in?"

"Looks like it."

Max spun to face the new addition to their little party. "Titus, what are you doing here?"

Cade answered for him. "He's the one who called it in."

"I was out walking Ned." He patted the

huge dog on the head. "As we passed by, I saw a weird light flickering on the second floor, most likely a flashlight. I'd heard the two of you went out to dinner while Rikki's boy was at Shelby's."

It spoke to how fast gossip spread through town that the most solitary man in Dunbar knew so much about everyone else's business. Meanwhile, Titus was still talking. "I continued walking in case someone was keeping watch. Once we were out of sight, I called Cade. By the time he arrived, they were already gone. No more flickering lights, and the back door was standing wide open."

"Thanks for calling it in, Mr. Kondrat."

Titus offered Rikki a small smile. "No need to be formal among neighbors. It's Titus, and you're welcome."

Max studied the house as flames of anger in his chest threatened to burn out of control. How dare someone invade the safe place that Rikki had created for herself and her son! He wasn't a violent man by nature, but right now he would cheerfully take a ball bat to whoever had done this.

"Have you been inside?"

Cade nodded. "Yeah, I wanted to make

sure Titus was right about the culprit or culprits being long gone. I called you right after that to let you two know what was going on."

"Do you want us to come inside with you?"

"Not yet. I want to ask you a few questions first, and then we'll do a quick walk-through so the two of you can check to see if anything is missing or damaged. I've also called the county to send their forensics people down here to work their magic for me. I'm not sure when they'll arrive, but it could take a while."

Max wrapped his arm around Rikki's shoulders and held her close. It wasn't actually all that chilly outside, but she was trembling. The additional support might not do much about her fear, but he had to do something to help her.

Cade studied her for a few seconds. "I'm going to call Shelby and let her know there'll be a delay before you can pick up Carter. She's good with kids and knows to keep him busy enough to not worry about where you are. To be honest, I'd rather have him hanging out with her than risk scaring him with all of this going on."

Max was glad that Rikki didn't hesitate.

"That would be great if it's not too much trouble."

"I'll let her know."

After making the call, his expression transformed from friendly neighbor to one that made it clear he was a cop on a case. "If you're up to it, we should get started."

"I'm fine."

When she shivered again, Max shrugged off his sports coat and wrapped it around her shoulders. At least Cade waited until then to start his interrogation. Max was feeling pretty darn protective right now, and it was all he could do not to plant himself between his friend and the woman who didn't deserve to have her home invaded. She smiled up at him in thanks for the jacket, and then stood straight and met Cade's gaze head on. "Ask away."

"It's never easy to know if a break-in like this is just somebody taking advantage of the owner being away for the evening to steal a few things to turn into quick cash or if they broke into your house specifically for some other reason."

After a brief pause, he asked, "Do you

know of anyone who might be out to get you?"

Rikki didn't say a word as her knees gave out and sent her plunging toward the ground. But all things considered, Max figured that was probably answer enough.

CHAPTER ELEVEN

Rikki couldn't have sorted out all of the emotions whirling through her head at that moment even if she'd wanted to. At least Max had caught her before she actually landed on the driveway, saving her some embarrassment. In a surprising show of strength, he swept her up in his arms and carried her over to his car. Titus did an end run to get there first and had the door open so Max could settle her into the front seat.

If that wasn't humiliation enough, all three men wanted to call the paramedics to come check her out. Darn it, she didn't want to be some damsel-in-distress ninny. Now that she'd had a chance to catch her breath, pure anger replaced the fear that had been her initial response to learning that someone had dared to invade her home.

"Please don't call them. I'm fine." She paused to draw another calming breath. When Max started to protest, she cut him off. "Really, I'm just upset by what's happened."

Max looked skeptical, but Cade finally nodded. "So I take it you do know someone who might want to cause you trouble."

She really didn't want to tell Cade all the sordid details of her past, especially with Max—not to mention Titus—standing there listening to every word. What if it changed how Max thought of her? How he looked at her? But the determined look on Cade's face made it clear that there was no avoiding the conversation.

"Can we go through the house first? Then we can sit down and talk about it. I'd rather not stand out here in the driveway where the whole world can listen in."

Okay, that was an obvious exaggeration, but several of her neighbors were standing out in their yards watching all of the excitement. It would be no time at all before phone calls were placed and emails sent to spread the news. The best she could do was to try to limit the damage. Not only was her own reputation at stake, but also that of her bed-and-breakfast. Those few bad reviews she'd gotten recently would be nothing compared to the damage to her business if people thought it wasn't safe to stay there.

Cade scanned the gathering crowd and sighed. "Let's go inside."

As she followed Cade and Titus to the front porch, she was grateful for Max's solid presence next to her. He had his arm around her, keeping her grounded. That didn't stop her from wanting to scream at the unfairness of it all. She'd worked so hard to put the past behind her and focus on the future she wanted to build for herself and her son.

Okay, she'd survived everything that people had thrown at her before; she would do so again. Bracing herself for what was to come, she took Max's hand as they stepped across the threshold into the building that had become the first real home she'd known in years, the place that represented all of her hopes and dreams. It would be easy to let this nightmare tarnish it, but she wasn't going to let it. No one was going to ruin all the work she'd put into making a success of her business.

Shoulders back, she led the group from one room to another as they looked for signs of damage or things that had gone missing. At first glance, she couldn't spot a single sign that anyone had touched anything at all. Max followed along in her wake, doing his own close inspection.

As he looked around, he said, "Other than the back door, I don't see anything that's out of place or damaged so far."

The library was the only room they hadn't yet checked out on the first floor. When she opened the door, she stared in shock at the mess scattered on the large table and floor. Whoever had come through had taken the time to totally wreck the model that Max and Carter had worked so hard on. The pirate ship had been smashed and the pieces flung helter-skelter across the room.

Max picked up a handful of broken pieces and muttered under his breath. "Carter is going to be devastated."

"Why would anyone trash a child's toy?"

Cade and Titus both looked every bit as furious as Max, but it was Titus who responded. "I can think of three reasons. They could simply be jerks who like to mess things up. Considering we haven't seen any other pointless damage, I'm doubting that's what is going on. It could also be because they knew how much it would hurt you because it will upset your son. Finally, if they somehow knew Max was involved, the destruction might have been aimed at him. Considering he's a temporary guest, that seems unlikely to me. Regardless, until Cade figures out who did this, there's no way to know which is the right answer."

As he spoke, his hands were clenched in tight fists, his eyes cold with anger. His dog whined softly and leaned in closer to his owner. Titus finally gently stroked Ned's head, acknowledging the dog's warm support.

Max stared at the mess, his expression bleak. "We'll need to replace some of the pieces, so I'll order us a new set. We can work on the Viking ship until it gets here."

She wanted to tell Max not to bother, that it cost too much money, but she knew he wouldn't listen. "Let's head upstairs. I want to get this over with."

Even though Cade had already made sure the house was empty, he insisted on leading the charge up the steps. After clearing each room, he let her and Max walk through. Nothing seemed disturbed in the first few rooms. The apartment she and Carter shared looked the same as it had when she'd left home with

Max. When they reached the green room where Debra Billings had been staying, Cade stopped to say, "This one looks like it's been occupied recently. Is your guest still in residence?"

"No, she checked out earlier today, but I haven't had a chance to clean the room or check the wardrobe to make sure she didn't forget anything. Ms. Billings has family in this area, so she often stays here when she comes over from Spokane for a visit. She's a private duty nurse and had to go back home to start a new job."

The men followed her into the room. They checked out the wardrobe, under the bed, and anywhere else they could think of. From there, they looked into the bathroom down the hall that was shared by the green room and the rose room. Finding nothing obvious out of place, they checked the third floor rooms with similar results.

That left Max's room in the turret. The door was ajar. He cursed under his breath and pushed past Cade to look around. His research had been ripped out of his notebook, and his books were scattered all over the floor. At least his laptop hadn't been stolen.

When he knelt to gather up the mess, Cade stopped him. "Sorry, Max, but this a crime scene. We have to leave everything as it is until the forensic team goes through it all."

She hated that for Max. One reason he preferred to take care of the room himself was that he didn't like anyone messing with his stuff. This time, she reached out to take his hand, reassuring him with her touch. He gave her hand a quick squeeze and then visibly relaxed. "I won't know if any of the papers are missing until I go through them. I can't imagine why my research into a century-old crime when my great-grandfather's gold was stolen would be of value to anyone but me. Once your crew finishes dusting my laptop for prints, I'll see if the intruder tried to access anything. It's password protected, so with luck they couldn't get in."

"We're done here for now. Let's go back downstairs so I can finish taking your statements." Cade's phone buzzed. After reading the message on the screen, he gave Rikki a long look. "I hate to say it, but I would suggest that you both pack what you'd need to spend the night at a hotel. The forensic crew can't get here until morning. I really need them to process the place before I can let you move back in."

Max nodded. "I keep a bag in my car that contains the basic necessities, so I'm good to go. Rikki, do you need help getting stuff together for you and Carter?"

"No, it shouldn't take me long." She looked back at Cade. "Can I take a few things out of the bathroom?"

He nodded. "Take what you need."

The men waited in the hall while she packed a bag for herself and Carter. After that, they finally adjourned to the living room downstairs. Titus stopped at the front door with Ned at his side. "Cade, if you don't need us any longer, I'm going to head out."

"Go ahead. Thanks for sticking around to help."

Titus turned his attention in Rikki's direction. "If you need anything, don't hesitate to call. Have Max bring you and your boy to my place tomorrow for lunch or dinner. It'll be on the house."

Then he was gone before she could respond. "He's already done so much. I should have thanked him again."

Cade chuckled. "The man isn't much of

a talker, and I suspect he gets embarrassed when people catch him doing something nice. My advice is to let him feed you. It's his way of taking care of people. When I threw Shelby in jail a while back, Titus showed up at the back door with food for her, me, and all of my officers. He took off before anyone had a chance to thank him then, too."

She'd run out of excuses to avoid telling Cade what he needed to know. Max would probably allow them privacy if she asked him to, but that would hurt his feelings. If what he heard changed how he viewed her, it was better to find out before she allowed herself to get further entangled with the man.

Cade sat on one of the upholstered chairs in front of the picture window while she chose the love seat that faced it. Max hesitated only briefly before positioning himself next to her, once again wrapping his arm around her shoulders. She let herself lean closer to him as she started talking.

"For you to understand what happened, I need to go back to the beginning. I apologize for how long this will take."

Cade looked up from his notebook. "Take your time, Rikki."

"I lived with my maternal grandmother in Boise from the time I was about ten. No idea who my father was, and my mother…well, let's just say there were good reasons why my grandmother got custody of me. We weren't rich by any means, but we got by okay. After high school, I enrolled in a local community college program that would give me the prerequisites for a four-year degree in hotel management at one of the state colleges. Grandma passed away in the summer between my first year and the start of my second. She left me enough money to pay the rent and my tuition, and I worked at a local hotel to get some experience and to keep food on the table. If I was careful, it would've been enough to see me through all four years."

Lost in the past, she stared out the front window and kept talking. "I met my ex-husband right after I started the first quarter of my second year. It was one of those whirlwind romances you hear about, and we got married six months after we met. I found out I was pregnant right before I finished up my degree at the community college. In brief, I thought the plan was that we'd have the baby, and then I'd go back to school. Joel had different ideas, and we got divorced. He's out of our lives completely."

Max interrupted her long enough to mutter, "Good riddance."

That made her smile. "No argument there. Anyway, I enrolled at the state college and rented a basement apartment from a man named Bill Spier. It was close to both the school and the hotel where I worked part-time. I had to be careful with my money, but Carter and I were doing okay.

"Anyway, my landlord was getting up there in years and didn't get out much. He was lonely, and so was I. Bill was such a nice man, and he enjoyed spending time with me and Carter. His only family was an adult niece and nephew who lived on the eastern border of Montana. They're twins named Traci and Casey. They rarely called him and almost never visited, not even for the holidays. Instead, the three of us—Bill, Carter, and I—celebrated special occasions together."

Once again, Max spoke up. "It was nice that you had each other."

"I thought so. Anyway, Bill passed away in his sleep near the end of my senior year. Traci and Casey immediately swept in to take over his estate. One of their first actions was to order me to move out at the end of my lease, which I did without protest. As his closest relatives, the twins expected to inherit everything. That's what I figured, too, but Bill surprised all of us. The twins weren't at all happy that I was asked to attend the reading of the will. Although the bulk of Bill's estate did go to the twins, he also set aside a sum of money for me. He included a letter to me that said how much he had appreciated all the time Carter and I spent with him, and that he also admired my fierce determination to succeed. He wanted to give me a financial boost to help me achieve my goals."

Cade heaved a big sigh. "Let me guess. The niece and nephew accused you of bamboozling their uncle out of his money."

"Got it right on the first try. Bill lived pretty simply, so I had no idea that he actually had quite a bit of money. When you add in what they got for selling the house and everything in it, each of the twins ended up with a seven-digit inheritance. He left me a small fraction of that amount, but they wanted every penny they could get. They got the police involved by accusing me of all manner of things. They even hired a private investigator to see if I'd been stealing stuff out of Bill's house and pocketing the money I got from selling it. Mr. Gable, Bill's lawyer, finally interceded on my behalf. He told the investigating officer that Bill had made it clear I had no knowledge of his decision to leave me some money until the will was read."

She couldn't help but smile a little. "He was pretty disgusted by the twins' behavior, which is why he billed the estate for the time he spent clearing my name. I'm quite sure Bill's relatives weren't at all happy about that."

"They didn't stop there."

There was an extra level of grit in Cade's voice, but she knew the anger wasn't aimed at her. "No, they didn't. They took it upon themselves to cause me all kinds of problems. They deliberately damaged my credit rating by reporting that I hadn't paid my last month's rent. I'd given them the check on time, but they held on to it for two months before they finally 'found' it. They caused me problems with my employer at the hotel to the point I was let go. They even tried to stir up trouble with the college. Luckily, one of my professors stood up for me."

Without warning, Max abruptly got up and left the room. She watched him go, unsure what was going on. Had her story been too much for him? It wouldn't be a surprise. How many men wanted to be involved with a woman with so much personal baggage? She might not blame him for walking away, but it really hurt. To her relief, he returned a few seconds later with a box of tissues in his hand. It wasn't until then that she realized she'd started crying at some point in her story. "Thanks."

After dabbing at her eyes, she picked up where she'd left off. "After I graduated, I got a job at a hotel in the same city where we'd been living, but Bill's relatives started harassing me again. Then…well, you get the idea. I finally packed up Carter and our belongings and started driving west. I figured I could get lost in a city the size of Seattle, especially since they lived in Montana. We stopped for lunch in Leavenworth after crossing the pass. Someone happened to have left a local newspaper on the table, so I browsed the help wanted ads while I waited for our food. I got pretty excited when I saw that Maude Travis, the woman who used to own this place, was looking for someone to manage her bed-and-breakfast. The salary wasn't all that much, but it also included the apartment where we live upstairs."

She smiled. "I decided it was worth checking into, so we drove straight here and talked to Maude. Bless her heart, she hired me on the spot. Because of health issues, Maude moved into a retirement home with progressive care soon afterward. A few weeks later, she decided to sell the business and gave me the first chance to buy it. I used the money Bill left me for a down payment and borrowed the rest. Up until recently, I had no reason to think that the twins had found me."

Cade leaned forward, elbows on his knees. "What's changed?"

"I've gotten some unexpectedly poor reviews on social media. Whoever is doing it doesn't identify themselves or offer any explanation of what they didn't like about their stay here. Just a one-star review or maybe a comment like 'avoid this place at all costs.' It's just the sort of attack campaign the twins would use to injure my reputation again."

By that point, Max looked thoroughly disgusted. So did Cade, who paused to jot a few notes. "I'll need their contact information if you have it handy, or after you get back tomorrow. In fact, why don't you lock up the house now and head over to Shelby's to pick up Carter? Check in somewhere close by and get a good night's sleep. Call me in the morning so I can update you on the investigation."

Max stood and held out his hand to tug her up off the love seat. "We should be able find a place up on Highway 2, so we won't be far away."

Rather than make Cade wait to get the information on the twins, Rikki headed into the entry where she kept her address book and wrote down their names, addresses and phone numbers. While she was at it, she also included the name and number for the attorney who had handled Bill's estate and handed the paper to Cade. "This is the most up-to-date information I have. They may have moved or changed their numbers since then."

He folded the paper and stuck it in his uniform pocket. "It's a place to start. And Rikki, I'm sorry this happened to you, and not only the break-in. I swear I can't understand what makes people act the way they do sometimes."

Cade's words and Max's solid presence at her side were bright spots in what had been a really dark night. For now, she needed to pick up Carter. The poor kid was probably wondering if she'd forgotten about him.

Max picked up her bag as the three of them headed out into the night. She locked the door on the way and wished it was just as simple to close the door on her past.

CHAPTER TWELVE

CARTER FELL ASLEEP within minutes after they buckled him into the back seat of Max's car. The poor kid had had a long night. After Shelby's other guests had left, she had enlisted Carter's help in making a batch of cookies to take home with him. When he proudly handed them over to his mother, Rikki had given him a big hug.

She'd made the decision not to tell Carter about what had happened other than to say that there was a problem at the house, and they were staying at a hotel until she could get someone in tomorrow to make repairs. He'd accepted the explanation with no questions other than to ask Max if he'd be staying at the same hotel.

Right now, Max watched as she briefly twisted around to check on Carter. Sighing, she turned back to look out into the night. "Poor guy, he's worn out. Sounds like he and the other kids had a good time with Shelby. I really dread telling him about what happened to the pirate ship. I can't understand why anyone would do something so mean."

Max was mad about it, too. Absolutely furious, actually. "He'll be upset, but we'll have a replacement within the next forty-eight hours. And like I said earlier, we can start on the other set while we wait for the new pirate ship to arrive."

Rikki offered him a half-hearted smile. "I know it won't do any good to say that you really don't have to buy another one. He'll understand."

That was not happening. "I can afford it, and I won't let anyone spoil our fun. Besides, having that to look forward to will give him something to focus on besides knowing a bad guy was in your house."

While he spoke, he watched her out of the corner of his eye. The ambient lighting from the dashboard emphasized the tense set of her jawline and how her eyebrows rode low over her eyes as she worried about what tomorrow would bring. Might as well get a tough discussion out of the way while they were alone. Well, except for the sleeping boy in the back seat.

"You were worried that neither Cade nor I would believe you about the money you got from your landlord."

She kept her gaze pinned on the road stretched out in front of them. "No one ever does."

Max pointed out the obvious. "The attorney clearly did, and you said your professor stood up for you."

"Yeah, but that's two out of who knows how many. After all this time, I still can't believe my boss at the hotel believed I was lying about it. I thought we were friends."

He didn't blame her for feeling bitter. "Actually, four people believe you if you count me and Cade. You also have Titus on your side, so that makes five. I realize you don't want to broadcast the situation all over creation, but the people who really know you would believe you."

She finally turned to face him. "That's just it. Since Joel and everything that's happened since, I've gotten in the habit of keeping people at arm's length. It hurts too much to make new friends only to have them believe enough of the twins' lies to leave them doubting my honesty and character. It's hard to get a good job when people don't trust you."

He tightened his fingers on the steering wheel, wishing for a second that he had the same death grip on the twins' scrawny necks for the misery they'd caused the woman sitting next to him. "You're amazing, Rikki, and so strong. I hope you know that."

"I'm glad someone thinks so." Her smile looked a little more genuine. "I do appreciate how you've stayed with me every step of the way this evening. That was really above and beyond what anyone can expect of a guest."

Okay, that hurt. Did she actually still think of him as nothing more than another paying customer? If so, she was fooling herself. He'd bet his last dollar that she hadn't gone out to dinner with anyone else who had stayed at her B and B, much less trusted them to watch over her son so she could spend an evening with the ladies in town. But now wasn't the best time for that discussion. They were both tired and upset about the break-in.

By that point, they'd reached the closest town. "Any preference which motel or hotel we check into?"

"Anything will be fine."

It took them two tries to find a place that had two rooms available. Luckily, they were next to each other, which made things more convenient. Rikki brought in their bags, while Max carried Carter. He helped her get him settled in one of the beds in her room. "Do you have everything you need?"

She offered him a tired smile as she followed him over to the door. "Yes, we'll be fine. How about you? Do you need anything?"

He was going to say no, but found that there was one thing he definitely needed— or at least wanted—before walking out that door. As it turned out, he wasn't going to wait until tomorrow to clarify a few things when it came to their relationship. He might pay for the use of the turret room, but he was not just another one of her guests. It was time for her to admit that.

"Yeah, there is one thing."

Before she could ask what that was, he had his arms around her, pulling her in close. "I want this."

He softly brushed his lips across hers, once and then a second time. Then he pulled back far enough to meet her wide-eyed gaze head on. "If you don't want this, if I really am just another guest, say so and I'll stop."

It was like throwing the dice and knowing everything worthwhile in his life was riding on the outcome. Rikki held his gaze for one heartbeat and then another, her clear gray eyes studying him. He had no idea what she was searching for. But when she tilted her face up, bringing their lips close enough for him to feel the warmth of her skin, he thought maybe somehow she'd found it.

He didn't know if he closed that last small distance or if she was the one who perfectly aligned her lips to his. All he cared about was that they were kissing, and he could finally learn the warmth and taste of this amazing woman. Her hands came up around his shoulders until her fingers brushed through the hair at the nape of his neck. He smiled against her mouth and deepened the kiss.

Rikki sighed and leaned back against the wall as if her legs would no longer support her. The small movement reminded Max of how much the woman had been through that evening. As much as he wanted to spend hours…maybe even days…right there in her arms, now wasn't the time. They both needed to call it a night and get some rest. Tomorrow could be another tough day.

Easing back, he rested his forehead against hers. "I should go now. Call when you're up and about in the morning. We'll stop for breakfast before we go back to the house. Sleep in if you can."

"Sounds like a plan." She let her hands drop back down to her sides, releasing her hold on him. "Thank you again for everything tonight."

"You're welcome."

He took a deliberate step back, knowing he might not find the strength to leave if he didn't go now. "See you in the morning. Lock the door behind me."

"I will."

He was unlocking his own room when Rikki's door opened again. She peeked out at him, her expression solemn as she whispered, "Just so you know, Max, you haven't been just another guest for a long time now. Good night."

Satisfied they'd settled that much, Max waited until he was safely inside his room before giving in to the urge to do a little happy dance. He was still smiling when he finally sought out his own lonely bed.

Rikki helped Carter out of the back seat of the car and waited for Max to join them before approaching the house. The three of them had slept until well after eight o'clock. They'd taken their time getting dressed before walking across the highway to eat a huge breakfast. While she personally showed some restraint at the waffle bar, Carter and Max hadn't even tried. Between the two of them, the pair had consumed a horrifying amount of whipped cream, maple syrup and chocolate chips on their waffles. At least they'd each made a token effort to eat something healthy by tossing a few blueberries on top of the heap.

She suspected Max was currently experiencing some regrets over the amount he'd eaten from the way he rubbed his stomach and frowned. Deciding to tease him a little, she asked, "A little too much breakfast?"

"I blame him," Max said, pointing at Carter. "He set a poor example for me. I've never had chocolate chips and whipped cream on a waffle before."

She arched an eyebrow. "Remind me again—which one of you is the adult and which one is the five-year-old?"

Rather than answer her question, Max immediately pointed down the street. "Oh, look, here comes Cade. He's right on time."

One reason they'd lingered over breakfast was that the forensics team had still been going through the house. Cade had warned her that there would be fingerprint dust or whatever they called that stuff on various surfaces that she'd need to clean up. Otherwise the house should be pretty much as she'd left it. At least they'd focused their attention on the few places where they knew for sure the suspect had touched things—the back door, the library and Max's room.

Cade pulled up out front but remained in his cruiser for several minutes talking on the phone. When he finally joined them, he said, "Sorry to keep you waiting so long. I was sympathizing with Shelby about the latest wedding crisis. Something about the florist not being able to get the right shade of pink roses for the bouquets. I suggested that she order the red instead."

He shuddered. "I'll never make that mistake again."

It was hard not to laugh as Rikki hastened

to reassure him. "We only just got here ourselves."

"I'm not sure how long I can stay, what with the flower crisis and all." He held out the set of keys she'd given him last night. "As you go through the house, make note of anything that is out of place or missing. Max, I'll be really interested if anything was taken from your room or if any attempt was made to hack into your laptop."

"It shouldn't take me long to check."

Carter eased closer to Cade. "Chief Peters, a bad person broke our pirate ship. Mr. Max ordered us a new one, and we have to start all over."

His chin wobbled a little as he spoke, which had Cade crouching down to his level. "I know, Carter. I'm sorry that happened. It was really mean of them, but I know you and Mr. Max will have fun working on the new one. I think he also mentioned something about a Viking ship, too. You'll have to invite me back to see them when they're all done."

That offer brightened her son's mood. "I will."

As Cade stood back up, he patted her son on the shoulder. "I can't wait."

Rikki took that as her cue to head to the front door. As soon as she unlocked it, Max eased past her to be the first one inside. He paused, his head tipped to the side as if listening for something, maybe to confirm they were alone in the house. "It's quiet."

She looked around the counter at her desk and was relieved to see that nothing had been disturbed. While she did that, Carter charged down the hall to the library. She wanted to stop him, but Max caught up with him first. "Remember, kiddo, we're going to make a new one. Don't let the mess upset you."

Then he let the boy open the door. Her heart nearly broke at the distraught look on his face. Finally, he sighed. "Don't worry, Mom. I'll clean it up."

It was tempting to tell him to leave it to her, but she hesitated. Maybe it would be better to give him something to do. "Sort all the blocks that are still good from the broken ones. You might be able to use them to build something else. I'll get you some containers to use."

By the time she got back, Max and Cade had headed up to the turret room, and Carter was already hard at work. After giving him the containers, she hustled upstairs to see if Max needed anything.

Cade stood leaning against the wall as Max finished gathering up the papers into a neat pile on the table he used as his desk. Using a washcloth from the bathroom, he carefully wiped the fingerprint dust off his computer and then booted it up. Rikki held her breath while he checked it out.

"As far as I can tell, no one managed to get past the security. That's a relief." He sat back in his chair, a frown on his face. "I'll run more thorough scans later to make sure."

He set the computer aside to make room so he could sort through his papers. She and Cade watched in silence as Max brought order out of the chaos left behind by who-ever had ransacked the room. It didn't take long. "Everything is here. I'll have to reprint a bunch of stuff and buy a new notebook, but that's easy enough. I still can't imagine what anyone hoped to gain from my research. It doesn't make sense."

Cade straightened up. "Well, unless all of this and the mess in the library were red her-rings."

Rikki frowned. "How so?"

"To distract us from what the person was really after. You know, to keep us focused on why they trashed Carter's model and Max's paperwork instead. If so, then we need to be looking for the real reason."

"How do we do that?"

The lawman was clearly frustrated. "All I can suggest is that you go through each room again. I know we did that last night, but you might spot something in the daylight that we didn't notice the first time through. If you find anything, let me know."

Max looked up from his paperwork. "I'd offer to help, but I'm not familiar with many of the other guest rooms."

He was right. She was the only one who would likely notice any changes. "That's okay. You've already done enough. It shouldn't take me long to do a walk-through."

Cade checked the time. "I need to get back to the office and check in with Shelby about the flower fiasco."

Max snickered. "Let me know if I can do anything to help. Maybe we can get some tissue paper in the right color and make some of those paper carnations they used to decorate the gym for the dances where I went to school. I can teach you and Titus how to make them. We'll make a night of it. I'll bring the pizza and beer."

That had the other man laughing. "I want to be there when you make that suggestion to Shelby. I'll make sure to have the EMTs on standby in case she doesn't take it well."

Max laughed, too. "Nice, Cade."

"You think I'm kidding? That woman has no sense of humor about the wedding, but I promise to say something nice about you at your funeral." He patted Max on the shoulder. "On that cheery note, I'm out of here."

Rikki followed Cade back downstairs. "Were you able to find out anything about the twins?"

"Not yet, but I plan to follow up this afternoon." He stopped in the entry near the door. "How are you doing, Rikki? I know all of this is a lot to deal with."

"I'm upset, but managing for the most part. I hate that my son is so unhappy about his ship, but you and Max have both helped him deal with that. I also have mixed feelings about you reaching out to the twins. In a way, it would be a relief to know that they were behind the break-in. But if it wasn't them, it might just put me back on their radar. The last thing I want is for them to start hounding me again."

"I reached out to the police in their area and asked them to make discreet inquiries about the twins' activities over the past few days. If they've been seen by friends, coworkers, or neighbors, then we'll have our answer."

"And if it wasn't them, then we're back to square one with no real suspects."

"Don't worry, Rikki. We'll do our best to find answers. Call if you find anything or if something else happens. And don't forget to take Titus up on his lunch or dinner offer. No use in working any harder today than you have to."

"I'm thinking we'll head there for dinner. After the breakfast we had this morning, I can't imagine any of us are going to want much in the way of lunch. I'm not sure how well Titus would take it if we showed up and then only picked at our food."

"Good thinking. No one wants to incur the man's wrath. I'd go into withdrawal if he ever cut off my access to his sweet potato pie or his chicken and dumplings."

"That would be a disaster." She followed

him out onto the porch. "Thanks again, Cade. I really appreciate everything you've done."

Back inside, she stood still and let the quiet settle around her. Should she start on the first floor and work her way up or the other way around? Finally, she checked in on Carter and then headed for the kitchen. She'd begin by washing the back door and scouring the kitchen counters. Even if the bad guy, as Carter had called him, hadn't touched anything, it was likely the forensics team had. Either way, she wouldn't feel comfortable cooking in there until she knew every trace of their presence was gone.

Gathering her cleaning supplies, she got to work and started reclaiming her home.

CHAPTER THIRTEEN

THE PAST TWO days had been filled with lots of cleaning. On Monday afternoon, Max made a trip to an office supply store in another town to replace the items that had been damaged or destroyed by the intruder. He'd taken Carter with him to give Rikki a break. The pair had returned with not just what Max had needed, but also a large sack of supplies for Carter to use. Once again, Max had spent more than he should have, but Carter was so pleased with his own "writing" materials that she couldn't bring herself to complain. Upon their return, the two had moved a small table and chair into Max's room for her son to use whenever Carter wanted to "write" with Max.

She continued to have mixed feelings about the deepening connection between her guest and her son, not to mention herself. She wasn't used to depending on anyone other than herself, and for good reason. Her own father had never been part of her life, and her mother had come and gone without warning. The only person who'd been there for her was her grandmother. Having Joel abandon her and their son had only made it that much harder for her to trust anyone.

However, her resolve to do anything about her qualms regarding Max's role in their lives had definitely started to fade. If Max eventually decided to disappear from their lives for good, well, all she could do was deal with the fallout.

After getting a call late the night before, Max had left for Montana at the crack of dawn on Tuesday morning to meet with a source for one of his freelance articles. Carter had been really disappointed when he woke up to find his buddy was gone again. Luckily, the unexpected arrival of an entire family later that afternoon had provided a nice distraction for her son. They had four kids, including two about Carter's age. The three of them had spent much of the evening hanging out in Carter's room.

The Quinns were now packing up to leave. Dale handed her his credit card. "Ms. Bruce, we've really enjoyed our stay. I also want to thank you for finding room for the whole family on such short notice. It was a true godsend."

She smiled at the older gentleman. "You're welcome. Be sure to take some of the muffins and rolls from the dining room if you want something to snack on while you're driving. I can also fill your to-go cups with coffee if you'd like. The offer is good for your son and his family as well."

"That would be great. I know he'd appreciate it. Meanwhile, we're going to head back to that diner in town for lunch."

She handed back his card. "I'll set out some juice boxes for the grandkids, too."

"That would be great."

He immediately went back upstairs to spread the good news. His family wasn't actually checking out until later in the day, so she'd have to wait until then before she could ready the rooms for her next guests. Not that she had any scheduled to arrive that day. It was probably a good thing, because Elizabeth Glines was hosting a surprise wedding shower for Shelby that evening. Her daughter, Liza, was going to keep an eye on Carter and several other children at the party so the adults could enjoy themselves.

The Quinn family's unexpected stay had been a real boon to her bottom line. The older couple and their son's family were on their way back home to Colorado after attending a family reunion up near the Canadian border. They'd meant to make it as far as Boise yesterday but their van developed engine trouble. The good news was, they found a repair shop that could fit them in, but only if the shop could keep the vehicle overnight. The owner had given them Rikki's number, and they'd booked five of her rooms.

After putting the coffee on, she packed up juice boxes, several bottles of water, and the muffins. Next, she stopped to peek into the library, where Carter was working on the new pirate ship.

"You doing okay?"

He held up the segment he was working on. "Yeah. Mr. Max will be amazed how much I got done when he gets back."

"He'll be proud of you, and so am I." She winked at him. "I'll be in the kitchen if you need me."

He nodded and kept on working. No sooner

had she started for the kitchen than the front door opened. She wasn't expecting anyone and hadn't heard any of the Quinns coming down the stairs. She did an about-face to see if she was needed.

To her surprise, Debra Billings stood waiting by the front counter, looking a bit sheepish. "Hi, Rikki. I know I should've called first, but you usually have rooms available. But judging by the cars in the driveway, I may have misjudged the situation."

Rikki mustered up her best professional smile. "Yes, I unexpectedly ended up with a full house yesterday afternoon."

"So none of the usual rooms are available?" Her expression turned hopeful. "I didn't see that writer's car out there. If he's out of town, maybe I could book that one tonight."

How many times did Rikki need to remind the woman that Max had paid for the room for weeks in advance? Whether he was actually in residence or not, the room wasn't available. Besides, he was due back tomorrow or the next day, not that it was any of Debra's business.

"I'm sorry, but that room remains unavailable. However, my other guests are leaving today. They paid for a late checkout, so they have the rooms until later this afternoon. If you're willing to wait, I can make up one of those rooms for you as soon as they leave. You'd be welcome to hang out in the living room until then. Otherwise, I can call you when the room is ready."

Then, as much as she really didn't want to make the offer, she added, "I can also call to see which of the motels on Highway 2 might have rooms available. That would save you the hassle of having to check yourself."

From the stony look on the woman's face, she wasn't particularly thrilled with either of those options. Finally, she sighed. "I'm sorry, and I know this really isn't your fault. I should've called first. My cousin was admitted to the hospital. When I heard she wasn't doing well, I panicked, threw a few things in my suitcase, and headed out."

"I'm sorry to hear that. I hope she feels better soon."

"Me, too. She's the one I'm closest to. Finding out that she was so sick hit me hard."

When Debra seemed stuck in place as if unable to make a decision on her own, Rikki tried to help her along. "Why don't I lock your luggage in the hall closet and then fix you a cup of tea? I also have some of those macadamia nut cookies you like so much. I'll bring them to you in the living room, and you can let me know if you want to wait for one of my rooms or if I should start making calls."

That seemed to do it. Debra smiled just a little. "I'll book one of your rooms for the next two nights to begin with. After I rest a bit, I'll go to the café for lunch. With luck, the room will be ready by the time I get back. If so, I might sneak in a nap before heading back over to visit my cousin. I stopped by to see her on my way here, but they were taking her for more tests. The hospital is some distance from here, so I don't know what time I will get back."

"In that case, remind me to give you one of the house keys. Carter and I will be gone this evening."

"Thank you, Rikki. I'm glad you're willing to accommodate me like this. I feel so much more comfortable staying here than I would at some impersonal hotel. Your place is so much…warmer and more welcoming."

"I'm glad to hear that. Now, I'll go fix that tea I promised you."

When she returned with the tea and cookies, Debra thanked her. "I apologize again for showing up with no warning. After the number of times I've stayed here, it's almost like my home away from home."

Rikki sat down, figuring it wouldn't kill her to spend a little time with one of her best customers. The Quinns still hadn't left, and she couldn't get started on her housekeeping duties until they did. "Are you between jobs again? The last time we spoke, you were going be taking care of a former client who had been in the hospital."

For a second Debra looked confused, but then she nodded. "Yes, she's fine. I rushed all the way back only to learn her daughter decided to come stay with her instead. I'm sure the patient was happy to have her there, but it's frustrating when I had to cut my trip short in order to help them out."

"That is too bad. Does that happen often?" Because that would be really frustrating.

"No, but it's always aggravating when it does." Debra set her tea aside. "It's one reason I've been thinking that I'd like to do something different job-wise. I've been a nurse for a long time, and it certainly never gets any easier."

She gave Rikki a considering look. "Actually, had I known this place was going to be on the market, I would've snapped it up in a heartbeat. I also stayed here a couple of times back when that older woman still ran it. What was her name? Mabel? Mary? It started with an *m*, didn't it?"

"Yes, her name was Maude. Maude Travis."

"That's it, of course. Anyway, she offered decent service, but I could tell the right person could do so much more with the place. For starters, I would really enjoy visiting with the people who stay here. But I know it's not as simple as I'm making it sound. Obviously, there's a lot of work going on behind the scenes. You're also young and fit and make it look easy. I would have to hire some help, but I'm sure there's someone here in town who needs to make a few extra bucks."

Where was Debra going with this discussion? Maybe it was time to make an excuse and find something more useful to do. "So far, I've been able to handle the workload by myself."

"It must keep you busy, what with being a single mom with a small child to care for." Before Rikki could respond, Debra added, "I hope you remember to take some time for yourself, Rikki. I speak from experience when I say that focusing too much on a career can be a mistake. I love nursing, but a career doesn't keep you warm on a cold winter night. If I'd been better at balancing my job with my personal life, I might still be married."

She stopped to study Rikki for a few seconds. "But maybe you know something about that, too."

Yep, it was definitely time to get back to work. Rikki might have shared details about her personal life with Max, but she and Debra did not have that kind of relationship. She stood up. "If you'll excuse me, I've got to check on Carter and do some of those chores we've been talking about."

"Just one more thing if you don't mind."

Rikki remained standing, hoping that would speed things along. "Sure."

"I know I've taken a roundabout way of getting to the point, but here's the thing. What I'm really saying is that I'd like to buy the bed-and-breakfast from you."

Rikki dropped back down in her chair as she struggled to process what the woman had just said. "I beg your pardon?"

Debra set her cup of tea aside. "I want to buy the bed-and-breakfast. It's exactly the sort of business I would like to take on." She waved her hand around in the air. "It's big enough to be profitable, but not so big as to make it hard to manage. I'd also like to move back to this side of the mountains to be closer to my family, which makes Dunbar the perfect location for me."

Rikki rose to her feet again and retreated a step toward the living room door. "I'm sorry, but I'm not interested in selling."

Debra kept right on talking as if she hadn't heard a word of what Rikki had just said. "I would, of course, offer what you paid for the place."

"That would be generous of you, Ms. Billings. But again, my home is not for sale. If you'll excuse me, I have work to do."

She'd almost made it to the door when her guest upped the ante. "I'm sorry, Rikki. I meant to say that my offer would be the price you paid for the house plus extra since the housing market has gone up in this area.

I would also pay an additional amount on top of that to compensate you for all of the work and money you've put into the business."

That so wasn't going to happen. The woman could offer all the money she wanted to, but nothing would compensate Rikki for all the sweat and care and pride she'd poured into the old Victorian house. It had become the home that both she and Carter needed and loved. No, she wasn't even remotely tempted by Debra's offer.

"I'm sorry, but the answer is still no. This is our home, and we plan to stay."

Debra picked up the last cookie on her plate. "You don't have to decide now, Rikki. I've made you a most generous offer. You should take some time to think about it."

Mustering up her most professional smile, Rikki shook her head. "Again, my answer is no. Now, I have work to do." She glanced at Debra's empty plate. "I'll bring you more tea and cookies."

Looking far less friendly than she had only a few minutes ago, her guest stood up. "Don't bother. I'll go have lunch, and we'll talk more about this later."

Maybe, but it wouldn't change Rikki's answer. Rather than indulge in a bit of snark on the subject, she once again fell back on her professional good manners. "I'll try to have your room ready before you get back."

Debra looked as if she had more to say, but Rikki headed that off at the pass by walking the short distance down the hallway to the library. She slipped inside until the front door opened and closed again. It was a relief when a car started and then drove away.

"Is something wrong, Mom?"

Rikki hated the worry in Carter's voice. He'd put the events of Sunday night behind him for the most part, but his question made it clear he was still worried the bad guy might show up again. As she joined him at the table, she hoped her smile was more genuine than it felt. "Nothing is wrong, kiddo. Ms. Billings left to go have lunch at the diner, and I'm expecting the Quinns to do the same. I heard the front door open, and I was listening to see if it was her leaving or someone else coming in."

Reassured that all was well, Carter went back to work on the pirate ship. Max had encouraged Carter to finish it even if Max wasn't there to help. Since Carter had spent so much time playing with their guests, he hadn't made much progress. She'd assured him that Max would understand.

"Looks like you've gotten quite a bit done today."

He stopped to study the ship. "It won't take us long to finish once Mr. Max is back."

She considered offering to hang out and work on it with him, but she actually did need to finish her chores. "I have a few things to take care of in the kitchen. After that, I'll be upstairs cleaning the rooms once the Quinns leave. If you need anything, come find me."

She swooped in to kiss his cheek before he could protest. He was going through a spell where he didn't want her to fuss over him, but sometimes she couldn't resist. "Help yourself to a reasonable snack if you get hungry."

He paused in his efforts to wipe away her kiss to give her an interested look. "Six of the macadamia nut cookies and a glass of milk?"

She crossed her arms over her chest. "One cookie and the milk."

"Mom. That's not reasonable. I'm a growing boy."

That had her laughing, but he was right. He was hungry a good part of the time no matter how much food she shoved in his direction. "Two cookies, a bunch of grapes, and the milk. That's my best offer. Do we have a deal?"

He rolled his eyes. "Yeah, we do."

"Good, and I'll even deliver it in a few minutes." With some effort, she resisted the urge to ruffle his hair before walking away. "Have fun."

Carter called after her, "When will Mr. Max be back?"

"He said it would be tomorrow evening at the earliest. I haven't heard from him, so that's all I know."

Carter looked up from his model. "I miss him."

"Me, too." She managed another smile. "But he'll be back. He promised."

And only time would tell if that was a good thing or not.

CHAPTER FOURTEEN

MAX WAS SO tired he ached. It was his own fault. He could've spent the night in Montana and left in the morning when he was more rested, but he'd finished his business earlier than expected and decided to head back toward Dunbar. The idea was to shorten how far he'd need to drive the next day.

But once he got started, he kept driving through town after town, each time thinking he'd stop in the next one. He couldn't remember when he'd reached the tipping point and decided to drive straight through to Dunbar. It wasn't the smartest thing he'd ever done, but he really wanted—no, he *needed*—to get back to Rikki and Carter. He missed them both, but that wasn't what kept him fueling up on coffee and driving through the night.

Whoever had broken into the house would be back. There were no hard facts to support that opinion, but that didn't matter. His instincts kept insisting that the intruder had been after something specific in Rikki's house, even though Max had no idea what it might have been. If simple theft had been the driving motive, why would they have left his laptop? There were also other easy-to-grab items all over the first floor of the house. Rather than rooting around in the darkness with a flashlight in unoccupied rooms on the second and third floor, why not take the easy stuff and go?

He thought about calling Cade to see what he'd learned about the twins who had caused Rikki so much trouble in the past, but that would have to wait until Max got back to town. Even if they were behind the break-in, there wasn't much Max could do about it. That was definitely outside of his purview.

But what he could do was be there to stand guard. He wasn't sure how Rikki would feel about that, but he didn't care. She and her son were his to keep safe whether they knew it or not. He suspected she wouldn't appreciate his caveman attitude, but they could argue about that once the threat was over.

With that in mind, he sped up and counted down the miles between him and the two people who had somehow become the center of his universe.

FIVE HOURS AND two more cups of coffee later, Max pulled into town. It was a good thing he was only a few blocks away from his destination, because caffeine had definitely lost its power to keep him awake. He'd done more than his fair share of marathon driving in his life, but he couldn't remember his eyelids ever feeling this heavy before.

He maintained a slow but steady pace. The last thing he wanted to do was accidentally run through one of the two stop signs in town and get pulled over by one of Dunbar's finest. He made it to the last turn and now had the B and B in his sights. Finally. He drove the last block and turned into the driveway. Relief that he'd made it back safely mixed with disappointment that all the lights in the house were off.

He wished he'd thought to get one of the house keys before he'd left on this trip. It was evidence of how muddled his thinking had become that he hadn't let Rikki know when to expect him. Now he'd either have to backtrack to Highway 2 and check into a motel for what remained of the night or else wake up Rikki to let him in.

In the end, it was a no-brainer. His mind was too fried with caffeine and exhaustion to make driving any farther a smart thing to do. He leaned back against the headrest and dialed her number. It rang several times before she finally answered.

"Rikki, it's Max. Sorry I woke you, but I'm out in the driveway."

When she didn't immediately respond, he winced. "Look, forget I called. I can sleep in my car until morning."

He squinted up at the sky to the east. There was the barest hint of light outlining the top ridge of the mountains. Dawn couldn't be all that far away. "I'll be fine. Go back to sleep."

After disconnecting the call, he wadded up his jacket for a pillow and leaned his seat back to a more comfortable angle. He'd barely closed his eyes when someone knocked on the window on his side of the car, startling him back awake.

"Who? What?"

"Max, wake up and come inside."

He blinked several times to bring his eyes into focus. Finally, he recognized Rikki's pretty face staring at him, looking confused and not a little worried. When she knocked a second time, he mumbled, "I'm awake."

He turned the key in the ignition far enough

to be able to roll down the window. "Rikki, I'm back."

She straightened up a little bit. "I can see that. Have you been drinking?"

"Yep—coffee. Lots and lots of the high-octane stuff."

He smiled at her. At least he thought he did, but maybe he was wrong about that judging by how worried she looked. "How long has it been since you slept?"

That required a great deal of thinking on his part, something he was ill-equipped to do at the moment. The best he could do was hazard a guess. "Monday…no, Tuesday. I drove straight home from Montana."

She looked even more concerned. "You drove all the way from Montana to Portland without stopping to sleep?"

Now she was the one making no sense. "Why would I drive to Portland?"

Rikki looked up at the sky as if praying for patience. "Because that's where you live, Max. You said you drove all the way home."

One of them was confused, but at the moment he couldn't have said for sure if it was Rikki or him. He tried one more time. "I did. I'm here, aren't I? In Dunbar, not Portland. If you were in the driveway at my condo, that wouldn't make any sense at all."

Rikki huffed a small laugh at that, but he wasn't sure why. She finally stepped back from the car. "Come on, Max. Let's get you out of there and inside the house. We can continue this discussion later after you've had some sleep."

"Good idea."

He rolled the window back up and then opened the door. She hovered close by as though ready to catch him if necessary. As wobbly as his legs felt when he stood up, it was probably a good idea. He reached back inside to retrieve his pack. "I need my laptop. The rest can wait until…"

When he couldn't finish that sentence, she stepped in to help him. "Until your brain starts firing on all cylinders again?"

"Yes, that."

He counted himself lucky that there was a hint of humor in her voice. She should've been reading him the riot act for dragging her out of bed at this hour. Whatever hour that might be. She took his arm and led him toward the house. "Don't forget to lock the car, Max."

After he fumbled a bit with the fob, the car beeped and the lights flashed to let him know it was mission accomplished. Rikki maintained her hold on his arm and stayed in step with him until the two of them were safely inside the house. "Do you need something to eat before you go upstairs to bed?"

"It might be a good idea. Nothing fancy, though. A muffin would be enough."

She led him down the hall to the kitchen. "We can do better than that."

After parking him at the table, she got busy making something. He wasn't sure what, but he knew it would be good and more than he deserved. It wasn't long before she set a plate in front of him containing a huge omelet and one of those muffins he'd suggested. "Thanks, Rikki."

"You're welcome. Now eat."

He did as ordered, feeling better as soon as the food hit his stomach. While he ate, Rikki made quick work of cleaning up. When he finally set down his fork, she joined him at the table. "Care to explain why you thought driving all this distance on no sleep was a good idea?"

They were stepping on shaky ground. "It seemed important at the time."

"Can you at least admit that it wasn't the smartest thing you've ever done?"

He squinted at her. "Would it help to know I've done dumber things in my life and survived?"

Oops, that was clearly the wrong answer. Rikki pinched the bridge of her nose as if his words had caused her physical pain. "Max, what if you'd fallen asleep at the wheel? You could have been badly hurt or even killed, not to mention you were a danger to other people out on the road."

He hung his head and offered the only excuse he had. "I needed to get back here fast."

"Why, Max? Telling your great-grandfather's story has waited this long. Surely an extra day's delay in working on your research wouldn't have put you that far behind schedule."

What was wrong with her? He hadn't rushed all the way back here for his book. "I came back because I thought…no, I *know* he'll be back." He paused before adding, "Or he could be a she since we don't know who broke in. Either way, I don't want you and

Carter to be here alone when that happens. Driving all night was worth the risk to make sure I was here to protect you."

The shock on her pretty face left him at a loss as to how to respond. Did she really think he'd leave them unprotected for a minute longer than necessary? Or was it that she thought he couldn't handle the job?

As if reading his mind, she answered the questions he hadn't asked. "While I appreciate the sentiment, that's not your responsibility. You're a guest, Max, not the police."

He wasn't sure if he was disappointed or angry that she'd brought up the whole guest thing again. Rather than risk making the situation even worse, he lurched to his feet. "Listen, I should just go to bed. Thanks for breakfast, and I apologize again for waking you up."

That she didn't try to stop him, not even to wish him good-night, hurt more than he could imagine. He trudged up the narrow steps to his room and locked the rest of the world outside.

RIKKI PACED THE length of the hall and back again, stopping periodically to listen for any sign that her star boarder was up and about. Lunch had come and gone with no sign that Max had dragged himself out of bed. Carter was thrilled to see his friend's car out in the driveway but disappointed that he couldn't run right upstairs to see him.

It might have been cowardly on her part, but Rikki had done her best to avoid her other guest as much as possible. Debra had appeared for breakfast a little before nine. She'd spent most of the time making calls to check in on her cousin. As soon as she finished eating, she'd left for the hospital. It had been a huge relief that she hadn't brought up the subject of buying Rikki's business again.

Hopefully, she wouldn't, but Rikki wasn't counting on it. The woman had sounded pretty darn determined. All she could do was keep refusing the offer until Debra believed her or left. Hopefully, that wouldn't damage their relationship to the point that she lost the woman as a customer. But if it came to that, so be it.

A familiar sound brought her pacing to a halt. That creaking step at the top of the stairs signaled Max was on his way down. It was about time. She wondered how much he'd remember from their early morning interaction. It would be great if he had no memory of their somewhat weird conversation after he'd woken her up to come let him in. Somehow, she didn't think either of them would be that lucky.

She retreated to the kitchen, not wanting to reveal how worried she'd been or that she'd been lurking at the bottom of the steps waiting for him. Although both of those things were actually true. After pouring two large cups of coffee, she heated up a large slice of quiche in the microwave and retrieved a bowl of fresh fruit from the refrigerator. Putting all of it on a tray, she carried it into the dining room and set it on the table.

Max appeared in the doorway a few seconds later. He looked marginally better than he had the last time she'd seen him. At least he'd shaved and showered, even though his expression still looked a bit confused. He stared at the food on the table and blinked as if he was still having trouble focusing. "Is that for me? Because it's way past breakfast, and you don't do lunches."

"That's true, but I'm making an exception today."

He ventured farther into the room. "Why?"

"Because I figured you'd sleep in and wake up hungry. If you don't like quiche, just say so. It won't hurt my feelings."

"Yes, it would." He frowned as he finally sat down at the table. "But I don't hate quiche. In fact, it sounds good right now. Filling without being too heavy. My stomach isn't happy after me mainlining nothing but caffeine and junk food until I ate that omelet you made for me."

They sat without talking as Max dug into the meal she'd fixed for him. Once he was done, he carried his dishes back to the kitchen. From what she could hear, he also loaded them in the dishwasher. It wasn't his job to bus tables, but she didn't bother to point that out. They had more important things to discuss.

He returned with a large glass of water in his hand and sat back down. "Thanks for that. Put it on my bill."

Okay, that was ridiculous. "I provide breakfast, Max. Nothing says I can't serve it in the middle of the afternoon."

His mouth was a straight line. "I'm guessing you won't like it if I point out that you served me breakfast once already today. As

I recall, it was around o-dark-thirty. You've already gone above and beyond for a guest."

He was right about that, but she didn't like that he sounded mad about it. "Considering you're paying for days when you aren't even here, we can let a few things slide, Mr. Volkov."

"I'll concede the point, Ms. Bruce, only to add that I appreciate everything you did when I showed up last night."

"Don't mention it." She gave him a stern look. "And I mean that. I don't want my other guests to get ideas. Also, don't do anything like that again. It's not your job to watch over the two of us. That's what the police are for."

He stared at her for a second before nodding, but not looking happy about it. "Agreed."

Then he fidgeted a bit. "There is something I do need to ask you about, though. Is there any chance that Carter decided to work at his desk in my room while I was gone? He's aware of the rules and is usually good about following them."

Then why would he ask that? Her first instinct was to defend her son, but she was pretty sure Max wouldn't have asked the question without good reason. "What's happened now?"

His eyebrows rode low over his eyes as he frowned. "Someone was in my room while I was gone."

She immediately relaxed. "Oh, that was me. I took advantage of your absence to vacuum and dust. I also changed the sheets and the towels. I tried to put everything back just as it was, but I might not have gotten it all exactly right."

"Okay, then. That makes sense." Despite his words, Max didn't look all that convinced as he finished his water. "I heard a car pull out this morning. I take it you have another guest."

"Yes. I'm sure you remember Debra Billings. Her cousin was admitted to the hospital, so Debra came back to be with her. She's staying in the green room again. I actually had a whole bunch of surprise guests in the short time you've been gone. A family passing through the area had an unexpected car problem. They rented several of my rooms on Tuesday night and hung around until yesterday afternoon for the repairs to get finished."

"I hope they appreciated your efforts."

"They did. Mr. Quinn left a huge tip on the dresser in their room with a thank-you note for offering them 'shelter in the storm,' to use his description." She smiled. "All guests should be as nice. His two youngest grand-kids were about Carter's age, so he had some unexpected playmates to hang out with."

"I bet Carter enjoyed that."

"He did. I told him you wouldn't mind that he didn't get a lot of work done on the new ship."

"I'll reassure him about that. Right now, I want to ask Shelby if I can work at the museum today while it's closed." He stopped to listen. "Is Carter up in his room? I'll let him know I'm back and want to work on the ship with him this evening after I get back from dinner."

"Actually, I think he's across the hall in the library."

"Perfect. I'll touch base with him and then head off to the museum." He stood up. "I'd also like to check in with Cade to see how the wedding plans are going."

For the first time, he looked amused. "I know Shelby can catch me up, but it's more entertaining to hear the chief of police bab-bling about florists and meeting the in-laws."

Rikki bet it was. Cade didn't seem the type to rattle easily, but pulling a wedding together in such a short time had clearly knocked both the bride and groom off-kilter. "I went to a wedding shower for Shelby last night. It was a lot of fun, and she seemed genuinely touched that everyone went to the trouble on such short notice. On the surface, she's calm, cool and collected, but Cade's not the only one getting more stressed as the wedding date gets closer. From what I could tell, she's pretty weirded out about not meeting his parents until the day before the wedding."

"They'll get through it." Max's expression turned serious again. "At least their families care enough to be there for them. That's more than a lot of people can claim."

Then he abruptly walked out of the room and out the front door. It was odd that he didn't stop to check in with Carter. He clearly hadn't appreciated being reminded that as a guest it wasn't his responsibility to watch over her and Carter. At the same time she also couldn't help but wonder what was behind that last remark about families not caring enough.

It was yet another reminder that while the

man had learned her most private secrets, most of his were a mystery to her. She'd heard that he was the last child in his great-grand-father's lineage, but that was all she knew about his family. And while his mailing ad-dress was a condo in Portland, Oregon, he didn't seem to spend much time there.

Suddenly, she was flashing back to their confusing conversation out in the driveway last night. He'd said he'd needed to get back home as fast as possible. At first, she'd taken that to mean he'd returned to Portland after leaving Montana. Instead, it turned out that he'd been talking about coming back to Dun-bar. Did he really think of the town as home? Surely not. No doubt he'd been talking non-sense due to the lack of sleep and too much coffee. Probably, anyway.

That's when that irritating small voice put in another appearance, whispering in her ear. *But what if he wasn't confused? What if he really is starting to think of Dunbar as home? He's been making friends and establishing new bonds, and not only with me and Carter. If he did decide to move here permanently, maybe there would be more dinner dates in our future, more kisses like the one we shared at the hotel. I'd like that, wouldn't I?*

Memories of their shared laughter over dinner and the warm strength of Max's embrace as he'd kissed her that night flowed through her mind, leaving her aching for more of the same. It had been years since she'd felt this kind of special connection with a man and wasn't sure how she felt about it. This time, however, she didn't order the voice to leave her alone. Instead, she filed away those thoughts to ponder later. Right now, she needed to give her son an update on his friend's plans and then get back to work.

CHAPTER FIFTEEN

MAX WALKED OFF his temper before heading to the post office. How many times did Rikki have to remind him that she thought of him simply as a guest before he believed her? Every time she put him in his place, it made him furious. Maybe he should take her at her word. If it came to that, he'd have to find someplace else to stay while he did his research. As he turned the corner, he realized he was rubbing his chest. The thought of moving out of the B and B was causing him actual physical pain.

There wasn't much he could do about that now. He wasn't going anywhere until he knew the threat to Rikki and Carter had been eliminated. She might not appreciate his tactics, but too bad. He'd deal with her anger when the time came. For now, he had places to go and people to see.

As he'd told Rikki, he needed to talk to Shelby at the post office. Before heading there, he stopped at Titus's café to buy several pieces of pie. However, when he finally reached the post office, it was obvious Shelby was too busy to chat. There were four women clustered around the counter with Shelby studying a bunch of papers. He could be wrong, but he bet whatever had all of them waving their hands in the air and talking over each other had to do with the wedding and not business.

No way he was going to get caught up in that mess even if he had come armed with a big slice of peach pie for the bride-to-be. Instead, he took a sharp right turn to cross the street and headed for the relative safety of the police department. Moira was covering the front counter this time. "Officer Fraser, I was hoping to see Chief Peters. Is he available?"

She glanced back over her shoulder as if to make sure the coast was clear and then leaned closer to him. "He'll probably appreciate the distraction and a friendly face."

"Bad day?"

"A couple of members of the city council dropped in unexpectedly, and things got a bit heated. Add in some problems with the wedding plans…it's been a tough one."

Poor guy. Max set the small picnic basket he'd borrowed from Titus on the counter. "At least I come bearing gifts."

He took three of Titus's mini pies out of the basket and set them on the counter. "I thought Cade might need some pie today and figured he might feel guilty eating in front of the rest of you. Take your pick and leave the rest for Oscar and the other officer."

She immediately latched on to the peach pie and tucked it out of sight behind the counter. "I'll put the other two in the fridge and text Oscar and TJ about your thoughtful gifts. You can go on back to Cade's office."

Max did as she suggested. He knocked even though Cade's office door was open. His friend was on the phone but motioned for Max to come in. He hung up a few seconds later, and immediately rubbed his temples as if to ease a headache. "What's up?"

"I need to talk to you about something, but why don't we start off with these?" He pulled out two full-sized slices of pie and not the minis he'd bought for the other officers. "I got Dutch apple because Titus said it was your favorite."

"Thanks." Cade eyed his slice greedily and

reached for the plastic fork that Max had set on his desk. "What's the occasion?"

Max settled back in his chair and prepared to start eating. "Since when do we have to wait for a special occasion to enjoy a piece of Titus's pie?"

"True enough. Besides, this might just be the highlight of my entire day. Between the city council and the wedding, I've been through the wringer."

"What's up with the council?"

Cade lowered his voice. "I informed them that Moira will be in charge of the department while Shelby and I are on our honeymoon. We'll be gone two weeks, and someone has to be the designated boss while I'm gone. Oscar is not the best choice if anything serious comes up, and Moira has way more experience than TJ."

"So what's the council's problem?"

Looking thoroughly disgusted, Cade muttered, "They think she's too young to handle the responsibility despite her experience on the job. I told them the county sheriff promised backup if Moira needs help. Besides, it's not like Dunbar is a hotbed of crime."

"What more do they want?"

"Well, for one thing, they want to make sure they can reach me if they need to. Evidently Shelby and I shouldn't go too far away on our honeymoon in case they want me to rush back at a moment's notice. You know, somewhere like Seattle." He sneered and shook his head. "I told them even if I have my phone with me, I won't be taking their calls."

"Good for you. I won't even ask where you're going, and I hope you haven't told anyone else even the general direction you're heading. You don't want the mayor or anyone else trying to track you down."

Cade finished the last bite of his pie. "We haven't told anyone anything. Apparently neither of our mothers appreciates the secrecy, but I don't care."

By that point, he was looking pretty smug about his sneakiness. "We only get one honeymoon, and I won't let anybody mess it up. Do you know that this is the first real vacation Shelby has ever taken since she was a kid? Someone else from the postal service is going to cover for her, and Ilse Klaus is taking charge of the museum."

Max almost choked on the bite he'd just taken. "Is that wise? Isn't Shelby worried that

that woman will decide to paint flowers all over the front of the building? That's what she wanted to do to the town's official vehicle when she was the mayor."

That had Cade laughing. "They negotiated a list of what Ilse can and cannot do as the acting curator. Shelby didn't mention if the subject of redecorating came up. She's so stressed already that I'm almost afraid to ask her."

Cade glanced at his computer, a hint that he needed to get back to work. In response, Max gathered up their trash and stashed it back in the basket. "I have a couple of quick questions. Did you learn anything about the twins who had hounded Rikki over her inheritance from their late uncle?"

"They live in eastern Montana almost on the North Dakota border, and the police chief knows them well. Both of them were home on Saturday, the day before the break-in, and the police chief saw them at church on Sunday morning. There's no way they could have driven all the way to Dunbar by the time of the break-in. And the brother showed up on time at work on Monday. I'm sorry, but my gut instinct is that they wouldn't have gone to all that trouble and expense simply to wander through Rikki's house."

Max sat up straighter. "Actually, I agree with you. From what I gather, they've left her alone since she moved to Dunbar. As far as we know, there's been no inciting incident that would have stirred them back into action."

Cade didn't look happy. "Which puts us back where we started. I haven't gotten any results back from the forensic team, but I'm not expecting any great revelations."

His frustration was clear, something Max understood. "It would've been nice if we could pin the break-in on them. But even if they'd been willing to make the trip, how could they have even known that Rikki's place would be empty on that night? We didn't make plans to go out to dinner until that afternoon. No matter how you look at it, it doesn't make sense for them to be the culprits."

Cade leaned back in his chair and put his feet up on the desk, hands behind his head. "So what do you think does make sense?"

"That whoever broke in was already in town. Even then, they took quite a risk. If we'd gone to the café for dinner, we would've arrived back at the B and B a lot earlier."

"So you think someone was watching the house."

That was one possibility, but Max pointed out another one. "Or someone was already *in* the house. I wasn't the only person staying at the B and B for part of the weekend."

That pronouncement had Cade dropping his feet back down to the floor and sitting up straight. "Who?"

Max figured Rikki would be furious with him for ratting out one of her regular customers, but he'd do far worse to protect her and Carter. "A woman named Debra Billings. From what I can tell, she's been staying at the B and B off and on for at least as long as Rikki has owned the place. I believe she has family in the area. Rikki could tell you more about her."

"Is there any specific reason you suspect her?"

"Only proximity. And to be fair, she wasn't the only one who stayed there that week. It would be easy enough for a guest to familiarize themselves with the layout of the place. If so, maybe they got lucky and stumbled on one of the few times that Rikki was gone for the evening and with no guests other than me staying there. Until recently, Rikki has pretty much kept to herself and is only just now getting involved in things like Shelby's book club and your wedding plans."

At least Cade wasn't jumping in to tell Max he'd gone off the rails with his assessment of the situation. "So that leaves the question of why break in at all. What could they be looking for?"

That was the one thing Max hadn't figured out. "I keep circling back to the possibility that messing up my stuff and smashing Carter's ship were distractions. If that's the case, then there must be something else in the house that's of interest. From what I can tell, the place came furnished when Rikki bought it. That leaves a lot of possibilities."

Cade reached for the stack of folders and pulled out the second one from the top. He flipped through several pages of handwritten notes until he found whatever he'd been looking for. "I thought it would be interesting to talk with the prior owner. Unfortunately, she passed away not long after Rikki bought her out. The lady's name was Maude Travis, and

I guess the house was passed down through the family to her."

"Another dead end." Realizing how that sounded, Max winced. "Sorry, no pun intended."

"Did you come see me simply to follow up on my investigation, or has something else happened that has you concerned?"

"Nothing specific. More like I've noticed a few little things that don't add up."

Cade picked up his pen and clicked it a couple of times. "Like what?"

"I got back to town in the wee hours of the morning and pretty much crawled upstairs to bed. When I finally rejoined the living, I realized some of the stuff in my room had been moved since I left. Normally, Rikki mostly leaves my room alone. I don't like her having to wait on me, so I make my own bed and things like that. I asked if someone had been in there, and she admitted she'd done some housekeeping and maybe didn't put everything exactly back where she found it."

"You don't believe her?"

"Of course I do, but there was something else."

"Which is?"

He shifted in his chair, his energy running hot as he tried to put everything in logical order. "Early last week I helped Rikki fix up another room she wants to rent. She'd already started working on it, so I didn't see the room before that. There was something weird, though. Someone had drilled small holes at regular intervals along at least one wall. Rikki had already patched them, so there's nothing to see. It wasn't simply the number of holes that seemed strange, but where they were located—about two feet off the floor, so not where you'd hang pictures or even a shelf. She thought maybe someone had been checking for termites or something even though there was no mention of any insect damage on the inspection done when she bought the place."

Max paused to give Cade a chance to catch up with his note-taking before continuing. "Anyway, while I was poking around in my room after I got up, I noticed that the dresser had been moved. I could tell because the old indentations in the carpet were about two inches away from where the legs are now. I pulled the dresser out from the wall. Can you guess what I found?"

"A row of holes?"

"Yep. They were the same distance off the floor and at about the same frequency. I looked behind several other pieces of furniture and found the same thing. The plaster dust was still on the rug, and the holes look fresh. If Rikki had moved the dresser to vacuum, she would've seen the holes."

"Did you tell her what you found?"

"Not yet. I wasn't sure if I should."

Looking up from the notes he'd been taking, Cade asked, "Why not?"

Max met his gaze head on, hoping the man understood his driving need to put an end to the threat against Rikki and her son. "Because I think it's time we set a trap to see if whoever is doing this will take the bait."

CHAPTER SIXTEEN

THE OTHER MAN'S expression turned predatory as he considered the idea. Max waited a second and then added, "There's one problem." Cade didn't look surprised. "Let me guess. You think Rikki won't like the idea."

"No, I'm sure she'll hate it." He held up his fingers to tick off the reasons for that. "Other than me, Debra Billings has been one of Rikki's best customers, which also makes her one of the most familiar with the house and Rikki's schedule. But if it turns out that she isn't behind the break-in, this could backfire and cause Rikki some big-time problems. She already worries about the occasional bad review. Can you imagine what it would do to her reputation if a guest posts a low rating because we accused her of a crime she didn't commit?"

He pointed to his second finger. "All we have to go on is some mysterious holes in the wall. That's not proof of anything, especially when we don't really know when or why they were made. Still, access is everything, and I can't imagine some random thief sneaking into the house with a power tool without being noticed."

And finally, he put up a third finger. "Rikki will never forgive me for doing something like this without consulting her. As she frequently reminds me, I'm merely a guest."

Cade gave a low whistle. "I bet that ticks you off big-time. That woman must not being paying attention if she hasn't noticed you have some strong feelings for her. Having only recently fallen fast and furious for the woman across the street, I recognize the signs."

"Yeah, I don't like it, but that doesn't matter. Guest or not, I'm going to end the threat." He realized that sounded like what he had in mind was vigilante justice. "With your help, of course. My role should be to get her and Carter out of the danger zone."

Cade's mouth quirked up in a small smile. "I'm glad to know you weren't planning on having all the fun without me and my officers, what with it being our job and all."

Max rolled his eyes. "I know that, Cade."

"How will you get her out of the house?"

"I need to meet with a history professor in Seattle on Saturday. I'll invite her and Carter to come with me and make a day of it. We can do something fun and then go out for dinner."

"That could work. Let me know when you've firmed up your plans." He made a couple of quick notes before looking up again. "Are you really thinking about keeping her in the dark about all of this?"

"It's tempting because I'm afraid she won't agree to the plan, and we need to do something to put an end to the threat. The trouble is that other than her late grandmother, she's never had anyone she could depend on. Even when she reminds me I'm just a guest, I think that's the fear talking. Regardless, we need to do this. If she kicks me to the curb, so be it."

Cade leaned forward, elbows on the desk. "So you're thinking it's better to ask for forgiveness than for permission?"

"Pretty much."

"I wish I could tell you that I think that's a good idea." Cade offered him a sympathetic smile. "But having said that, if necessary, I'd do the same if it was the only way I could keep Shelby safe."

Max couldn't help but tease the other man. "I figure it will be easier for Rikki to give me a pass for being overprotective than it was for Shelby to get past you tossing her in the slammer. The fine citizens of Dunbar hated my guts for threatening their beloved Trillium Nugget. Even so, they weren't half as upset about that as they were about you locking Shelby up. From what I heard, you almost had a riot on your hands."

"Not my finest moment, that's for sure. Thank goodness Shelby has such a forgiving nature." Then Cade smiled. "Actually, when I screwed up with Shelby, it was Titus who shared some helpful wisdom."

Okay, that was a shocker. "He seems like an unlikely source of advice for the lovelorn, but I'm game. What did he tell you?"

"I'm paraphrasing here, but whatever happens, don't give up on Rikki or yourself too easily. Forever is a long time to live with those kinds of regrets."

The thought of facing his life without Rikki and her son in it was incredibly bleak. Max even understood her reluctance to rely on other people. Thanks to his parents, he had his own issues in that department. Right now he needed to deliver Shelby's pie and see if he could work in the museum for a couple of hours.

"I'll keep that in mind while I figure out how to convince Rikki that we need to take action." He gathered up his pack and the basket he'd borrowed from Titus. "For now, I'm heading over to the post office. Any messages for Shelby?"

"Tell her to call when she'd like a ride home."

"Will do."

Before he reached the door, Cade stopped him. "One more thing, Max. As the chief of police, I did my due diligence in researching your background when you first presented your demand for the Trillium Nugget. What I learned had no bearing on the case and was nobody's business. I haven't shared it with anyone, and I won't. But if you want Rikki to trust you, you might want to think about trusting her first."

And after delivering that little bombshell, he picked up a file and started reading.

IN THE END, Max delivered Shelby's pie and Cade's message. His discussion with Cade had left him too restless to concentrate on his research, so he took a long walk instead. After looping around the heart of the town twice, he gave up on finding any peace of mind and decided to find what solace he could in one of Titus's dinners.

He still hadn't gotten used to walking into the café and actually being greeted with a few hand waves and a friendly smile or two. Before the matter of the Trillium Nugget had been settled, he couldn't go anywhere without garnering hostile looks and the occasional sign-waving protestor following his every footstep.

Titus stepped out of the kitchen just as Max walked in. He glanced at the clock and frowned. "It's a little early for dinner, isn't it?"

Max realized it wasn't even five o'clock. "Yeah, I guess it is. I didn't get back from my road trip until right before dawn, so I'm off schedule. I thought I'd eat early and then head back to the B and B for the evening. I promised Carter that we'd work on our project together."

Although it just now occurred to him that he'd left the house without actually speaking to him. Hopefully Rikki would've told him. If not, Max would have to apologize to his young friend. Meanwhile, Titus led him through the café to the far corner next to the window, where he dropped a menu on the table. "Your server can tell you which entrées are currently available. I've got a couple of things to check on in back, and then I'll join you for a little bit."

"That would be great."

Max picked the chair that afforded him a view of the café as well as out the window. Cade had given him a lot to think about, especially with his closing remarks. It probably shouldn't have come as a surprise that the lawman had done a deep dive into Max's past considering the threat he'd presented to the town Cade was sworn to protect. He was right about the whole trust issue. At this point, the only facts that Rikki knew about Max were his occupation, his great-grandfather's history in Dunbar, and that he liked playing with Legos.

It wasn't much and didn't speak well of him.

The chair across from him scraped across the floor as Titus sat down. "The last time I saw someone acting so pathetic was the day Cade arrested Shelby. It's the classic 'I've got woman troubles' look. It's sad, really."

"Very funny." Max looked around the café, hoping to derail the conversation. "The server never came by."

"I ordered for you."

"Thanks… I guess. It all depends on what you chose."

Rather than respond to Max's implied question, Titus crossed his arms over his chest and gave him a hard look. "Have there been more problems at the B and B?"

"Funny you would ask. Cade and I were just talking about that very subject."

He fiddled with the salt and pepper shakers while he explained the plan he and Cade were considering and what had triggered Max's desire to take action. "If it had only been the papers on my desk, that would be one thing. However, someone moved the furniture, too. They drilled some holes in the walls about two feet off the ground."

Titus hadn't exactly been relaxed before, but the tension in his expression soared to a new level. "Were the holes big enough for one of those camera scope things to pass through?"

Well, wasn't that an interesting thought?

"Now that you mention it, yeah. There were also holes in another room, but Rikki thought maybe the prior owner had someone check for termites."

"So you think this has to be an inside job."

Max nodded. "That's my take on it. Rikki and Carter are the only ones who are there most of the time. If Rikki had reasons to drill holes, she would've said so."

Titus almost smiled. "There's also you."

"True, but I hope you don't think I'm dumb enough to set a trap for myself."

"That remains to be seen." He looked toward the kitchen. "We should suspend this conversation. Rita is headed this way with your meal."

Max could hardly believe it when she set a huge plate of chicken and dumplings down in front of him. "It's Thursday?"

Titus shook his head. "What day did you think it was?"

"Actually, I'm not real sure. This week has been a bit of a blur. I left for Montana early Tuesday morning. I met with my source on

Wednesday and then decided to drive straight through rather than stopping somewhere along the way. I arrived back in Dunbar right before dawn this morning."

"Why the big hurry to get back?" As soon as he asked the question, Titus rolled his eyes and said, "Sorry, stupid question. You were worried whoever broke in would try again."

"Yeah, not that Rikki appreciated my efforts. All it garnered me was a lecture about the stupidity of driving on no sleep and a lot of caffeine."

Titus obviously found that amusing, the jerk. Sadly, all it took was a single bite of dumpling for Max to forgive the man for pretty much anything. "Maybe you get sick of hearing this, but you're one heck of a cook."

"Yeah, well, let's get back to your problem. Who else has had frequent access to the house?"

"I'd rather not mention names, but there is one lady who comes and goes pretty frequently."

Titus didn't ask for a description, but Max was willing to bet that he had a reasonable suspicion about who it was. After all, this was the only place in town to get a meal. Debra was bound to have eaten there multiple times while staying at the B and B. Instead, Titus went right to the heart of the matter. "And what does Rikki think about the idea?"

Suddenly, the savory chicken no longer tasted quite as good. "I'm not sure I should tell her."

Titus's laughter rang out across the café, drawing the attention of the scattering of diners. Most were looking at him as if they'd never expected to see the surly chef do something so out of character. Max's temper flared hot. "What's so funny?"

"It must be something in the water supply here that makes men act stupid around strong women."

Max didn't particularly appreciate being insulted. "What makes you say that?"

"Didn't anyone tell you how Cade decided to break the news to Shelby that you were after the Trillium Nugget? He asked her to go hiking with him and even called it a date. I'm guessing she was pretty excited about that. After all, half the single women in town had been bringing him casseroles and flirting up a storm hoping to catch his eye. Then when he had her a couple of miles up a trail, he broke the news that while he really had wanted to ask her out, the reason he'd picked that particular day was to tell her about you."

As much as Max wanted to deny there was any similarity between the two situations, he couldn't. "Shelby forgave him."

"Yeah, and he counts himself darn lucky that she did." Titus stared across at Max. "Do you really want to throw the dice and see if Rikki does the same?"

Then he pointed at Max's plate. "Eat up. If your plan blows up in your face, who knows when you'll ever have another chance to enjoy my Thursday special."

Max watched him walk away and then did as he was told. By the time he finished eating, he still hadn't made up his mind how to tell Rikki about his plot to catch a criminal.

RIKKI HAD ALREADY been worried about Max when he'd left earlier without talking to Carter. That wasn't like him. Maybe it was because he hadn't quite recovered from his foolish drive across nearly three states to get back to Dunbar, but she had to wonder if something else was going on.

Looking back, she realized he hadn't ex-

actly been satisfied with her explanation for
why some of the things in his room hadn't
been in the correct spots when he'd returned.
He didn't think she was lying to him; she was
sure of that much. It was more like he thought
there was more to the story. But what?

When he'd finally returned, she and Carter were about to sit down to dinner. She'd
invited him to join them, but he'd already
eaten at the café. Even though he'd accepted
Carter's invitation to keep them company,
Max wasn't his usual chatty self. Even Carter
picked up on it and worriedly asked if Max
had changed his mind about helping with the
ship. He was relieved when his buddy assured
him he'd been looking forward to it all day.

It was almost a relief when Carter polished
off the last of his dinner and led the charge
down the hall to the library. She left them
alone for more than an hour, and then she
brought them each a small hot fudge sun-
dae. She'd brought one for herself, too, thinking that would give her a legitimate excuse
to hang around long enough to gauge Max's
mood.

They'd obviously been working hard, because the ship was almost complete. She

wouldn't be surprised if they asked if Carter could stay up until it was done. Instead of waiting for them to plead their case, she admired their work. "It's really looking great. If I were you, Carter, I'd keep working until you finish it. That way, maybe the two of you can start the longship tomorrow."

"Really? I can stay up late?"

"It's fine with me, but only if Max wants to continue. He didn't get back here until just before sunrise, and he might want to go to bed earlier than usual."

Carter turned a hopeful look in his friend's direction. "Can we? Please, Mr. Max?"

Rikki knew she wasn't the only one who couldn't withstand Carter's hopeful expression. "I don't think it will take us long if we work hard."

At that, Carter started shoving ice cream in his mouth as fast as he could. Max reached out to stop him from taking another bite. "Slow down, kiddo. We've got time to enjoy our dessert before we go back to work."

When he released his hold on her son's arm, both man and boy continued eating at a much more reasonable pace. When they were done, she stacked their dishes. "I'll be in the living room if you need me for anything."

She'd almost reached the door when Max caught up with her. Speaking in a subdued voice, he said, "There's something I need to tell you, but it would be better if we talked after Carter goes to bed."

When she didn't immediately respond, he added, "It's important or else I wouldn't ask."

Even if the worry in his words hadn't already had her concerned about the nature of what he needed to tell her, the tension in his stance would've clinched the deal. "I'll come back down as soon as I tuck him in."

Max closed his eyes and drew a slow breath, making it difficult to tell if he was relieved that she'd agreed or if he'd been hoping for a reprieve. That seemed odd since he was the one who'd made it sound imperative that they talk sooner rather than later.

"Thank you."

"You're welcome." Although he didn't actually sound all that grateful, which was also worrisome. "Max, what's wrong?"

For a second, she thought maybe he would give her at least some hint about what was troubling him. Instead, he offered her a rather sad excuse for a smile. "We should talk in the kitchen. Your other guest never goes in there, so it might be more private than the living room."

"Okay."

Which was a stupid thing to say when it was clear that nothing was okay at all. She didn't even try to smile as she walked away, hoping their model practically put itself together. Anything to speed things along. For now, she would read in the living room.

She made herself a cup of chamomile tea. Not her favorite flavor, but it might take the edge off her nerves. After several failed attempts, she finally managed to get lost in the cozy mystery she was reading. She was about to find out whodunit when the front door opened and jarred her out of the story.

When Debra Billings stepped into the entryway, Rikki crossed her fingers that she would head straight up to her room. Between the woman's earlier refusal to accept that Rikki wasn't interested in selling the bed-and-breakfast and the added stress over whatever Max wanted to talk about, she was in no mood to play gracious hostess. Sadly, Lady Luck wasn't in the mood to cooperate.

Debra sailed into the room, a huge smile on her face. "Oh, there you are. I was hoping we could continue our discussion from earlier. After this scare with my cousin, I am more determined than ever to move back to this side of the state."

Oh, brother. Could she be any more melodramatic?

Rikki closed her book. "Will you be staying with her once she's discharged from the hospital to help out?"

"Not right away. They plan to move her to another facility to give her time to more fully recover before sending her home."

Debra came closer and sat down facing Rikki. "So about our conversation…"

Rikki tried to head her off at the pass. "If you're talking about me selling the bed-and-breakfast, I've already given you my answer. There is no cause for further discussion."

"But you haven't heard my final offer. I think you'll be pleased with how generous I'm being."

As she spoke, Debra settled back in the chair. No doubt she thought if she kept upping the ante that Rikki would eventually give in, but that was not going to happen. She was done with being pushed around by bullies. The harder they pushed, the more determined she was not to give an inch.

"No matter how generous the offer, Ms. Billings, I'm simply not interested. Please accept that." She paused to look around the room. "This is my home. It's not for sale."

Debra's smile faltered briefly, but then she upped the wattage as if that alone would sway Rikki's decision. "Think of your son. How much time do you actually have for him with the full burden of running this place resting on your shoulders? How many nights do you lie awake worrying about your bottom line? I have to admit that I'm surprised you make any kind of profit with the number of vacant rooms you have. You might make tasty muffins and keep the place fairly clean, but marketing is clearly not in your bailiwick."

She mimicked Rikki's perusal of the room. "You're in over your head. I'm willing to offer you enough to start over somewhere else. Maybe in a bigger town where you can find a job more suited to your skills."

Screaming at a customer was probably pretty high on the worst mistakes a small business owner could make, but right now

Rikki didn't care. She drew a deep breath and prepared to unleash her displeasure with Debra, her less than subtle insults, and her unwanted offer. Unfortunately...or maybe actually fortunately, Carter picked that moment to seek her out. He was holding the pirate ship with a proud smile on his face.

Rikki ruthlessly wrestled her temper back under control as she set her book aside and joined him by the door. "You finished the ship! It will look great sitting on the shelf in your room. Shall we take it upstairs?"

Falling back on her good hostess manners, she glanced back at her guest. Proud of her control, she even managed a small smile. "If you'll excuse me, it's Carter's bedtime."

"I'll wait here so we can finish our chat."

Okay, maybe Rikki's control wasn't as strong as she'd hoped. She ditched the smile completely and kept her response short and to the point. "Don't bother. The answer is still no. Good night."

CHAPTER SEVENTEEN

WHAT THE HECK was that all about? Max ducked back down the hallway where he couldn't be seen. He'd seen Rikki aggravated before, mostly at him, but he'd never heard her wield words like weapons. Clearly something had happened between her and the Billings woman that had put them at odds. Short of threatening Carter somehow, he couldn't imagine what she could've done to make Rikki that angry.

It was no surprise that Rikki's entire demeanor changed as soon as she was alone with Carter. She praised him for all his hard work on the model. They disappeared up the steps still chatting about where they should put it in his bedroom that would keep it safe. Their voices faded in the distance, but he lingered as he waited to see what the other woman did next.

A few seconds later he heard her talking to

someone. It was a one-sided conversation, so she had to be on the phone.

He couldn't make out the words, but the tone was clear. The woman was furious and taking it out on the person on the other end of the line. The call didn't last long, because Debra was up and moving. It was too late for him to take shelter in the library. Instead, he retreated down the hall to the next doorway. If she spotted him, he would start forward as if he had been in the dining room for some reason.

Rather than heading upstairs to her room, Debra turned in his direction. What was she up to now? When he stepped into sight, she jumped and gave a small squeal. He was feeling petty enough to take some pleasure in it. "Sorry, Ms. Billings. I didn't mean to startle you."

She drew a sharp breath and then smiled. "No problem, Mr. Volkov. My mind was a million miles away, and I didn't notice you there. I see that you and young Carter finished the project you were working on. It's so kind of you to spend so much of your valuable time with him. It will be difficult for Rikki to manage without you babysitting her son when you finally leave Dunbar."

Before now, he might have believed her smile and her concern were genuine, but there was a sharp undertone in her voice that set his teeth on edge. That didn't mean he wanted her to know that. "Yeah, he's a great kid. Luckily, I still have a lot of research left to do, so I won't be going anywhere soon. That's why I've rented a room here for the foreseeable future."

"I know. I had hoped to rent the turret room myself sometime this summer. I know it may seem odd, but I've wanted to try out all of Rikki's rooms. They all have different views and styles of furniture, so it varies the experience of staying here."

Ah, so that was the excuse she'd come up with for wanting to change rooms each time she came. Interesting. "I'm sure you would enjoy the turret room. The view of the mountains is great from there."

"I won't lie. I'm jealous, but eventually I'll get a chance to stay in that room." She stepped to one side of the hall, turning her back to the wall to give him room to pass by. "Well, I didn't mean to keep you. I was going to see if Rikki had left any snacks out in the dining room."

"I'll save you the trip. Sorry, but I ate the last of the cookies an hour ago. I'd forgotten that Rikki had another guest."

He was lying on both counts, but she didn't know that. Maybe Rikki really had put cookies out at some point, but he hadn't bothered to check since she'd brought him and Carter ice cream. For sure he hadn't forgotten that Debra Billings was staying there. "Nice talking to you. I think I'll go read in the living room for a while."

She muttered something under her breath when she thought he was out of hearing. While he might not have understood the words, the anger laced through them was perfectly clear. A few seconds later, she headed upstairs, hopefully to turn in for the evening. If she was the one who had broken into the house and searched his room, he doubted she would risk making another foray as long as he and Rikki were up and about.

He sat near the front window and stared out into the night. At any other time, it would have been a peaceful moment. However, knowing Rikki would reappear soon, his mood had taken a definite turn for the dark. There was no telling how the upcoming discussion would go, but he knew it wouldn't be all sweetness and light.

But after mulling over what both Cade and Titus had told him, he had come to the difficult decision to be truthful with Rikki, no matter what. Titus might have no idea what secrets Max had been living with, but evidently Cade had learned far more about Max's past than Max was comfortable with anyone knowing. It was one reason that he chose to travel so much in his job, only touching base at his condo in Portland when he ran out of clean clothes or excuses to keep driving.

Even so, Cade hadn't thought what he'd learned would necessarily be a deal breaker with Rikki, but only as long as Max was honest with her. After years of avoiding close relationships, Max had backed himself into this corner by letting himself care about Rikki and her son. How could he ask her to let him become part of their lives for the long term if he was afraid to let her see who he really was?

If she rejected him, so be it. He would still help Cade remove the threat presented by whoever had broken into the house. After that, when Rikki and Carter were safe, he'd pack up and hit the road again. At least this time he'd know he'd done something good.

"Max?"

The softly spoken word jerked him out of his dark thoughts. He rose to his feet and dredged up a smile. "Sorry, I didn't hear you come down the steps."

"You must have really been concentrating on something. That was the third time I said your name."

"I think I'm still feeling the aftereffects of last night. My brain isn't firing on all cylinders right now." He pointed up at the ceiling. "I'm pretty sure Ms. Billings has retired for the night if you'd rather sit in here than in the kitchen to talk."

"Actually, I was thinking about making some hot chocolate. How does that sound?"

He stepped closer to her. "That depends. Do we get marshmallows?"

She nodded. "If that's what you prefer. I also have whipped cream. It's your choice."

"I might just have both. It's been that kind of day."

He dared to put his hand on her lower back as they walked down the hall together. That she didn't complain or shy away helped calm his nerves. He let it drop away when they entered the kitchen.

"Have a seat at the table. This won't take long."

He watched as she stood on tiptoe and stretched as far as she could to open the cabinet above the huge stainless steel refrigerator. It was a reminder of how petite she was. Sometimes he forgot because she was such a powerhouse when it came to personality and sheer determination. Clearly whatever she wanted was out of her reach. When she started for the stepstool tucked away in the far corner of the room, he blocked her way. She didn't need to be climbing up on something when he was right there to help. "What do you need? I can reach it for you."

She pointed to the canister sitting right in front. "That's the good stuff. I keep it for times like this."

He handed her the canister. "And what kind of time would this be?"

She waited until she'd put a saucepan on the stove, filled it with milk and turned it on before answering. "The kind for dealing with frustrations and having late-night serious talks."

"Who's frustrating you?"

Because he was pretty sure it wasn't him this time. He knew he was right when she gave the ceiling a dark look. "I shouldn't talk badly about one guest with another one, but we both know you're not a run-of-the mill guest."

Well, at least she'd finally conceded that much. "I couldn't help but hear the very end of your conversation with her right before you went upstairs with Carter. I didn't mean to eavesdrop, but I was standing right out in the hall. All I heard was you telling her that your final answer was no."

Rikki shoveled a generous amount of the hot chocolate mix into the pot and started stirring. "For some reason she's suddenly decided she wants to buy my business. I don't mind her asking, but that she won't accept no for an answer is nothing short of rude. She wants to give up private duty nursing and live closer to her family. Her plan is to buy me out and then hire someone to run the place or at least to do most of the heavy lifting."

Rikki glanced up at him, her eyes gleaming with a sheen of tears. "Evidently I do a good enough job with baking muffins and cleaning, but I'm not quite up to snuff when it comes to marketing. I'm also neglecting my son by leaving it up to total strangers to play with him so I can scrape together enough time to do my job. Not that you're a total stranger."

By that point, the words were tumbling out of her mouth faster and faster. Debra Billings's thoughtless comments had really hit a nerve. Rather than try to offer comfort, he let Rikki vent until she ran out of steam before responding. It didn't take long. As soon as she went silent, he shut off the burner under the saucepan. With that done, he gently turned her around and held her close. He softly stroked her back, trying to ease her pain and stop her trembling.

Touch alone wasn't getting the job done, but maybe words would help. After all, he made a decent living using his skill at stringing the right ones together. "Rikki, honey, please don't cry. That woman doesn't know what she's talking about."

If anything, Rikki cried harder. He tried again, this time leaning back enough so that he could tip up her chin and look directly into her stormy gray eyes. "You're an incredibly strong woman, Rikki. You've made a good home here in Dunbar for you and your son. He's a bright, happy kid and has everything he needs to be successful in life. Believe that if you can't believe anything else."

Her cheeks were blotchy from crying, her eyes red and irritated from the tears, but she'd never looked more beautiful to him. He gently cradled her face in his hands, using his thumbs to wipe away her tears. "I'm so sorry she upset you. If I didn't think it would cause more harm than good, I'd be escorting her out of the house even as we speak."

"She's leaving tomorrow. That's soon enough."

"Will you let her come back?"

After a couple of sniffles, Rikki nodded. "Probably. She wasn't wrong about me having too many empty rooms."

He wanted to argue, but it was her decision to make. "You've already told her that you weren't interested in selling. Hopefully she got the message."

"If necessary, I'll make that part of the deal

if she wants to book one of my rooms again. I don't need her business that badly."

That comment offered a glimmer of the feisty woman he liked so much. Now more than ever, he was dreading that talk he'd mentioned earlier. All the hot chocolate and marshmallows in the world wouldn't brighten her mood after that. If there was time, he would've postponed the discussion rather than piling on more trouble when Rikki had already had a tough night of it.

She drew a ragged breath. "Sit down while I fix our drinks."

Knowing Rikki, waiting on a guest—even one who wasn't the run-of-the-mill kind—would help settle her nerves. He stepped away from her even though it hurt to do so. In short order, she presented him with an oversized mug filled with hot chocolate crowned with a mountain of mini marshmallows and topped with a swirl of whipped cream. And if those things didn't contain an overabundance of sugary goodness, she set out a plate of macadamia nut cookies.

"I would point out that consuming all this sugar before bedtime is probably not a good idea. If it hits me like it would Carter, this will be the second night in a row that I won't get to sleep until dawn."

She eyed him over the rim of her cup. "We can always counteract the sugar buzz with some of the scotch I have up in that same cabinet."

"I'm game if you are."

Especially since he knew what was coming next. He set his mug aside. Normally hot chocolate warmed him from the inside out, but right now he wasn't sure if anything would lessen the chill in the pit of his stomach.

Her cup landed next to his on the table. "You're worrying me, Max. No matter what it is you're afraid to tell me, please start talking. The tension is killing me. I can't promise to understand, but I swear I'll try."

"That's all I ask."

The only problem was that he couldn't figure out where to begin. Finally, he gave up and just started at the beginning, not that he relished the idea of dredging up the worst memories of his life. "I've never talked about my past or my family. Well, except for Lev."

She offered him an encouraging smile. "I've noticed, but you're entitled to your privacy, Max. If you don't want to share the gory details, it's okay."

He winced. Rikki had no idea how apt her description was. "I only knew one of my grandparents—my mother's mother. She's the one who owned the cookbook I gave you. My parents ran off and got married against the wishes of their families, so they were pretty much ostracized by both sides. They were only eighteen at the time, so I can understand why their folks thought they were too young."

"No arguments there, although I don't have any right to talk." Rikki met his gaze. "I wasn't much older when I got married, and look how that turned out."

It wasn't the same at all. "Your husband is the one who walked away, Rikki. You ended up with a great kid and a life you love. My parents may have stayed together, but we would've all been better off if they'd gone their separate ways."

He sipped his drink, hoping it would clear the lump of pain that was lodged in his throat. "At least they both managed to finish college. Dad got lucky when he took a job with a start-up company that hit it big, which meant money was never a problem. From what I could tell, everything was great until they made the mistake of having me."

Rikki slammed her hand down on the table. "Don't ever talk about yourself that way, Max. I don't know what their problems were, but you weren't a mistake."

Her defense of him was heartwarming. Maybe if she said that often enough, he might even come to believe it. "Let me rephrase. For the most part, my mother wasn't the problem. It was more that my father didn't like sharing her attention. I never really understood their relationship. All I know is what I heard from other people, which was that my folks were happy right up until they weren't. The only difference between that divide was adding me into the mix. After that, they'd have these huge fights and then make up. I think on some level they both loved all the melodrama, but I hated it. As time went on, Dad resented the time she spent with me more and more. Eventually, I started spending summers with my grandmother until I went to boarding school when I started eighth grade."

Darn, he really hated the horrified look on Rikki's face. "Don't feel sorry for me. I was happier at the school."

"But you were so young."

"So were all the other kids." He reached across the table to take her hand in his, needing that small connection to keep himself grounded. "Fast forward a few years. I majored in journalism in college and was all set to look for employment somewhere back east. You know, the dream job that all journalism students want and so few get. It also would've put a lot of welcome distance between me and my folks. I actually had a decent shot at that kind of job, but then my mother begged me to stay in Portland. Dad had taken to drinking a lot, and it was getting to be too much for her to handle alone."

Rikki set her cup down a little harder than necessary. "So she expected you to give up your dreams for a man who was jealous of his own son."

"No, I expected it of myself, Rikki. If I hadn't, then I would've been no better than he was."

She didn't look any happier. "You are a better person than I would have been under the circumstances."

"I doubt that, but back to the sordid details. I took a job at a small newspaper and started writing freelance pieces on the side. My relationship with Marti was already falling apart. She was right about me not opening up to people. The last thing I wanted was for anyone to feel sorry for me because I had such a screwed-up family life. Lots of people had it worse."

This time it was Rikki who gave his hand a squeeze. "I have some experience with that myself."

"It didn't help that I kept getting calls from Mom at all hours of the day begging me to come help her with Dad. He was getting more and more difficult to deal with. After Marti left me, I tried moving back home, but that only made the situation worse."

When he drifted to a full stop in the narrative, Rikki left the table and set the stepstool in front of the refrigerator. After grabbing a half-empty bottle from the cupboard above, she returned to the table and topped both of their cups with a hefty dose of scotch. He took a sip and grimaced before taking a much larger drink. It tasted awful, but he hoped the alcohol would take the sharp edge off his pain.

"To finally get to the point, Mom called

one night, and I didn't come running. The paper had sent me to a formal dinner for some political bigwig where we were asked to mute our phones. By the time I got her message, it was already too late. From what the police pieced together, Dad had insisted on going out for more booze."

Max struggled to breathe past the pain of that night. "I don't know how many times I told her to get out of the house when Dad was out of control and then call 911 first and then me. Instead of doing the sensible thing, she got in the car with him."

The pain in his heart was always too familiar. He'd been living with it ever since that fateful night. "I still have no idea why she did that. Maybe Dad forced her. Maybe she went willingly. I keep asking myself which of those two options is worse, but I'll never know the answer."

By that point, his eyes burned with the need to cry, but he'd already done enough grieving for the disaster that followed. "The officers who investigated the accident said it was impossible to tell if Dad lost control and then hit the tree or if he actually aimed for it. Either way, he died at the scene. Mom lasted until she reached the hospital, but I got there too late to say goodbye."

"I'm so sorry, Max."

She meant it, too. It was there in her pretty gray eyes and her gentle touch. Even so, she had to be wondering why he chose this particular moment to air all of his family's dirty laundry.

"I failed my mother, Rikki."

When she started to protest, he stopped her. "I know she was an adult and made her own choices, but sometimes logic and facts get trumped by emotions. My head knows that she made a huge mistake, but my heart keeps telling me that I could've made her listen if only I hadn't muted my phone or if I'd fought harder to put Dad in care."

He ran his fingers through his hair in frustration. "If, if, if… There were so many chances to change the trajectory of how things played out, all of which brings me to why I'm telling you all of this. I failed to keep one woman I loved safe. I can't…no, I *won't* fail another one. This time I can't take no for an answer."

Rikki's face went pale as she stuttered, "Wh-what are you saying?"

He drew a ragged breath and chugged down the last of his chocolate and scotch. Then he met Rikki's gaze head on. "If that wasn't clear enough, let me put it another way—come heck or high water, no matter what it takes, I have to make sure you and Carter are safe from whoever has been sneaking around in your house. I've already talked to Cade about setting a trap."

Rikki looked stunned by that pronouncement. "Why would you do that without consulting me first?"

"Weren't you listening? I don't know how you feel about me, and right now it doesn't matter. No matter what, I want to help Cade put a stop to whatever has been going on. As far as why I would do that, I would think it would be obvious—I love you, and I love your son."

CHAPTER EIGHTEEN

RIKKI STOPPED BREATHING, stopped thinking, stopped everything as she struggled to get her head around what Max was trying to tell her. There was an awful lot to unpack. His story about his family life made her heart hurt. So did the fact that he couldn't let go of his guilt over his mother's death. And knowing him, probably his father's, too.

But that last bit—that he loved her and Carter—well, that was more than her already tired brain could comprehend right now. She had some strong feelings for him as well, ones that scared her. They were the reason she'd tried so hard to keep redrawing that line between them to keep him firmly on the other side as a guest, as someone who would eventually leave and never return as so many others had done before. If she didn't define how much she cared about him, maybe it wouldn't hurt so much when he went back to his real life.

When she tried to free her hand from his grasp, he held on for several seconds before finally releasing his hold on her. Good. She didn't want to fight about it, but right now she needed some space. Rather than confront the emotional part of his declaration, she focused on the other half. "Why set a trap?"

"Do you want to live with this threat hanging over your head for who knows how long?"

Rather than give her a chance to respond, he kept right on talking. "The thing is, I was so afraid you wouldn't agree to the plan that I wasn't going to tell you. But it doesn't take a genius to know that would have been a mistake of epic proportions. This is your home and your business, not mine. I don't have the right to make that kind of choice for you. It has to be your decision, no matter how I feel about the two of you."

"Thank you for that much, Max. Now explain to me what you and Cade were thinking."

She was worried that he would be angry that she didn't immediately acknowledge his declaration of love, but he looked more relieved than anything as he launched back into his explanation. "On Saturday, I want to take you and Carter to Seattle for the day. I have to meet with a professor at one of the colleges to pick up some research he's helping me with. After that, we'll do whatever you and Carter want to do. We can go to the zoo or maybe even go whale watching."

"We've never done that, and it sounds like fun. We can let Carter decide." Then she frowned. "That is, if I think this is a good idea. Start explaining why you want to do this."

Max quirked an eyebrow and offered her a small smile. "Anyone ever tell you that you're a stubborn woman?"

"Yes, but I won't apologize for not being a pushover. I have my son and my business to think about. I can't afford any more bad press."

That had him frowning. "You've had more bad reviews?"

"Yeah, there has been a flurry of them. Same as before—one-star reviews but with no explanation offered. It makes me furious. Either someone is trying to torpedo my business or it's the twins stirring up trouble for me again."

Max got up and poured them each some water. "Has Cade had a chance to tell you what he learned about the twins?"

"No."

He set a glass in front of her and sat back down. "I saw him earlier. I know he hasn't heard back from forensics yet, so that may be why he hasn't called. Regardless, he did contact the chief of police where the twins live. As it turns out, the man he spoke to goes to the same church as they do. He saw them there Sunday morning, and the brother was at work on Monday morning. Also, since our decision to go out to dinner was a last-minute deal, they wouldn't have known the house would be empty on that particular night."

"So even if they've been giving my B and B low ratings, they weren't the ones who broke in."

"Looks that way."

Once again, he took her hand in his. "I think—and Cade agrees with me—that the person or persons we're looking for had to have been close at hand that night. It's the only way they would've known there was a limited window of time when the house would be empty."

She sipped the water to buy herself time to mull over that much. "Even if that's true, what makes you think that person is still wanting to get inside the house?"

"Because they've already been back at least once."

Seriously? "What makes you think that?"

Because if he'd suspected something was going on and had told Cade instead of her, there was going to be heck to pay. The way Max's gaze shifted to the side before he answered told her everything she needed to know. It was time to demand answers. "When you asked if Carter had been in your room, I told you that it had been me. That I was the one who moved your stuff around to dust under it. Did you think I was lying about that?"

Max looked insulted by that. "No, of course not. But you cleaning my room doesn't explain the rows of holes that have been drilled into the wall behind the dresser and the bedside tables. They're just like the ones you patched up in the green room."

That's what had him all stirred up? "They were probably done at the same time as the others. There's no reason to think it just happened."

"Yeah, there is. I could tell the furniture

was moved recently, because whoever did it failed to put everything back exactly the way it was. There are marks in the carpet where the dresser used to sit, not to mention the drill left plaster dust on the floor. I'm sure you've vacuumed behind the furniture at some point since you took over the business. Maybe not the dresser, but at least the smaller pieces."

He was right. She had, which gave credence to his argument and left her feeling a bit sick. "But who could it be?"

"You're not going to like this, but logic says it has to be someone who has access to the house on a regular basis. I think you can rule out any guests who have only been here once, especially if they live some distance away like the family that came through while I was gone."

She hated the way he only dropped breadcrumbs, hoping she'd follow the trail he was laying out for her step by step until she bought into his theory. Well, it was time he put it all on the table. "Stop hinting around, Max. Tell me what you and Cade are thinking. You must have someone in mind."

"Yeah, we do, but we're sure you won't like it. And honestly, up until today I would've had a hard time believing it myself, but we both know the possibilities are pretty limited."

There was only one person who fit the criteria—Debra Billings. She might not be all that happy with the woman right now, but Rikki couldn't picture her wandering through the house in the dark, drilling holes in the walls. Even if she had, why would she take the time to destroy all of Max's and Carter's hard work?

"But Debra Billings wants to buy this place. Leaving bad reviews and damaging the walls would only cost her in the long run. It makes no sense."

"It does if she was looking for something specific the night of the break-in. I'm guessing she didn't find it. Otherwise, she would've disappeared and never come back." He held up his hand. "And before you ask, I have no idea what it might be. Even so, it's the only explanation that makes sense."

"And Cade is actually buying into this wild theory?"

"Enough so that he's willing to set a trap to catch the culprit. While you, Carter, and I spend the day and evening away, Cade is going to set up a stakeout to see if he can catch the culprit in the act. We're not completely convinced it's Ms. Billings, but she's one of the few people who've had access to the house."

He paused. "Now that I think about it, she's also had the key to the front door."

"She's always returned the key."

Max leaned in closer to her. "That doesn't mean she hasn't had a copy made."

Rikki couldn't remain still a second longer. She picked up their empty mugs and returned for the water glasses. After dumping the cookies back into the cookie jar, she stashed the empty plate and everything else in the dishwasher before wiping off the table.

For the second time since they'd started this talk, tears were streaming down her cheeks.

"I hate this, Max. I don't like not being able to trust people. And while I'm mainly talking about whoever has been messing around in my house, I'm also talking about you. You should have told me everything before you talked to Cade. I'm not fragile, and I prefer to make my own decisions."

When he tried to hold her again, she took a quick step back out of his reach. He winced, making it clear that her rejection hurt him. Right now she couldn't seem to help herself. "All I wanted was to build a good life for my son. I think we deserve that. Is that really too much to ask?"

"No, it's not, and that's why I'm going to do everything I can to help things get back to normal for you and Carter. If our plan works, that could be as soon as Saturday night. Then, if you want, I'll leave so the two of you can get on with your lives. I'll talk to Cade first thing tomorrow and get back to you on the logistics of everything."

Then he turned his back to her and walked away without waiting to make sure she'd agreed to cooperate. His gait was stiff, as if he was holding himself together by the thinnest of threads or anticipating a blow that would send him reeling.

And heaven help her, she let him go.

LAST NIGHT HAD gone about as well as Max had expected. It had been a rough ride for both of them. Oddly enough, he'd slept better than he had in ages. He wanted to put it down to sheer exhaustion, but there was more to it than that. For some reason, spewing all of the dark details of his family's sordid past had left him feeling...*empty* wasn't the right word. *Unburdened* came closer. *Relieved* closer still.

Rikki now knew more about him than people who had known him for years. Heck, he'd been practically engaged to Marti, and he hadn't told her a tenth of what he'd shared with Rikki. No matter how things played out between the two of them, he would always appreciate how she'd listened without making him feel like he was just trying to elicit sympathy.

He couldn't help but notice that she hadn't said a word about his other confession—the one where he'd admitted how he felt about her and Carter. It was pretty darn disappointing that she hadn't immediately thrown herself into his arms to profess her own undying love for him. Not that he'd expected that to happen.

Not really, anyway.

He rolled over onto his back and sat up after punching his pillow into a more comfortable shape. "Okay, Max, you're being overly dramatic here. This isn't some made-for-TV love story where the hero rides to the

rescue. It's Rikki's way of life and her live-
lihood on the line. If this all goes haywire,
you can walk away. She can't. No wonder she
wasn't inclined to leap across the table into
your waiting arms."

The one-sided conversation wasn't getting
him anywhere. All he could do at this point
was to make sure they were all on the same
page and then take care of the final details
necessary before putting the plan in motion.
They wouldn't need reservations for the zoo,
but he was pretty sure they would need them
to go whale watching. Seeing orcas up close
and personal had been on Max's bucket list for
a long time. From what he understood, there
was also a chance of seeing gray whales, bald
eagles and seals along the cruise up through
the San Juan Islands.

If they didn't do that tomorrow, well,
maybe they could some other time. It would
all depend on if Rikki would consider hanging out with him once this was all over. It was
probably too much to hope for, but he wasn't
ready to give up quite yet. Max glanced at the
clock on the bedside table. By the time he got
himself organized for the day, Cade should be
in his office. The sooner they talked, the bet-

ter. Afterward, he would explain everything to Rikki. No, after what she'd said, he would confer with her, not dictate the terms of how things would work. Even then, she might still decide not to participate. If that happened, he wasn't sure how he and Cade would handle the situation.

Rather than lie there and stew about it, he'd make sure that he and Cade came up with a detailed plan, one that would have an answer for any objection that Rikki might have. She was a smart woman. He was sure she would see reason. Eventually, anyway. For now, he needed to get moving.

As it turned out, Cade suggested they meet at his house, saying there was less of a chance for anyone to listen in. It wasn't that he didn't trust his officers. They were professionals and would carry out their duty, but there were people in and out of the police department all day long. That meant there was no telling who might accidently overhear something Cade preferred to keep just between the two of them.

Well, evidently between them and Titus, since he was already sitting on Cade's front porch when Max arrived. Interesting that Cade would invite him and not another member of the small Dunbar police force. Max looked around and frowned. "Am I early or is Cade late?"

Titus chuckled. "He got called to the church to meet with the pastor and Shelby. Something about pre-wedding counseling. It was the first he'd heard about it, so he wasn't sure how long it would take. He texted to tell me he's running late but hoped to get here soon."

Max dropped into the chair next to Titus's. "Where's Ned?"

Titus shook his head, looking disgusted. "The lazy critter was sleeping when it came time to leave. I told him no treats for him if he's going to stand me up at the last minute like this. It wasn't much of a threat since he knows my staff will give him snacks whenever he wants one."

"So he's getting friendlier?"

"Fat chance of that." Titus snorted at the very idea. "No, he simply stands and stares at his intended target. Eventually, that person gets so twitchy that they give him a treat and hope he bothers someone else the next time he feels peckish."

Okay, that was pretty funny. "Gotta respect a dog that knows how to get what he wants."

Their conversation was interrupted by the sound of another vehicle pulling into the driveway. Cade got out of his cruiser and slammed the door with far more force than necessary. Max glanced at his companion. "Somehow I think the session didn't go well. I'm almost afraid to ask what happened."

Titus put his feet up on the railing as if settling in to listen to a long tirade from the police chief. "Considering the man looks ready to blow, we're bound to get an earful whether we want one or not."

Sure enough, Cade came stomping their way, his expression thunderous. "Can you believe it? What was he thinking? Don't get me wrong. The pastor is nice enough, and I get why he wants to make sure people are getting married for the right reasons."

Max felt as if they'd been dropped into the middle of an ongoing conversation. Were they supposed to already know what had happened at his meeting with the pastor? While Max would've let Cade rant and rave, Titus was far braver than Max was. "Sounds reasonable. I'm guessing he sees a lot of folks who haven't figured out that 'until death do us part' is a long time."

Cade shot him a disgusted look. "I know that, but he normally meets with the couple over a period of months. The trouble is that Shelby and I don't have months. We're down to about eight days. He's been out of town, and now he insists on cramming all of the required sessions in anyway. We don't have that kind of time. How am I supposed to do my job, get ready for my parents and hers to descend on us, and still meet with him? There aren't enough hours in the day as it is."

He yanked off his hat and ran his fingers through his hair as he stared out at the woods for a few seconds. Finally, he sat down, heaving a huge sigh as he did. "Sorry about that. The pastor is such a soft-spoken guy that I couldn't bring myself to tell him how I really felt."

Max fought the urge to grin. "Plus, you want him to think you're mature enough to handle marriage for the long term. He's probably known Shelby forever and wouldn't want her to saddle herself with a raving lunatic."

"That, too." He leaned his head against the back of the chair and closed his eyes. "I really wish it wasn't too late to elope. I asked Shelby if that might still be a possibility on the way out of the church. She didn't even bother to respond."

"I'm surprised she didn't whack you on the head for even asking." Titus's amusement was clear. "You can handle another week of total chaos. Once the wedding is over, you two can head off on your trip to some mysterious destination."

There was an impish glint in his eyes when he added, "Did you know that there's a betting pool on where you're taking Shelby on the honeymoon?"

Cade groaned. "Seriously?"

"Yep. Two of the city council members picked Seattle, saying they'd told you to stay close by in case the town needed you back sooner than planned."

"Fat chance of that happening."

"That's what I thought. I didn't want to ask them what they're so worried about. I've heard good things about the county sheriff, so there's no reason to think she and her deputies can't handle anything that might happen while you're gone."

"That's true, and she already knows my replacement might need some backup if something unexpected happens."

Titus looked puzzled. "Is the town hiring some outsider to cover for you?"

"No, there's no reason for that. I'll tell you the same thing I told them. Moira Fraser is a good cop and has plenty of the kind of experience necessary to handle the job for two weeks."

For a brief moment, Titus's expression turned rock-hard. "I'm surprised the council agreed to that. I don't doubt for an instant that Moira's up to the job, but she needs more backup than a kid right out of the academy and a man who is overdue to retire."

"She knows to call the sheriff's office if she needs help."

Titus glared at Cade, his hands flexing as if he wanted to punch something—or someone. "Yeah, but they have their own caseload. How fast do you think they can get here if they're out on a call of their own?"

"I worry about that, too. All I can say is that they'll do their best. That's all anyone can ask."

Titus didn't respond. He settled back in his chair, clearly not happy. Why was the man getting so worked up about the situation? It certainly wasn't helping Cade's already questionable control over his temper. It was time to steer the conversation back to calmer waters. "So, Titus, what were the most popular picks in the betting pool?"

Titus eventually relaxed enough to start talking. "Paris, a camping trip in Glacier National Park, New Orleans, New York, Hawaii, and an Alaskan cruise. There were a few outliers, as well. A couple of people thought Shelby would want to spend the trip visiting other small-town historical museums to get new ideas for ours."

When Cade shuddered, Titus offered him some rough comfort with a light punch on his arm. "I wasn't the only one that suggested that idea was insane. Personally, I put my money on a road trip where you have no planned agenda and stay at random cheap motels along the interstate."

Max could understand why Cade looked a bit offended about that particular idea. "That sounds pretty tacky."

"Maybe so. But if you keep moving, they can't find you."

Even Cade had to laugh at that. "I'll keep that in mind."

"Good. I have ten bucks riding on it."

Max reached for his wallet. "I want to put twenty down on the cruise. I hear cell phone reception isn't always good. That would limit how often he'd have to take a call from the mayor, although I'm sure Otto would only call if there was a real emergency."

Titus laughed at that. "You mean like when he broke down and cried when you were trying to take the Trillium Nugget away from the town?"

"Yeah, like that."

Evidently, Cade had reached his limit on them making fun of his problems. Donning his most intimidating cop face, he said, "Okay, Max, tell me what you've got in mind. Go over everything that's happened and where we go from here. We need to get this all nailed down so I can get back to the office."

The explanation didn't take long. Within a few minutes, Max had his marching orders. Just as he'd thought, his only job was to get Rikki and Carter out of town for the day. The longer they stayed away, the better. It seemed unlikely that the culprit would strike in daylight, but it was always a possibility. As of right now, Rikki wasn't expecting to have any new guests to worry about, so that should help simplify things.

Meanwhile, Cade would have his officers drive by the house while out on patrol, but not so often as to set off alarms if someone was actually watching the house. Titus was going to help out by walking Ned through the neighborhood a few times over the course of the day. Well, if he could convince the dog he needed that much exercise.

They all agreed it was far more likely the culprit would slip in under the cover of darkness. With that in mind, Cade and Titus planned to set up a stakeout where they could keep an eye on the house. Max had to wonder why Cade would involve a civilian rather than one of his own people, but he figured he had his reasons. It could be something as simple as not having enough staff to cover the day-to-day routine calls if he pulled them off their regular duties.

Max only cared that they were doing everything they could to end the threat to Rikki and her son. They went through everything one more time to make sure they were all on the same page. When they were done, Cade asked, "How is Rikki doing with all of this?"

"She's not happy that the situation has come to this, but she's on board with the plan. She's relieved that we're getting her and Carter out of the line of fire for the day. It's hard learning that she might not be able to trust everyone who stays at the B and B. If it does turn out that someone she welcomed into her home has betrayed her like this, she's always going to wonder who else might break her trust."

"Or worse yet, be a threat to her son."

Titus wasn't wrong about that. "She already worries about how upset he'll be when I leave town because of how attached he and I have gotten. She knows I'd never deliberately hurt him, but there's no getting around the fact he won't be happy when it's time for me to go. Neither will I, for that matter."

Titus stood up and stared down at him. "So don't leave. It's clear you care about both her and the boy. Tell her."

That lump in Max's throat was back again. "I did. I already told her I love both her and Carter."

"What did she say?"

Max didn't really want to talk about this,

but these men had become friends. Maybe one of them would have some helpful advice. "She changed the subject."

Cade and Titus exchanged glances, but he had no idea what they were thinking. Finally, Titus said, "Stop by for pie, your choice of flavors. Not sure what good it will do, but it can't hurt."

Max slumped down in his chair. Great, he wasn't the only one who thought the situation looked hopeless. Regardless, it was nice to know he had some place to go if he needed to lick his wounds. Doing his best to smile, he accepted Titus's generous invitation.

"Thanks, I'll do that."

CHAPTER NINETEEN

RIKKI WIPED HER hands on the dish towel and took great care to hang it up neatly. Max watched in silence as she fussed until the towel was exactly aligned with the other one on the rack. He understood her need to focus on something, anything other than the matter at hand. He'd give her all the time she needed even if it was taking a toll on his own nerves.

All in all, Rikki had asked remarkably few questions as he relayed the gist of his conversation with Cade and Titus. She didn't even seem surprised that the usually reclusive café owner had volunteered to help guard her home. When she finally resolved the towel issue, she poured each of them a fresh cup of coffee and joined him at the table.

Rikki stared down at her coffee for several seconds before finally lifting her gaze to meet his. "I hate all of this, but what choice do I have? I need to make my home safe for my son."

He wanted to touch her, offer her some little bit of reassurance that all would be well. Unfortunately, he was pretty sure the overture wouldn't be welcome right then. "You do have a choice, Rikki. Say the word, and we'll call it off."

"No, I don't think we should." Her chin took on a stubborn tilt. "It's time to end this. I woke up to more negative reviews this morning. Same kind as before with low ratings and no explanation. If it's not the twins posting them, then I have to believe it's the same person who has been messing with the house."

Seeing her look so frustrated had Max curling his hands into fists. He wasn't a violent man by nature, but right now he very much wanted to punch something or, better yet, someone. Preferably whoever was trying to destroy Rikki's business. "I'm so sorry this is happening."

Rikki drummed her fingers on the table, the only indication that her emotions were running hot. "It's not your fault, Max."

At least she didn't say that it also wasn't his problem to solve. Even if that might technically be true, it didn't feel that way to him. He had a powerful need to protect her and Carter, to the point he'd already decided to stick close to home instead of going to the museum to work on his research. He also wasn't going to hole up in his room with his laptop. Until they eliminated the threat, he'd either work in the living room or hang out in the library with Carter. After all, that Viking longship wouldn't build itself. He wanted to make sure it was finished in case Rikki did send him packing.

"So, what's next?"

Finally an easy question to answer. "Maybe ask Carter what he'd like to do on our adventure tomorrow. If we decide to go whale watching, we'll need to get an earlier start than if we hang around Seattle."

For the first time since they'd started talking, there was a brief flash of excitement in her eyes. Then she frowned. "Unless you think we should stay on dry land in case Chief Peters needs us to come running for some reason?"

Max couldn't argue with her logic. Maybe they should, but he wanted to give her an experience that she'd never had before. "He was pretty sure that if someone does try to break in tomorrow, they'll most likely wait until after dark. If you want to go whale watching, that's what we'll do."

The urge to touch her became too strong to resist. He gently rested his hand on hers, keeping it light. "I'll make the reservations."

Before she could say another word, the kitchen door swung open with a bang. Carter charged in and headed straight for Max. The noise startled Rikki into almost dropping her coffee. "Carter! That's not how you enter a room."

Looking much put-upon, he offered a grudging apology. "Sorry, but I've been waiting for Mr. Max a long time. I got bored."

Max held out his arms to his young friend. "Sorry, big guy. Your mom and I have been making some fun plans for tomorrow, and it took longer than I expected."

Carter accepted Max's hug and apology. "What kind of plans?"

"That's up to you and your mom."

Rikki had been about to sip her coffee, but she set the cup back down on the table. "Well, Mr. Max has to drive to Seattle early tomorrow morning to meet with a man for a few minutes. Since his meeting won't take long, he thought the three of us could do some fun stuff together afterward."

Carter frowned. "What kind of stuff?"

"We thought you might like to go whale watching. We'd get on a big boat that would take us up through the San Juan Islands to where the orcas hang out."

The boy's eyes were huge as he looked from his mother toward Max and then back to her again. "Really? We'd see whales?"

Max figured they shouldn't make promises they might not be able to keep. "The captain of the boat can find the orcas most of the time, but no one can control where the whales go and what they do. That means no one can guarantee that we'll see them, but we might also see bald eagles and seals. I bet cruising for a few hours will be a lot of fun. We can eat lunch on the boat, too. I think they serve hot dogs and a few other things. On the way home, we'll stop for dinner someplace."

By that point, Rikki had the same big smile on her face as her son. "It's been a while since we've taken a whole day to have fun. So what do you say, Carter? Do you want to do this?

Max said we could go to the zoo or the aquarium if you'd rather do one of those things."

Both adults held their breath as they waited for Carter to decide. It didn't take long. "I want to see whales."

Before they could discuss it further, Carter slapped his hand over his mouth. "Sorry, I forgot, Mom. That lady who comes all the time is waiting at the counter to check out."

Then he tore back out of the kitchen before either of them could stop him. By the time they caught up with him, Carter was practically bouncing as he explained to Debra Billings that he and his mom and Mr. Max were going to see whales and orcas tomorrow. And he wanted to have waffles for dinner on the way home.

Rikki waited until her son paused to breathe to intervene. "Carter, I'm sure Ms. Billings is happy for you, but she's probably wanting to finish checking out so she can leave. She has a long way to drive to get back home."

Max hung back to watch how the woman responded to Carter's big news. Her smile seemed genuine when she spoke. "I've been whale watching a time or two and loved it. I hope you get to see lots and lots of whales. It's really amazing when they jump out of the water and make a huge splash. I think they call it breaching."

While she spoke, she handed Rikki her credit card. "That's nice that you're taking my advice about finding some balance between your personal life and your professional one."

She glanced at Max and then back to Rikki. "I'm sure Mr. Volkov will show you a real good time."

Before Max could decide if that was a note of snark he heard in her voice, she added, "And Carter, too, of course. The weather is supposed to be nice, so it should be a great day out on the water."

Rikki handed back her card. "I'm sure it will be fun. Have a safe drive, and I hope to see you again soon."

"Don't worry, you will. I'll be coming back to check on my cousin as soon as she's released from care."

When she reached for her suitcase, Max beat her to it. "Here, let me take this out to your car for you."

"Oh, you don't have to do that."

When she reached for it, he didn't give her

the option to take it from him. Instead, he headed straight outside and set the suitcase next to her car for her.

She unlocked the trunk and stepped back while he set her suitcase inside. "Sounds like quite the expedition you have planned for tomorrow, Mr. Volkov. Too bad Rikki couldn't get a babysitter for the day. I'm sure the two of you would have a lot more fun without her son to chaperone, if you know what I mean."

Where was she going with this? Was she simply trying to get a rise out of him for some reason? Deciding he really didn't care, he simply said, "Like Rikki said, have a safe drive."

Then he slammed the trunk closed and walked away.

SATURDAY HAD DAWNED bright and clear just as the weatherman had promised. After a quick breakfast, they set off on their adventure. Rikki could only hope that she had enough energy to make it through the day. It was never a good thing to start off on an outing already tired, especially when it was her own fault. Part of the problem was that she'd worked hard all day Friday, trying to stay too busy to think or worry.

Thankfully, there was always cleaning and paperwork waiting to be done. At the same time, Max and Carter had concentrated on their latest project. Around the middle of the morning, Max had invited her and Carter to walk down to the café, saying something about Titus owing him a piece of pie. She'd declined the invitation but allowed Carter to go after warning him he'd be eating extra vegetables with lunch.

After dinner, Chief Peters had called to confirm all the details for Saturday with her. After she'd tucked Carter in for the night, she'd given Max a brief rundown of their discussion. Needless to say, she hadn't slept much after that. Too many things to think about and too many things that could go wrong.

If that weren't enough, she still hadn't figured out how to respond to Max's declaration of how he felt about her and Carter, not that she doubted him. Instead, she doubted herself and her own judgment. After all, she'd foolishly believed that Joel had loved her. Even if he had, at least a little at first, that hadn't kept him from walking away without so much as a backward glance.

She'd survived the experience, mainly because she'd had no choice. One of them had to take responsibility for their son. She never regretted having Carter in her life, not for one instant, but there had been plenty of times when she doubted her ability to give him the kind of life he deserved.

She also knew that despite his own rocky past, Max was nothing like her ex-husband. Her heart was convinced that once Max made a commitment, he'd see it through. No, it was her brain that was the problem and why she hadn't been able to sleep. It kept playing endless scenarios of possible disasters in her head. What if he did leave? What if the trap failed? What if she let Max walk away and spent the rest of her life regretting that decision?

Finally, she'd given herself a long lecture on not living in constant fear of what might happen and then reminded herself that she had a lot of good things in her life to be grateful for. She was no longer isolated. Cade and Titus were willing to step up and help her eliminate the threat to her business. The women in the book club had made her feel welcome, and she had high hopes that she and Shelby Michaels would become close friends once Shelby got past the madness of arranging a last-minute wedding.

And she had Max.

"You're being awfully quiet over there. Everything okay?"

"Mostly." She turned to face him. "It's hard to not worry about stuff, but I'm doing my best to put it all aside. There's nothing I can do about it now, and I don't want to let all of that business back in town cast a shadow over today."

As he often did, Max took her hand in his. "I'm really looking forward to boarding the boat. I've been wanting to do something like this with the two of you since the first time I stayed at the B and B. I was pretty sure you wouldn't even consider it back then."

"You'd have been right." Giving him an arch look, she said, "After all, you were a guest in my fine establishment. It would've been inappropriate."

"And now?"

He deserved her honesty. "You're so much

more than a mere guest, Max. I hope you know that."

His handsome face lit up with a hopeful grin. "That's progress. Any chance that you might eventually see me as something more than a guest in your life?"

As soon as he asked the question, he shook his head. "No, forget I asked that. Now isn't the time for that discussion. We're only a couple of blocks from where we meet the boat. Let's put everything else on hold and simply enjoy the day."

"It's a deal."

AN HOUR LATER, they stood near the railing, faces to the wind. Both Max and Carter were fascinated by all aspects of the boat and had investigated everything on the lower deck before looking for the best vantage point for seeing whales. After buying all three of them cups of hot chocolate, Max shepherded them up the steps to the upper deck to stake out a spot at the railing. As the boat picked up speed, it got pretty breezy. Max quietly slipped his arm around Rikki's waist and tucked her into his side to protect her from the wind.

She leaned into his strength and soaked up his warmth. It felt so natural, so right to be with him like this. His patience with Carter's endless questions was nothing short of amazing. He'd even brought binoculars and let her son take charge of them. While she was no expert, she bet they were top-of-the-line. "Are you sure you want to trust Carter with those?"

Max shrugged. "What's the worst that can happen?"

She pointed out toward the water that surrounded them. "If he gets too excited, he might accidently drop them overboard. I'm doubting the cruise line has divers on standby to retrieve lost items."

Max clearly wasn't worried about the possibility. "I can always buy a new pair. It's days and memories like these that can't be replaced. If it makes him happy to have them, then that makes me happy, too."

Wow, he couldn't have given her a better answer if someone had scripted it for him. "You're so good with him. Where did you learn how to win over five-year-old boys?"

He smiled, his eyes crinkling at the corners. "Mostly by having been one myself.

That was about twenty-five years ago, but it's all coming back to me."

Before she could respond, the loudspeaker on the wall behind them crackled. They stopped to listen as the naturalist made an announcement. "Ladies and gentlemen, I have good news. The captain just received a radio message that an orca pod has been spotted just ahead. Keep your eyes to the left or port side of the boat. If you spot something, wave your hands over your head and then point."

A few seconds later, an enormous orca breached in the distance, sending up a huge splash of water. Max lifted Carter up onto a nearby bench that ran along the railing to give him a better view. After that, all three of them got lost in the wonder of such powerful, beautiful animals frolicking in the waters surrounding the San Juan Islands.

Like Max said, such days were rare. Rikki would've gone so far to say they were priceless. When Max smiled down at her, she gave in to temptation and kissed him. They kept it PG-rated, but that didn't make it any less special. She might be sending him mixed signals, but at the moment she couldn't seem to help herself. Besides, he'd told her to leave her problems onshore. For now, that was what she was going to do.

IN THE WAY of all good things, the cruise finally had to come to an end. Max glanced in the rearview mirror to check on Carter. He had fallen asleep holding the toy orca Max had bought him in the boat's small gift shop. After all of the excitement out on the water, it was no surprise that the little guy had conked out within minutes of them getting in the car. Max didn't blame him. He could use a nap about now, too.

The cruise had been fun, but it was Carter's infectious joy that had made the day special. Every time a new whale appeared, the little guy had cheered and then run from one side of the boat to the other to get the best view. He'd been almost as thrilled when they'd spotted seals sunning themselves on a rocky shore or when a bald eagle had soared high overhead. Heck, the kid had even waved at every seagull that flew past the boat. As they tied up at the dock, the naturalist declared this particular cruise had been exceptional for how many orcas they had seen.

When Carter had asked if they could go whale watching again soon, Max had left it up to Rikki to respond. At least she hadn't explicitly told her son that it was a one-off, never to be repeated. Instead, she'd simply said that cruises were special treats and not something people did all the time. Carter hadn't been happy with that answer, but Max understood why she'd err on the side of caution. It wouldn't do to promise Carter that the three of them would make a habit of hanging out together until Rikki made up her mind to let Max remain a part of their lives beyond the time it would take him to finish his research.

Right now, it was actually almost a relief that the kid was asleep. For the space of a few hours, Max was pretty sure that Rikki had been able to leave all of her worries onshore. But as soon as they'd disembarked, he could almost see her picking up the pieces. The silence in the car grew more tense the farther they got from the pier. By the time they reached the highway that led toward the mountains, it was almost unbearable.

Finally, she glanced at her phone and

sighed. "I haven't heard from Cade. Have you?"

Max had stuck his phone in the holder on the dash. "He hasn't called, and I haven't received any texts. If he doesn't reach out to us by the time we stop for dinner, I'll check in with him."

She'd been staring out the passenger side window, but she gave him a quick glance. "Maybe we should skip dinner and drive straight home."

He'd actually been expecting her to suggest that. "Wouldn't it be better to stick to the plan unless Cade says otherwise? If we show up too early, we might blow the whole operation."

"We ate a big lunch on the boat, and I'm not particularly hungry."

He was tempted to point out that her "big" lunch had consisted of a hot dog and a small bag of corn chips, which was hardly a feast. Instead, he played his trump card. "We promised Carter he could pick where we were going to have dinner. As I recall, he asked for waffles."

"Fine. I guess we can stop at that place just

before we get to the turnoff to Dunbar. You know the one."

She sounded resigned to her fate, if a little bit angry that things weren't going her way. He understood she was upset and worried, but none of this was his fault. Not exactly, anyway. Yeah, he'd been the one to suggest the plan to Cade in the first place, but someone had to put a stop to the ongoing threat.

"Look, Rikki, I know it's hard when things in your life aren't in your control, but you're not alone in this. This isn't like when your ex-husband walked away and left you to raise Carter all by yourself. It's also not like when the twins stirred up all kinds of trouble for you and hardly anyone stood up for you. Now you have friends you can trust."

"Chief Peters might be your friend, but he's only helping me because it's his job."

Now she was just being contrary. "I don't think that's how he feels about it. Besides, Titus is helping, and it's definitely not his job. And then there's me. Even if all you feel for me is simple friendship, I'm not going anywhere until this is settled. Even if we get this resolved tonight, I'm not leaving unless you tell me to go."

"You'll have to leave eventually. Your home is in Portland, not Dunbar."

Okay, that was rich. His words took on a bitter edge as he tried to explain. "My condo provides a roof over my head and a mailing address. I only have enough furniture to have a place to watch television and a bed to sleep in. That's about it. The truth is that Portland hasn't felt like home since I left for boarding school when I was thirteen."

He suspected she was finally looking at him, but he kept his own gaze centered on the road ahead. There was no way he wanted to deal with her pity. "After my parents died, I closed up their house and let it sit. I paid someone to keep up the yard so the neighbors wouldn't complain. I only did the bare minimum, because I could barely stand to walk into the place. Everyone kept asking me why I didn't move in, but I couldn't. Too many bad memories, I guess. I finally forced myself to go through everything in case I wanted to keep a few mementos. That's when I ran across the stuff I had about Lev Volkov. I donated everything else to charity and then sold the house."

He paused while he changed lanes. They'd

almost reached the exit to the restaurant. "I spend as much time on the road as possible and only go back to Portland when I'm between assignments. The truth is that I've spent more time at your bed-and-breakfast than I have in any other single place in years. It might not be my mailing address, but somehow it and Dunbar have become as close to a home as I have."

She drew a sharp breath, her shock obvious. Before she spoke, the third member of their group spoke up. "Mom, are we there yet? I'm hungry."

Max wasn't sure which of them was more relieved by the interruption, but at least Rikki managed to sound calm when she twisted around to look at her son. "Yep, we're only a few blocks away from the restaurant. It's not too late to change your mind if you want something other than waffles for dinner. There are several other places close by."

"Nope, Mr. Max and I want to eat at the waffle bar again. He really liked the ones we had last time."

Max glanced at Carter in the rearview mirror. "I sure did. I can't wait to see what you decide we should pile on our waffles this

time. I think I'd like to try strawberries instead of blueberries, but I'm open to sugges-
tions."

Rikki gave an exaggerated sigh. "Okay,
guys, waffles it is."

CHAPTER TWENTY

MAX MADE GOOD on his promise to her son and piled everything on his waffle that Carter suggested. She wasn't sure how he managed to eat all of it, but then maybe she was the only one who was stressing over what might be happening back at the house.

One look at Max's face as he paid the bill told her that she was wrong about that. Maybe it was her turn to reassure him that everything would be fine, but she wasn't so sure that was true. She settled for holding his hand as they walked out of the restaurant. "No matter what happens, we'll be fine."

He nodded and helped Carter get settled in the back seat. Once he closed the door, he leaned against the car. "Before we go, I'll check in with Cade for an update."

After making the call, he held out his other arm to Rikki and cuddled her in close at his side while they waited for Cade to answer.

When he did, the news wasn't good. "Okay, thank everyone for trying."

He listened several more seconds before saying, "We'll be there soon."

When he disconnected the call and shoved his phone back in his pocket, she asked, "So was all of this for nothing?"

"Not for nothing. We had fun watching the whales."

He was right about that. It was disappointing that they still didn't know what was going on at the house, but they really had enjoyed their time out on the water. The truth was that while the whales had been amazing, what really had made the day special was getting to spend it with Max. "Yeah, we did. Thank you again for taking us."

"Anytime." He kissed her on the nose and then released his hold on her. "Let's get you two home. I don't know about you, but I'm ready to call it a day."

It took them less than fifteen minutes to reach the turnoff into Dunbar and another five minutes after that to get back to the bed-and-breakfast. Max slowed down as they approached the driveway, looking from one side of the road to the other. "Cade said he was still in the area, but I don't see him. I don't see Titus, either."

That was worrisome. "I wonder where they went."

Max pulled into his usual spot and parked the car. "Beats me, but he said it was safe to go inside. I'm guessing he'll come knocking in a few minutes."

His phone rang just as he turned the engine off. "Hey, Cade. We just got home. What's up?"

Max's expression immediately turned dark. "Okay, I hope everything is okay. We'll talk later."

Her heart pounding out a quick rhythm, she asked, "What's happened?"

Max looked disgusted. "Two of his officers are dealing with a car accident. Then someone else called in a complaint, and Cade had to respond."

He typed out a message and held out his phone so she could read it.

Someone on the other side of town was taking potshots at mailboxes.

Well, that explained why he didn't want to offer up the details in front of Carter. "What kind of person would do such a thing?"

"I don't know. Maybe some teenagers out for some fun, or maybe some of the rowdies at the bar out that way. They'll be sorry if Cade catches up with them."

Before they started for the house, someone stepped out of the shadows under the trees along the side of the yard. Rikki immediately picked up Carter as Max positioned himself between her and the perceived threat. A second later, Max glanced back over his shoulder. "It's okay. It's Titus and Ned."

Even if he hadn't been able to identify Titus by his lean build and the way he moved, there would've been no mistaking the huge dog at his side. Max waited for the other man to join them. "Is everything still quiet?"

"I don't know. I just got here." He looked around at their surroundings. "I guess Cade is out chasing someone, so he called me to come back. Ned and I will circle the house and then check in with you."

After glancing at Rikki, he nodded. "Sounds good. We'll wait inside."

MAX TOOK CARTER from Rikki and let her lead the way to the front door. At first glance, everything seemed to be in good order, but they'd only gone a few steps when there was a loud thump that came from somewhere over-head. Max froze and stared up at the ceiling.

"What was that?" Rikki leaned in close and kept her voice to a low whisper—a low, terrified whisper.

Before he could answer, it happened again. He handed Carter back to her. "There's someone upstairs."

"What should we do?"

After a brief hesitation, Max headed for the library. After looking around inside, he stepped back out of her way. "Stay in here with Carter. I'll find Titus and call Cade. I'll be right back."

Once he reached the front porch, Max pulled the door almost shut. Titus was just coming around the corner. Max held his finger up in front of his lips, warning the man to stay quiet. Then he pointed toward the upper floors of the house.

When Titus grimaced and nodded in acknowledgment, Max called Cade. "Someone's in the house. I've got Rikki and Carter stashed in the library. We'll hole up there until you arrive."

Cade muttered a few questionable words under his breath and then said, "I was al-

ready on my way back. The call must have
been a distraction to make sure I was on the
other side of town. Give me about five minutes to get there. I won't come in with lights
or sirens."

That was a relief. No use in setting off a
panic by drawing the neighbors' attention.
"Good. Titus and Ned are with us. The front
door is unlocked, so come on in. In case you
don't remember from the last time you were
here, the library is on your left, second door
down the hall. The first one is a closet."

"Stay safe."

When the line went silent, Max made his
way back inside. Both he and Titus moved as
silently as possible, but the distant sound of a
drill running helped cover the little noise they
did make. Great, more holes. Hopefully this
would be the last ones they'd have to patch.
All things considered, that was a stupid thing
to be worried about right now.

Max slowly opened the library door. He
didn't want to startle Rikki, whom he half
expected to be waiting just inside the room
armed with one of the heavy bookends that
were scattered around the bookshelves in the
room. Instead, she was seated at the table,

helping Carter work on the longship. He also liked that she'd lit a couple of candles rather than turning on the bright ceiling fixtures. The softer light was more soothing, but it also wouldn't show as much under the door if the person moving around overhead decided to come back downstairs.

Rikki murmured something to Carter before looking directly at Max, her pretty face pale. He crossed to squat down next to her so they could talk. "Cade is on his way back. Should be here in a few minutes. I told him to come straight in, so don't be startled when the door opens."

Ned gave the room a thorough sniff before abruptly pushing his way in between Carter and Rikki. He gave Carter's arm a quick lick and then laid his big head in the boy's lap, clearly demanding to be petted. Carter happily obliged him, a huge smile on his face. Max was already fond of the big mutt, but he flat-out loved him right then for providing a welcome distraction from the situation they were all in.

Meanwhile, Titus positioned himself next to the door. Once again, Max wondered about Titus's mysterious past. For an owner of a small-town café, he looked pretty darn comfortable standing guard. He leaned his right shoulder next to the door, his hand hanging down at his side and carefully tucked out of sight between his body and the wall. Max was pretty sure he stood that way to keep Rikki and Carter from noticing his gun.

The silence continued until there was a soft knock on the door. Titus opened it just a crack and then wider to let Cade slip inside. He caught Max's eye and nodded toward the far corner of the room, probably wanting to talk away from Carter. Max tugged on Rikki's hand and led her over to where Cade waited. If Max hadn't happened to glance in Titus's direction at that exact moment, he wouldn't have seen the man slip his sidearm back into the holster on his belt. After tugging his T-shirt down to make sure it was covered, he joined the rest of them.

Cade pitched his voice low and quiet. "Any changes?"

"No, we still hear occasional footsteps. Whoever is up there is busy drilling lots and lots of holes."

Cade cocked his head to the side as he listened. After a few seconds, he nodded. "I've called the county for backup, but they don't know how soon Deputy Flores will arrive. You all stay here while I head upstairs."

Max wanted to protest. There was no telling what kind of situation Cade would be facing. It might be his job, but he shouldn't have to do it alone. After all, the man was getting married in a matter of days and shouldn't be taking any unnecessary risks. Before he could say anything, Titus jumped into the conversation. "Deputize me."

It was interesting that Cade didn't exactly look shocked by the offer. "You sure?"

Titus looked as if he'd just bitten into something bitter, but he met Cade's gaze head on. "Yeah. Shelby would kick my backside if I let you have all the fun. Ned can stay with Rikki and Carter."

Max swallowed hard. They might need someone who knew his way around the maze of rooms on the upper floors. "I'm coming, too."

Rikki gasped. "Max, no."

He gave her a quick kiss, not caring that the other men were watching. "I'll be okay. I promise. We'll text you when it's over and when it's safe to come upstairs if we need you for anything."

Her eyes soft with worry, she kissed him again. "Okay. Keep in mind that nothing in this house is worth you getting hurt."

Then she turned to face Cade and Titus. "The same goes for the two of you. Walls can be fixed, things replaced. Promise me you'll remember that. I'd rather whoever it is upstairs go unpunished than have any of you put yourself in unnecessary danger."

Cade smiled at her, but Titus looked as if he had no idea how to respond. He finally gave Rikki an awkward pat on the shoulder before heading for the door. Cade followed on his heels, leaving Max to trail along behind. When they reached the steps, Cade looked back at him. "You hang back. If things go sideways, get back downstairs and stay with Rikki and Carter. Call 911 and update the county on the situation."

Max really hoped it didn't come to that. Before they started up the steps, he tugged on Cade's sleeve. "Avoid the third step from the top. It creaks."

Their weapons drawn, both of the other men moved almost in unison as if they'd done this particular dance together before. Max followed behind at what he hoped was a safe distance. Their target had done them all one favor by leaving the guest room doors open along the length of the hall. All it took was a quick peek in each one to see that they were empty without risking the noise of doors opening and closing them. Even so, seeing the wanton destruction that had been left behind in one room made Max furious. It would take a lot of work to restore it in time for the guests arriving for Cade's wedding.

They finally reached the last room. Cade slipped past the open door while Titus positioned himself on the near side. At Cade's signal, Max retreated to the top of the staircase. That small distance didn't keep his pulse from racing and his hands from shaking. He hoped the other two didn't notice; it was embarrassing when both of them were so clearly calm. Thanks to Cade's years in the military police, he had plenty of experience under his belt. It was also proof positive that Titus hadn't always made his living flipping burgers and baking pies. The mystery was where and when he'd picked up this more deadly skill set. Right now Max didn't care and wasn't about to ask.

Cade held up three fingers and did a quick countdown. Max remained frozen in place while Cade and Titus charged into the room. Two seconds later, after several loud thumps, the screaming started.

CHAPTER TWENTY-ONE

A DISTANT SHRIEK startled Carter. His eyes wide with fear, he dropped the blocks he'd been putting together, scattering them off the edge of the table and onto the floor. "Mommy, what's that noise? Is someone hurt?"

Rikki hoped not, but right now she had no idea what was going on upstairs. There was a lot more thumping, something heavy hitting the floor, and at least one more furious scream that echoed through the house. As soon as she heard it, she clapped her hands over Carter's ears, but it was already too late.

Ned abandoned his post next to Carter and stalked over to the door. He stood guard, a low growl rumbling deep in his chest. Oddly enough, Rikki found the dog's fierce attitude comforting. Someone would have to be either incredibly brave or foolish to face off against a dog that size and packing that much attitude. She let him monitor the situation outside the door while she tried to reassure Carter.

"Chief Peters, Mr. Titus, and Mr. Max are upstairs checking out the noises we heard earlier. We're pretty sure that someone came into the house while we were gone today, and Max asked his friends to help him find out what was going on."

By that point, there had been nothing but silence for several minutes. She hoped that meant the guys had everything under control, but she would breathe easier when she could see with her own eyes that Max had come through unscathed. Cade and Titus, too, but mainly Max. The thought of him getting hurt while defending their home made her sick.

Wait…when had she decided that it was *their* home? As in his and hers and Carter's?

Before she could chase down an answer to that question, she realized someone was moving around out in the hall. Whoever was out there opened the closet door and then closed it. Another few steps brought the intruder that much closer. Ned's growling kicked it up several decibels.

After a soft knock, a deep voice called out, "Ms. Bruce, I'm Deputy Flores from the county sheriff's office. Please restrain your dog and open the door."

Rikki hated walking away from Carter, but she didn't want him anywhere near Ned right now. She risked putting her hand on the dog's collar, but she didn't fool herself into thinking she could stop him from going on the attack if the deputy decided to force his way into the room.

She did her best to speak calmly and clearly. "Deputy, Chief of Police Cade Peters and two other men are up on the second floor. They asked me to wait here in the library with my young son and the dog until they came back for me."

"Are you and the boy all right?"

"Yes. There was some hollering not long after they went upstairs, but it's been pretty quiet for a while now."

"All right. I'll check things out. If everything is under control, I'll come back and let you know."

"Thank you. I would appreciate that."

She was prepared to wait for however long it took, but the deputy was back within five minutes. "Ma'am, this is Deputy Flores again. Chief Peters asks that you join them upstairs.

I can stay with your son if that would make you feel better."

After a brief hesitation, he added, "And if it's okay with the dog."

"Actually, Ned belongs to Titus Kondrat. I'll see if he'll come with me. Give me a minute to explain things to my son."

"Take as long as you need."

She breathed a huge sigh of relief as she hurried back over to where Carter sat, his eyes huge as he stared past her at the door. "You heard the deputy, Carter. Everyone is fine, and they need my help with something. Deputy Flores will sit with you while I'm upstairs. I bet he'll enjoy hearing all about your longship. Is that okay?"

He nodded and even let her hug him without complaining. Having reassured Carter, she turned her attention to Ned. "Well, dog, let's go find your owner."

Ned studied her for several seconds before sitting down, looking far more relaxed than he had since Titus left the room. Even so, Rikki latched on to his collar again before she opened the door. "We're coming out."

The deputy had backed up to the opposite wall to give her and Ned some space. As she passed, he held up a small bear dressed in a uniform just like his. "I'd like to give this to your son if that's okay."

"I'm sure Carter would like that. He's excited to show you the Viking longship he's been working on."

Then she led Ned down the hall toward the steps. She released her hold on him and then followed in his path as he bolted upstairs to find his owner. When she spotted Max waiting for her at the far end of the hall on the second floor, she ran straight into his arms. "Are you all right?"

"We all are, but you're not going to like what we found." Looking disgusted, he added, "Or who, for that matter."

Before she could pepper him with questions, he led her into the already crowded bedroom where Cade and Titus flanked their prisoner. Despite the streaks of dirt on her clothes and face, it was easy to recognize Debra Billings, although her choice of clothing was out of character for her. In lieu of one of her casual chic outfits with tasteful jewelry, she was wearing cheap black sweats with a matching stocking cap pulled down over her hair. At least the black zip ties holding her wrists together at her waist in front were a perfect match for her ensemble.

The woman might have been restrained, but she clearly wasn't cowed. She glared at Rikki and then tried to kick Titus. Ned didn't like seeing his owner being attacked and stalked forward, snarling with his impressive set of teeth on full display.

"Keep that vicious animal away from me!"

When Ned barked, Debra stumbled right into Titus and lost her balance in the process. Considering the woman had just tried to kick him, Titus deserved credit for steadying the woman rather than letting her fall.

In the meantime, Cade pointed toward the ragged hole in the wall next to the window. "Again, what were you looking for?"

Debra sneered. "None of your business."

Rikki had had enough. "Well, it is my business. What on earth possessed you to do something like this?"

When the woman didn't respond, Max stepped up next to Rikki. "Cade, what kind of time is this woman looking at for multiple counts of breaking and entering, vandalism, and attempted theft? I'm betting you can add making false 911 calls to the list."

The smile Cade directed at Debra was anything but friendly. "I'm guessing ten years, give or take a few."

"And if the defendant were to cooperate?"

Cade crossed his arms over his chest, looking pretty darn intimidating. "I'm sure the judge would take that into consideration."

Max was looking pretty tough himself. "So, Ms. Billings, with that in mind, you might want to answer the lady's question. What were you looking for?"

Debra ignored the men to glare at Rikki and continued to bluster. "If you'd simply agreed to sell me this place, none of this would've happened."

That was beyond ridiculous. "Seriously? You break into my home, tear the place to pieces, and somehow it's my fault? Not only that, but I bet you're the one leaving all those bogus reviews hoping that would make me more willing to sell this place." She stepped closer to inspect the damage. "What is wrong with you?"

By that point, Debra was looking a bit crazy. "I'll tell you what happened. Years and years of waiting hand and foot on people who didn't appreciate a single thing I did for them. Do you have any idea how draining it is to listen to nonstop complaints about how bad something hurts or how tired someone is or why it took me so long to fetch whatever stupid thing they wanted next? Just last week I drove all the way back to Spokane to take care of a client only to have her daughter meet me at the door to say they didn't need me after all."

Debra stared at the hole in the wall. "Maude, the lady who used to own this place, was another one. Imagine my surprise when I was hired to care for her after she moved out of this place. She started rambling on and on about her crazy old uncle who told stories about hiding a treasure somewhere in a bedroom wall when he was a kid. She never knew if the story was true or if it was his dementia doing all the talking. Apparently she ran across a picture when she was packing up to move out that made her think the treasure was real. Rather than look for it herself, she liked the idea of whoever took over the business finding it someday."

Seriously? Debra had clearly gone off the deep end herself. "And you believed her."

By that point, Cade's prisoner had run out

of energy, or maybe the seriousness of her current predicament had finally sunk in. "Look for yourself."

Max followed Rikki over to the hole in the wall. Using the flashlight on his phone, he illuminated the interior of the wall and let her look inside. For the first time, her pulse picked up speed because of excitement, not fear. "There's a wooden box in there."

Max reached for the crowbar lying on the floor at their feet. "Do you want me to get it out?"

She didn't even hesitate. "Might as well. Cade is probably going to need it for evidence."

Even if that wasn't true, it didn't make sense to seal it back up in the wall now that they knew it was there.

It didn't take Max long to rip out enough of the wall to be able to reach the box. He handed it to Rikki. "You should do the honors."

She started to carry the box over to the bed to open it when Debra broke free and lunged for the box. "That's mine. I found it."

Max jumped between her and Rikki, knocking the determined woman sideways. They stumbled back into the bed. Max fell hard, hitting his head on the bedside table as the box tumbled onto the floor. Its lid popped off, scattering the box's contents everywhere. Rikki started to pick up the resulting mess when she realized that Max was bleeding.

"Max, are you all right?"

"Not really." He winced and held his hand against his head.

Seeing blood trickling out between his fingers, Rikki bolted down the hall to the bathroom to get clean towels. Then she knelt at his side and wiped away the blood with one towel before pressing the second one against the wound. "He might need stitches."

Titus was already on the phone calling for the EMTs. Then he helped Max back up off the floor and onto a nearby chair while Cade wrestled Debra back under control. After parking her in another chair, all of them silently stared down at the mess on the bed and floor. Nothing about the situation was funny, but Rikki found it hard not to snicker just a little when she realized what they were looking at.

She gave Debra an incredulous look as she pointed at Max and then at the damaged wall. "Seriously? All of this pain and all this damage for a bunch of stupid baseball cards? Who would consider this treasure other than the kid who collected them?"

Tears streamed down Debra's cheeks as she moaned, "I can't believe it. I'm going to prison for nothing."

Titus picked up several and studied them. After showing them to Cade, he passed them off to Max before picking up several more. Rikki watched as the three men exchanged big grins. What were they seeing that she wasn't?

Still holding his head, Max finally showed them to Rikki. "Please tell me that when you bought the bed-and-breakfast from...what was her name?"

Rikki filled in the blank for him. "Maude."

"Yeah, her. Tell me the contract you signed when you bought this place said all of the contents were included."

Where was he going with this? "Yes, I did. I don't remember the exact wording, but that was the gist of it. Maude took what she wanted when she moved out and made it clear in the contract that anything left after that became mine. Why?"

Max spread out the cards like a poker hand

so she could see them. "Because individual baseball cards can be worth a lot of money, especially old ones like these. It can vary a lot based on who the player is and the condition of the card."

He pointed at a couple. "Here's one of Babe Ruth, and this one is Dizzy Dean."

Titus held out two more. "I've got a Jimmie Foxx and a Lefty Gomez."

Max gave a low whistle. "You'll need to find a dealer who specializes in such things. My best guess is that by the time he tallies up the value of this collection, you're not going to have to worry about making ends meet for a long time to come."

Then he shot Debra a disgusted look. "Good news, Ms. Billings. You're going to prison for trying to steal a fortune after all. I hope that makes you feel better."

Debra moaned again as Cade helped her back up to her feet and led her out of the room. He stopped in the doorway. "I'm going to turn her over to the county. I'll send the EMTs up when they get here."

Rikki offered him a grateful smile. "We'll be here."

After he was gone, Titus gathered up the

rest of the cards and handed them to her. As she stacked them back in the box, she struggled to get her head around the abrupt change in her fortune. The funny thing was that it wasn't the cards or money she was thinking about. No, it was the man who had not only thrown himself between her and a crazy woman with no regard for his own safety, but who had also handed Rikki his heart with no strings attached.

Maybe it was time she gave him hers in return—if she could find the courage.

CHAPTER TWENTY-TWO

RIKKI ACHED FROM head to toe with exhaustion by the time everyone left. Cade had told her that he'd appreciate her and Max stopping by his office in the morning to finalize their statements about the night's events. He'd also told her that while he couldn't make any promises, a lot of cases like Debra Billings's were settled with a plea bargain, which meant there wouldn't be a trial. Only time would tell, but she really hoped that was how things played out.

Titus had surprised everyone by offering to bring Ned and hang out with Carter while she and Max met with Cade. She'd have to do something nice for the man to thank him for everything he'd done. At the moment, she had no idea what that might be, but then, she wasn't doing her best thinking at the moment.

It had taken over an hour for her and Max to convince Carter that it was safe to go to bed. The poor kid had finally fallen asleep, clutching the small bear that Deputy Flores had given him. She would have to send him a thank-you note for his thoughtful gift.

That just left one man to talk to. It might be tempting to crawl into bed and postpone the discussion until tomorrow, but Max deserved better than that. The trouble was, she didn't know where he was at the moment. Maybe he'd turned in for the night, but it wasn't like him to simply disappear without a word. She'd still been sitting by Carter's bed when Max slipped out of the room. She'd been so focused on her son that she hadn't thought to ask where he was headed.

Satisfied that Carter was down for the count, she left his room and pulled the door closed. Before hunting for Max, she stopped in her room to run a brush through her hair and wash her face. Why hadn't anyone told her that she had blood—Max's blood—splattered on her shirt? She tossed it in the trash and put on a clean one before heading upstairs to Max's room.

After knocking several times with no response, she used her key to let herself in. Normally, she wouldn't have violated a guest's privacy. However, this was Max, and he'd taken a blow to the head earlier. What if he'd lost consciousness? It took her only seconds to verify his room was empty. Only slightly relieved, she took a quick peek into the room where they'd found the "treasure" in case he was taking another look around.

Max wasn't there either, so he must have gone downstairs to make sure the house was locked up and secure. She finally found him in the kitchen, heating something on the stove. He smiled at her when she walked in. "I hope you don't mind me helping myself to your secret stash. The EMTs told me to avoid alcohol, and hot chocolate sounded good."

"It does." She set mugs next to the stove for him and got out the marshmallows before sitting down at the table. "Are you all right?"

He filled the mugs and topped them off with the marshmallows. "I have a bit of a headache, but that's all. How about you?"

She'd been better, but right now she wanted to focus her attention on him. "I didn't get a chance to thank you for throwing yourself between me and Debra earlier. I'm so sorry you got hurt in the process."

"Don't worry about it."

That was easier said than done, especially with the white bandage on his temple as a reminder of what had happened.

Max joined her at the table, setting down the mugs next to the plate of cheese and crackers he'd already put together for them. "I thought we both could use a snack before calling it a day…or a night…whatever it is. I seem to have lost all track of time. Anyway, I hope you don't mind me making myself at home in here tonight."

She wrapped her hands around the warmth of the mug. "Actually, that's what I wanted to talk to you about."

He'd been about to sip his drink, but he set the mug back down on the table. His expression went from relaxed to rigid as he met her gaze from across the table. "That I'm a guest and don't actually live here? Don't worry, I haven't forgotten."

Ouch. The sudden chill in his voice cut like a knife, but she probably deserved it. Looking back over the past few weeks, she suspected her need to protect herself by drawing that line between them had hurt Max more than she realized. "Yeah, about that."

She set her own cup down next to his and

forced herself to meet his gaze. "I've been a fool and a coward, and I apologize for that."

He blinked as if her words surprised him. "For what exactly?"

"For letting the bad behavior of people like the twins and my ex-husband get in the way of us. I let old hurts and fears rule my decisions instead of leaving them in the past where they belong."

Max sat back in his chair, arms crossed over his chest. "I'm listening."

"I've been so focused on the past that I haven't given much thought to what I want my future to look like." She looked around the old-fashioned kitchen that she loved so much. "I want this house to be more than a business. I want it to be a home for me and Carter, a safe place where he can grow up happy."

"There's nothing wrong with that, Rikki. He's a lucky kid to have a mother like you."

She knew without asking that Max was thinking about his own mother, a woman who had chosen her husband over her son time and time again. It was amazing that Max had turned out to be the generous-hearted man that he was. She drew a slow breath.

"The thing is, this house is big enough to be a permanent home for more than just Carter and me."

She walked around to Max's side of the table and tugged on the back of his chair, asking him without words to scoot it out from the table. As soon as he did, she sat down on his lap and wrapped her arms around his neck. Staring into the brilliant blue of his eyes, she laid it all out there for him. "What I hadn't realized was that my heart is big like that, too. There's plenty of room in it for someone other than my son."

When he started to speak, she placed her finger across his lips. She needed to finish what she had to tell him first or she might not find the courage again. "I haven't forgotten what you said the other night—that you love both me and Carter. I should've told you then and there how I feel about you."

He tugged her hand away from his face and kissed her palm, sending a shiver of anticipation dancing along her skin. "I'm still listening."

Suddenly she knew this was going to turn out okay despite her mistakes and fears. "I love you, Maxim Volkov. I want you in my home, my heart, and in my life, now and forever. The turret room is yours for as long as you want it."

Then she risked giving him a small kiss, a promise of more to come. "I think it would make a good office for a writer. You could get a real desk and some bookshelves. Whatever you need."

"I admit that's a tempting idea, but I'd have to find somewhere else to sleep." His smile turned sly. "I'm thinking with my wife would be the perfect place."

He kissed her, this one filled with heat and promise. "That is, if you'll have me. Will you marry me, Rikki Bruce?"

She positively melted. "I will, but only if we elope."

"It's a deal!" Max's laughter filled the room. "In fact, we have a few days before the guests for Cade and Shelby's wedding start arriving. What do you say the three of us head off to Las Vegas on Monday?"

"I'll start packing when we get back from talking to Cade tomorrow."

"While you do that, I'll make the reservations. We'll have to drive to Portland first to pick up my DJ equipment for Cade and

Shelby's wedding, and I'll also need my tux. Then we can fly to Las Vegas and get married! We'll fly back to Portland on Wednesday morning and drive back to Dunbar. How does that sound for a plan?"

She hesitated before pointing out the obvious. "Are you okay with taking Carter with us?"

Bless the man, he didn't even hesitate. "Of course he has to come with us. He's going to be my best man. We'll book a suite with two bedrooms."

He kissed her again. "For now, we'd better head upstairs. Tomorrow is going to be a long day, and I can't wait."

Before heading for their individual rooms, they checked on Carter one last time. Max stared down at her son for the longest time before speaking. "Just so you know, I plan to adopt Carter and officially make him my son, too. Okay if I ask him tomorrow if he'd like that?"

Her heart was already full to bursting. She hadn't thought this night could turn out any better, but once again Max had surprised her. "He'll love calling you Dad."

"I'll love it, too."

Then he kissed her one last time outside of her bedroom door. She watched as he headed up to the turret room, soon to be his office. She called after him, "How mad do you think Cade's going to be because you're getting to elope and he didn't?"

Max paused on the bottom step, a huge grin on his face. "I don't know, but I can't wait to tell him. But considering the amount of stress he's under, maybe I should hold off until the reception next weekend."

"Good idea."

He was still laughing as he disappeared from sight.

EPILOGUE

TITUS WATCHED THE happy couple enjoying their first dance as husband and wife. He didn't know much about weddings, but he thought Shelby and Cade had gotten the one they both deserved. Despite a few rough spots along the way, they were almost disgustingly happy. When the second song started, Shelby danced with her father while Cade waltzed with his mother. In a gallant move, Cade's father asked Shelby's mother to partner with him.

By all reports, the two sets of in-laws were getting along well, the fathers looking proud and the mothers a bit teary-eyed. Several people had already stopped by to compliment Titus on the array of food that he and Bea had created for the wedding guests. She'd even hinted that maybe they could start a catering business together. The very idea almost sent him bolting out the door.

When the music ended, Max tapped the microphone to get everyone's attention before starting the next song. "We all know it was a group effort to get Cade and Shelby safely married off."

He paused to let the crowd laugh and call out a few comments before picking up where he'd left off. "On behalf of the bride and groom, I've been asked to thank everyone who helped make this event such a huge success."

People started moving onto the dance floor, clearly ready to get the party started. But apparently Max wasn't done. "I have one more announcement."

Interesting that he motioned for Rikki Bruce to join him. "I would like to dedicate this next song to Rikki, who made me one of the two happiest men in this room when she did me the honor of becoming my wife earlier this week in Las Vegas."

Cade stepped up next to Titus, looking a bit dumbfounded. Staring across the room at the other couple, he asked, "Am I hearing things or did Max announce that he and Rikki eloped? Did we know they were planning this?"

"Yep, he did, and no, we didn't." Titus couldn't help but smirk a little. "I'm guessing Max decided to keep things simple after watching you and Shelby jump through all those hoops to pull off this lovely extravaganza. At least both you and him got what you wanted."

For a minute, Titus thought Cade might explode, but then the man stared at his own bride standing a few feet away and smiled. He headed straight for her as he called back, "I've got no regrets, but good for him, the lucky jerk!"

Max wasn't the only lucky jerk in the room, and Titus couldn't help but envy the happiness the two men had found. He watched as Max gave Rikki a quick kiss while he waited for the uproar to fade. Then he grinned and said, "Enjoy this next dance. I know I will."

As the two sets of newlyweds joined in the dancing, a movement over near the entrance of the church hall caught Titus's eye. Moira Fraser had just walked in. She must be on duty since she wore her police uniform. He'd heard that Cade had told her and the other officers to trade off coming to the reception for a short time so none of them had to miss out completely on the celebration.

She hovered near the doorway as if looking for someone. Just before her gaze would have swept past him, he did an about-face and headed for the nearest exit.

He slipped out of the building, his conscience arguing that he should've hung out at the reception long enough to congratulate Max and Rikki. Maybe even claim a dance with each of the brides. That wasn't happening, and he'd apologize later if necessary. Besides, a slice of one of his pies would buy him a lot of forgiveness.

At least out here, under the stars and away from the heavy press of the crowd back in the hall, he could finally fill his lungs with fresh air. When the world crowded too close like this, the best thing he could do was rev up his motorcycle and tear down the highway until he outran his memories.

Besides, it was the last chance he'd have for a while. With Cade leaving on his honeymoon, Titus planned to stick close to town for the next two weeks. He didn't doubt Cade's claim that Moira could handle being in charge of the police department while he was gone. It wasn't her Titus didn't trust. No, it was her backup. Knowing her, she wouldn't appreciate having a self-appointed guardian lurking in the shadows.

But she was going to have one anyway.

* * * * *

Get 3 FREE REWARDS!

We'll send you 2 FREE Books plus a FREE Mystery Gift.

FREE Value Over **$20**

Both the **Love Inspired**® and **Love Inspired**® **Suspense** series feature compelling novels filled with inspirational romance, faith, forgiveness and hope.

YES! Please send me 2 FREE novels from the Love Inspired or Love Inspired Suspense series and my FREE gift (gift is worth about $10 retail). After receiving them, if I don't wish to receive any more books, I can return the shipping statement marked "cancel." If I don't cancel, I will receive 6 brand-new Love Inspired Larger-Print books or Love Inspired Suspense Larger-Print books every month and be billed just $6.49 each in the U.S. or $6.74 each in Canada. That is a savings of at least 16% off the cover price. It's quite a bargain! Shipping and handling is just 50¢ per book in the U.S. and $1.25 per book in Canada.* I understand that accepting the 2 free books and gift places me under no obligation to buy anything. I can always return a shipment and cancel at any time by calling the number below. The free books and gift are mine to keep no matter what I decide.

Choose one:
☐ **Love Inspired**
Larger-Print
(122/322 BPA GRPA)

☐ **Love Inspired**
Suspense
Larger-Print
(107/307 BPA GRPA)

☐ **Or Try Both!**
(122/322 & 107/307
BPA GRRP)

Name (please print)

Address   Apt. #

City   State/Province   Zip/Postal Code

Email: Please check this box ☐ if you would like to receive newsletters and promotional emails from Harlequin Enterprises ULC and its affiliates. You can unsubscribe anytime.

Mail to the **Harlequin Reader Service:**
IN U.S.A.: P.O. Box 1341, Buffalo, NY 14240-8531
IN CANADA: P.O. Box 603, Fort Erie, Ontario L2A 5X3

Want to try 2 free books from another series! Call 1-800-873-8635 or visit www.ReaderService.com.

*Terms and prices subject to change without notice. Prices do not include sales taxes, which will be charged (if applicable) based on your state or country of residence. Canadian residents will be charged applicable taxes. Offer not valid in Quebec. This offer is limited to one order per household. Books received may not be as shown. Not valid for current subscribers to the Love Inspired or Love Inspired Suspense series. All orders subject to approval. Credit or debit balances in a customer's account(s) may be offset by any other outstanding balance owed by or to the customer. Please allow 4 to 6 weeks for delivery. Offer available while quantities last.

Your Privacy—Your information is being collected by Harlequin Enterprises ULC, operating as Harlequin Reader Service. For a complete summary of the information we collect, how we use this information and to whom it is disclosed, please visit our privacy notice located at corporate.harlequin.com/privacy-notice. From time to time we may also exchange your personal information with reputable third parties. If you wish to opt out of this sharing of your personal information, please visit readerservice.com/consumerschoice or call 1-800-873-8635. **Notice to California Residents**—Under California law, you have specific rights to control and access your data. For more information on these rights and how to exercise them, visit corporate.harlequin.com/california-privacy.

LIRLIS23

Get 3 FREE REWARDS!

We'll send you 2 FREE Books <u>plus</u> a FREE Mystery Gift.

FREE Value Over **$20**

Both the **Harlequin® Special Edition** and **Harlequin® Heartwarming™** series feature compelling novels filled with stories of love and strength where the bonds of friendship, family and community unite.

YES! Please send me 2 FREE novels from the Harlequin Special Edition or Harlequin Heartwarming series and my FREE Gift (gift is worth about $10 retail). After receiving them, if I don't wish to receive any more books, I can return the shipping statement marked "cancel." If I don't cancel, I will receive 6 brand-new Harlequin Special Edition books every month and be billed just $5.49 each in the U.S. or $6.24 each in Canada, a savings of at least 12% off the cover price, or 4 brand-new Harlequin Heartwarming Larger-Print books every month and be billed just $6.24 each in the U.S. or $6.74 each in Canada, a savings of at least 19% off the cover price. It's quite a bargain! Shipping and handling is just 50¢ per book in the U.S. and $1.25 per book in Canada.* I understand that accepting the 2 free books and gift places me under no obligation to buy anything. I can always return a shipment and cancel at any time by calling the number below. The free books and gift are mine to keep no matter what I decide.

Choose one: ☐ **Harlequin**   ☐ **Harlequin**   ☐ **Or Try Both!**
            Special Edition   **Heartwarming**   (235/335 & 161/361
            (235/335 BPA GRMK)   **Larger-Print**   BPA GRPZ)
                                (161/361 BPA GRMK)

Name (please print)

Address   Apt. #

City   State/Province   Zip/Postal Code

Email: Please check this box ☐ if you would like to receive newsletters and promotional emails from Harlequin Enterprises ULC and its affiliates. You can unsubscribe anytime.

Mail to the **Harlequin Reader Service:**
IN U.S.A.: P.O. Box 1341, Buffalo, NY 14240-8531
IN CANADA: P.O. Box 603, Fort Erie, Ontario L2A 5X3

Want to try 2 free books from another series! Call 1-800-873-8635 or visit www.ReaderService.com.

*Terms and prices subject to change without notice. Prices do not include sales taxes, which will be charged (if applicable) based on your state or country of residence. Canadian residents will be charged applicable taxes. Offer not valid in Quebec. This offer is limited to one order per household. Books received may not be as shown. Not valid for current subscribers to the Harlequin Special Edition or Harlequin Heartwarming series. All orders subject to approval. Credit or debit balances in a customer's account(s) may be offset by any other outstanding balance owed by or to the customer. Please allow 4 to 6 weeks for delivery. Offer available while quantities last.

Your Privacy—Your information is being collected by Harlequin Enterprises ULC, operating as Harlequin Reader Service. For a complete summary of the information we collect, how we use this information and to whom it is disclosed, please visit our privacy notice located at corporate.harlequin.com/privacy-notice. From time to time we may also exchange your personal information with reputable third parties. If you wish to opt out of this sharing of your personal information, please visit readerservice.com/consumerchoice or call 1-800-873-8635. **Notice to California Residents**—Under California law, you have specific rights to control and access your data. For more information on these rights and how to exercise them, visit corporate.harlequin.com/california-privacy.

HSEHW23

THE NORA ROBERTS COLLECTION

40% OFF!

Get to the heart of happily-ever-after in these Nora Roberts classics! Immerse yourself in the beauty of love by picking up this incredible collection written by, legendary author, Nora Roberts!

YES! Please send me the **Nora Roberts Collection**. Each book in this collection is 40% off the retail price! There are a total of 4 shipments in this collection. The shipments are yours for the low, members-only discount price of $23.96 U.S./$31.16 CDN. each, plus $1.99 U.S./$4.99 CDN. for shipping and handling. If I do not cancel, I will continue to receive four books a month for three more months. I'll pay just $23.96 U.S./$31.16 CDN., plus $1.99 U.S./$4.99 CDN. for shipping and handling per shipment.* I can always return a shipment and cancel at any time.

☐ 274 2595   ☐ 474 2595

_____
Name (please print)

_____
Address   Apt. #

_____
City   State/Province   Zip/Postal Code

Mail to the **Harlequin Reader Service:**
IN U.S.A.: P.O. Box 1341, Buffalo, NY 14240-8531
IN CANADA: P.O. Box 603, Fort Erie, Ontario L2A 5X3

*Terms and prices subject to change without notice. Prices do not include sales taxes which will be charged (if applicable) based on your state or country of residence. Canadian residents will be charged applicable taxes. Offer not valid in Quebec. All orders subject to approval. Credit or debit balances in a customer's account(s) may be offset by any other outstanding balance owed by or to the customer. Please allow 3 to 4 weeks for delivery. Offer available while quantities last. © 2022 Harlequin Enterprises ULC. ® and ™ are trademarks owned by Harlequin Enterprises ULC.

Your Privacy—Your information is being collected by Harlequin Enterprises ULC, operating as Harlequin Reader Service. To see how we collect and use this information visit https://corporate.harlequin.com/privacy-notice. From time to time we may also exchange your personal information with reputable third parties. If you wish to opt out of this sharing of your personal information, please visit www.readerservice.com/consumerschoice or call 1-800-873-8635. Notice to California Residents—Under California law, you have specific rights to control and access your data. For more information visit https://corporate.harlequin.com/california-privacy.

NORA2022

Get 3 FREE REWARDS!

We'll send you 2 FREE Books plus a FREE Mystery Gift.

FREE Value Over **$20**

Both the **Romance** and **Suspense** collections feature compelling novels written by many of today's bestselling authors.

YES! Please send me 2 FREE novels from the Essential Romance or Essential Suspense Collection and my FREE gift (gift is worth about $10 retail). After receiving them, if I don't wish to receive any more books, I can return the shipping statement marked "cancel." If I don't cancel, I will receive 4 brand-new novels every month and be billed just $7.49 each in the U.S. or $7.74 each in Canada. That's a savings of at least 17% off the cover price. It's quite a bargain! Shipping and handling is just 50¢ per book in the U.S. and $1.25 per book in Canada.* I understand that accepting the 2 free books and gift places me under no obligation to buy anything. I can always return a shipment and cancel at any time by calling the number below. The free books and gift are mine to keep no matter what I decide.

Choose one: ☐ **Essential Romance**
(194/394 BPA GRNM)

☐ **Essential Suspense**
(191/391 BPA GRNM)

☐ **Or Try Both!**
(194/394 & 191/391 BPA GRQZ)

Name (please print)

Address   Apt. #

City   State/Province   Zip/Postal Code

Email: Please check this box ☐ if you would like to receive newsletters and promotional emails from Harlequin Enterprises ULC and its affiliates. You can unsubscribe anytime.

Mail to the **Harlequin Reader Service:**
IN U.S.A.: P.O. Box 1341, Buffalo, NY 14240-8531
IN CANADA: P.O. Box 603, Fort Erie, Ontario L2A 5X3

Want to try 2 free books from another series! Call 1-800-873-8635 or visit www.ReaderService.com.

*Terms and prices subject to change without notice. Prices do not include sales taxes, which will be charged (if applicable) based on your state or country of residence. Canadian residents will be charged applicable taxes. Offer not valid in Quebec. This offer is limited to one order per household. Books received may not be as shown. Not valid for current subscribers to the Essential Romance or Essential Suspense Collection. All orders subject to approval. Credit or debit balances in a customer's account(s) may be offset by any other outstanding balance owed by or to the customer. Please allow 4 to 6 weeks for delivery. Offer available while quantities last.

Your Privacy—Your information is being collected by Harlequin Enterprises ULC, operating as Harlequin Reader Service. For a complete summary of the information we collect, how we use this information and to whom it is disclosed, please visit our privacy notice located at corporate.harlequin.com/privacy-notice. From time to time we may also exchange your personal information with reputable third parties. If you wish to opt out of this sharing of your personal information, please visit readerservice.com/consumerschoice or call 1-800-873-8635. **Notice to California Residents**—Under California law, you have specific rights to control and access your data. For more information on these rights and how to exercise them, visit corporate.harlequin.com/california-privacy.

STRS23

COMING NEXT MONTH FROM

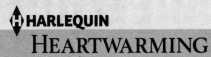

HARLEQUIN
HEARTWARMING

#487 THEIR SURPRISE ISLAND WEDDING
Hawaiian Reunions • by Anna J. Stewart
Workaholic Marella Benoit doesn't know how to have fun,
even at her sister's Hawaiian wedding! Thankfully surfer
Keane Harper can help. He'll show Marella how to embrace the
magic of the islands—but will she embrace his feelings for her?

#488 A SWEET MONTANA CHRISTMAS
The Cowgirls of Larkspur Valley • by Jeannie Watt
Getting jilted before her wedding is bad enough, but now
Maddie Kincaid is unexpectedly spending the holidays on a
guest ranch with bronc rider Sean Arteaga. 'Tis the season to
start over—maybe even with Sean by her side...

#489 HER COWBOY'S PROMISE
The Fortunes of Prospect • by Cheryl Harper
The history at the Majestic Prospect Lodge isn't limited to just
the building—Jordan and Clay have a past, and now they're
working together to restore the lodge's former glory. But it'll
take more than that to mend their hearts...

#490 THE COWBOY AND THE COACH
Love, Oregon • by Anna Grace
Violet Fareas is more than ready for her new job coaching
high school football. But convincing the community that she's
capable—and trying to resist Ash Wallace, the father of her star
player—is a whole new ball game!

**YOU CAN FIND MORE INFORMATION ON UPCOMING HARLEQUIN TITLES,
FREE EXCERPTS AND MORE AT HARLEQUIN.COM.**

HWCNM0823

HARLEQUIN
PLUS

Try the best multimedia subscription service for romance readers like you!

Read, Watch and Play.

Experience the easiest way to get the romance content you crave.

Start your **FREE TRIAL** at
<u>www.harlequinplus.com/freetrial</u>.

HARPLUS0123